MW00775204

THE FIVE SENSES
OF HORROR

Anthologies Edited by Eric J. Guignard

A World of Horror (forthcoming) (Dark Moon Books, 2018)

After Death... (Dark Moon Books, 2013)

Dark Tales of Lost Civilizations (Dark Moon Books, 2012)

+Horror Library+ Volume 6 (Cutting Block Books/ Farolight Publishing, 2017)

Pop the Clutch: Thrilling Tales of Rockabilly, Monsters, and Hot Rod Horror (forthcoming) (Dark Moon Books, 2018)

Exploring Dark Short Fiction (A Primer Series) Created by Eric J. Guignard

#1: A Primer to Steve Rasnic Tem (Dark Moon Books, 2017)

#2: A Primer to Kaaron Warren (Dark Moon Books, 2018)

#3: A Primer to Nisi Shawl (forthcoming) (Dark Moon Books, 2018)

#4: A Primer to Jeffrey Ford (forthcoming) (Dark Moon Books, 2018)

Fiction Written by Eric J. Guignard

Baggage of Eternal Night (JournalStone, 2013)

Crossbuck 'Bo (forthcoming, 2019)

That Which Grows Wild: 16 Tales of Dark Fiction (Cemetery Dance Publications, 2018)

THE FIVE SENSES OF HORROR

EDITED BY
ERIC J. GUIGNARD

PSYCHOLOGICAL COMMENTARY BY
JESSICA BAYLISS, PhD

ILLUSTRATIONS BY
NILS BROSS

DARK MOON BOOKS
Los Angeles, California

THE FIVE SENSES OF HORROR
Copyright © Eric J. Guignard 2018

All stories are copyrighted to their respective authors,
and used here with their permission.
An extension of this copyright page can be found at the end of this book.

All rights reserved. No part of this publication may be reproduced in any form
or by any means without the express written permission of the publisher,
except in the case of brief excerpts in critical reviews or articles.

Edited by Eric J. Guignard
Interior layout by Eric J. Guignard
Cover design by Eric J. Guignard
www.ericjguignard.com

Psychological commentary by Jessica Bayliss, PhD
www.jessicabaylisswrites.com

Interior illustrations by Nils Bross
https://muninsheim.deviantart.com

First edition published in July, 2018
Library of Congress Control Number: 2017937253
ISBN-13: 978-0-9988275-0-6 (paperback)
ISBN-13: 978-0-9988275-1-3 (e-book)

DARK MOON BOOKS
Los Angeles, California
www.DarkMoonBooks.com

Made in the United States of America

This book is dedicated to the Five Senses.
Without you, life would be rather dreary and markedly brief.

This is dedicated also, as always and with love,
to my family—Jeannette, Julian, and Devin—
who ensure I experience each of the senses daily
to their greatest and richest extents.

And to all authors who contributed such
dark and marvelous tales: Thank you.
Your imaginations are a wonder
and an inspiration to readers the world over.

TABLE OF CONTENTS

PREFACE: THE FIVE SENSES OF HORROR

BY ERIC J. GUIGNARD

I T'S SAID THAT ALL THE UNIVERSE can be can be classified into four categories: space, time, energy, and matter. Yet it is our five senses that interpret these things, providing unique meaning and expectations to that which we encounter. Hearing, Sight, Touch, Smell, and Taste: The stream of input from these senses is constant, forming our impressions of the world.

And so too is everyone's composite view of existence—like our fingerprints—without duplicate, a mélange of individual sense interpretations, which no one but the interpreter can fully understand in all its glorious and divergent nuance.

So we must content ourselves to wonder why or what causes other people to see or think things differently than ourselves. For there has always been an allure to understand the world through the experiences of others, whether of faraway and unfamiliar cultures or just the neighbor in that cluttered, noisy house next door.

Which brings us to writing.

Even before understanding any science or psychology behind it, suffice it to say, I—and many others—simply find ourselves most fascinated to read tales that stimulate our imaginations, this by way of the world in exciting or fictive terms, of impossible lands and adventures, what may have been or could yet be, the thoughts and experiences of "bigger-than-life" characters and their heroic, or erotic, or horrible, or otherwise thrilling or mysterious endeavors that are different from our own.

And what way to experience these things in our minds, than to have them enlivened, by writing, through the five senses?

Of course a stance of such scope can apply to any form of expositional prose, but being a fan of horror and dark fantasy, I wanted to explore the interaction and relationship of the five human senses on this particular genre.

So, a few quick thoughts about my defining criteria: I chose to focus on the short story rather than longer forms of writing. Besides personal preference, research and past conversations tend to revolve around grand, epic tomes, while smaller pieces—though no less effective—are often dismissed based solely on word count. Also within an anthology format, short stories can be included in their entirety, rather than only "excerpted," which doesn't always provide as comprehensive a picture. Further, I sought to explore only modern works within the last seventy-five years (1940–2015), because the same horror authors who are generally given any academic credibility are from generations ago—namely Poe and Lovecraft—while today's writers, although less studied, do incorporate more of our modern sensory perceptions.

Now with all that in mind, I've curated for you, dear reader, an anthology I hope you'll find immersive and enjoyable. The stories I selected can be categorized as either horror fiction based on scientific fact or condition, or horror fiction based on fantasy, but in all cases, each is meant to excite the imagination with thrill or wonder, while embodying unique and diverse perspectives of the senses.

I also structured this book not only for entertainment but to be a resource for learning, meant to appeal to readers, writers, and students alike. Included is companion academic and literary insight as well as psychological commentary examining the physiology of our senses, why each of our senses are engaged by dark fiction stories, and how it all inspires writers to continually churn out ideas in uncommon and invigorating ways.

Whether hearing the song of infernal caverns, tasting the erotic kiss of treachery, or smelling the lush fragrance of a fiend, enclosed within the following pages are fifteen horror and dark fantasy tales that will quicken the beat of fear, sweeten the flavor of wonder, sharpen the spike of thrills, and otherwise brighten the marvel of storytelling that is found resonant through our five senses.

Midnight cheers,

—Eric J. Guignard
Chino Hills, California
February 24, 2017

INTRODUCTION: WHY DO HORROR STORIES WORK? THE PSYCHOBIOLOGY OF HORROR

BY JESSICA BAYLISS, PHD

AS A WRITER, I often think about the experiences I want to evoke for readers through my stories: various emotions, thoughts, and sensory impressions. As a clinical psychologist, I think about these same things, trying to understand each individual I work with from their own unique perspective. My goal is to see the world through their filter—how their thoughts influence their emotions and behavior—and the patterns those thoughts take, helpful or unhelpful. Once I have accomplished that, I can guide them in gaining insight into how they make sense of the world, how they react to it now, and help them learn to respond in more helpful ways in the future.

The therapeutic process does not stop there, though. Another important and ongoing element consists of helping each person understand the things happening to them on a physiological level. The places where conscious awareness interfaces with unconscious processes. How the external and internal come together on a biological level.

That is what I want to talk about here.

Many things contribute to our sensory perception, and horror fiction plays on every single one of them. Our internal reactions to scary stories are a complex array of interrelated processes that involve our entire bodies: the brain and nervous system, the sensory organs, our skin, our cardiovascular system, our lungs, even our digestive tract. All of it responds to the things that go bump in the night.

We experience horror fiction with our whole bodies because we process fear with our whole bodies.

Why is fear so big?

The answer to this question is multifactorial, and it starts with evolution. Humans have been on this earth for approximately 200,000 years, and one of the reasons we have survived so long is because of our rapid and adaptive ability to respond to, and learn from, fear-related stimuli. The human brain—the most complex organic brain on the planet—is a living computer that is capable of both conscious and unconscious learning. We can register horrors consciously, but even if we somehow miss the monster hiding in the corner, our bodies and brains process endless data outside of awareness. Humans have other strengths, such as the ability to consciously process our world via thoughts and the ability to use language. I will get to those soon, but first, the physiology of fear.

When we encounter fear triggers, our bodies go into action. Sensory data is sent to our brain—from our ears, eyes, nose, mouth, and skin—ultimately hitting the amygdala, a structure in the temporal lobe, and the hypothalamus, which are important parts of our natural threat response. This is called the sympathetic response or, simply, the fight-or-flight system. Chemicals like cortisol, adrenalin, and oxytocin flood our blood streams, activating the cardiovascular system. We need all that blood flowing to our arms and legs so we have the strength and stamina to fight off the threat or to run away from it. Since blood carries heat, we sweat. Our breathing changes as the stimulants in our blood help our lungs take in more air. Digestion shuts down. Have you ever given a speech and needed water to combat dry mouth? That is the sympathetic response. We do not need to use our bodies' resources to digest food if we have a threat to cope with, therefore digestion is bypassed, which includes saliva production.

Sound familiar?

The fight-or-flight response can be triggered in a brief, transient way in response to a discrete stressful event—like if we finally discover what has been lurking in the dark, dank basement. We have all felt the burst of fear that comes with these moments. It can be intense, so intense, it may be difficult to control. But it is not all panic attacks and violent rages (yes, the same process responsible for fear is also responsible for anger); we frequently experience lower levels of these emotions in response to the everyday demands of modern life. The same fight-or-flight system is at work, just more chronically and with less intensity. Because we use mental representation to imagine stressful or frightening events that have not yet occurred, we can also initiate this process just by imagining these events. This anticipatory anxiety (i.e., worry) allows us to prepare for a threat, and it is why we can enjoy a good horror story.

So, this is how stories create fear in the body, but why do stories, and the scenarios they contain, scare us?

This question has a complex answer, too. Many scientists believe that we are actually born with an innate fear of certain things, particularly snakes and spiders, which are two creatures that can be deadly for humans. Scientists have conducted research looking at how quickly we are able to discriminate between a threatening stimulus and a non-threatening one. We are significantly faster at spotting something like a snake versus an inanimate object. This finding has been replicated in children, and it is enhanced when the snake is rendered as though it is about to strike. These fears are carried down through our genes. *No*, there is no snake phobia gene, but there are genes that contribute to our reactivity to things in the environment around us, our hypervigilance to danger, just how much our fight-or-flight system turns on when we encounter a dangerous situation, and the likelihood and degree to which we use avoidance as a coping strategy.

It may make sense from an evolutionary perspective to fear snakes and spiders. It even makes sense that we would pass down the ability to avoid these creepy crawlies to our offspring (after all, if the people with no fear of spiders died of spider bites, then they could not pass their own genes down to us, right?); but there were no killer clowns in the early days of human existence. Or ax murderers. Or axes, not at first, anyway.

The thing about these automatic processes is, they can become conditioned to various stimuli in our environment. *Any* stimuli in our environment. A psychologist named Dr. John Watson and his student, Rosalie Rayner, proved this in 1920 in a famous and infamous experiment known as the Little Albert Experiment. Little Albert was a one-year-old boy, healthy and well-adjusted in every way, with no apparent fears. What Dr. Watson did was to prove that phobias can be incited via the process of Classical Conditioning (CC), which is otherwise known as Instrumental Conditioning; this is the same process that Pavlov discovered when he realized dogs in his experiment were automatically drooling in response to a bell. CC is accomplished when a neutral stimulus is paired with a stimulus that means something to the organism (in this case to Albert). Watson took a neutral stimulus—a white fluffy object—and while Albert was looking at it, he made a loud noise near Albert's head. Of course, the poor kid was immediately upset. His fear response had been triggered by the noise, but when this was repeated over and over, all it took was seeing a white fluffy object for Albert's fear to turn on.

Voilà! A classically conditioned phobia. And I will tell you, horror fan that you are, if you want to see something very creepy, check out the Little Albert videos on YouTube.

The threat does not even have to directly involve us to cause a fear response. Social psychologists have long known that we can develop vicarious fear just by watching frightening events happen to others. Our thoughts play a role in this. We know that something is dangerous, and if we witness that event happening to someone near us—or even hear about it happening to someone we know—we can become sensitized to that stimulus. The thing is, we do not have to consciously think about it for the fear connection to form. Much of this happens outside of our conscious awareness, and classically-conditioned anxiety can occur vicariously.

So, how can a human brain automatically interpret an event happening to someone else as frightening? We can thank our mirror neurons for that.

Our brains are constantly reacting to the world. When we perform actions and take in sensory data, cells in our brains fire. For example, a pianist's cortex will light up when she is performing. Mirror neurons are sets of interconnected brain cells that also react when she *observes* someone *else* playing the piano. These neurons are considered one of the foundational components of our ability to experience empathy.

Empathy is the ability to enter into and experience the emotions of others. We can feel emotions with the people around us. Without mirror neurons and empathy, all fiction would be doomed to fail. Why would someone else's story be compelling if we could not connect to our own emotions when we experience it? But we can, and so it is.

Taken together, fear is a complex physiological process that involves intricate brain connections, neuro-chemicals, and multiple organ systems. What is deemed scary is taught to us throughout our lives in multiple ways, directly and indirectly. Directly, such as when we are scared half to death by a clown jumping out from behind a wall in a haunted house. Indirectly, such as when we hear a friend talk about his fear of clowns, or when we use our mirror neurons to interpret facial expressions of that same friend when we witness him confront a clown. And, of course, we learn what is scary through the stories we read, hear, and tell.

It is almost as if we were built for sitting around and telling stories in the dark.

In fact, our brains *are* wired for storytelling. We automatically process stimuli around us, putting them into order, creating a narrative. We find patterns and connections automatically, and we carry them around with us in our heads in the form of cognitive schemas, which we use to make sense of the world all the time, every day. It is our internalized schema that tells us what will happen if we are invited to a birthday party. We should send our RSVP by the required date, bring a gift, and we can rest assured that there will be food, particularly cake ... which someone will set on fire. But that is okay, because our schema includes this. We would not expect a zombie to burst out of said cake, because zombies are not part of our birthday party schema. (And now I want to write a story about a zombie busting out of a birthday cake!)

Horror fiction preys upon these shared stories of what is frightening or dangerous. The sound of a hook scratching against the door of a car. A ghostly cry in the night. A zombie horde. These threats are wired into our brains, partly through our environmental influences—those direct and vicarious stimuli—and partly by evolution. These forces have literally shaped us to avoid certain things so that we do not get eaten by the predator and so that we carefully handle the remains of our dead to prevent sickness.

When you really think about it, a talented writer has a few tasks before him: to artfully play with the established schemas shared by our society; to augment them in new ways to get a bigger fear response out of his reader; and, if he wants to be really effective, to figure out how to create entirely new sets of ideas by tapping into things we already find frightening. An ax is not terribly scary when dad is walking toward a fallen log. Sure, it is a tool that can cause injury—that is a schema we have learned—so best to be careful. That same ax is *way* scary when dad is walking toward *us* with it in his hands. Or chasing us through the house, busting open doors to find our hiding place.

The horror genre abounds with such scenarios that communicate to us that we are in for something terrifying.

Schemas are thoughts, and the Cognitive Behavioral Model is based on the idea that thoughts generate emotions. This theory is so robust, it has formed the basis of several psychotherapies with solid scientific evidence backing them. Life situations cause us to make interpretations, appraisals, judgments, assumptions, reactions, and then we experience an emotion. Dad with the ax by a wood pile (*Thank goodness he's taking care of the chores and hasn't bugged me*, equals relief, happiness, and pleasant anticipation of all the good books I'm going to read) versus Dad with the ax, trying to get into a room where Mom is screaming for help (*OMG, run for your life, call for help!*, which equals terror).

You might be thinking that I have just described two very different processes—the ones rooted in physiology and the ones rooted in our thoughts—but, actually, they are linked.

Two theories help us understand how. The James-Lange Theory explains how our internal physiological reactions can be interpreted by the brain to contribute to the experience of emotion. This is unconscious. If you remember, sensory data comes in, stimulating various parts of the brain—including the amygdala and hypothalamus—and this turns on the fight-or-flight process, which is a series of physical changes inside our bodies. According to William James and Carl Lange, this physical response triggers us to make an interpretation as to what emotion we are feeling. James, in particular, focused on this cognitive processing of the physical data we can feel inside our bodies. This theory is compelling, but only half right. Later, scientists Jerome Singer and Stanley Schachter added a layer of complexity. According to the Singer-Schachter Two-Factor Theory, we first look to the environment for clues as to what emotion we should experience, and we use that sensory data to settle on the emotion.

This distinction is important for a couple of reasons.

Firstly, as mentioned above, different emotions are remarkably similar within the body. Singer and Schachter conducted an experiment where they injected participants with epinephrine (though they didn't tell them that), then the participants were either shown people acting in happy, exhilarated ways, angry ways, or fearful ways. Guess what... the context, what the actors were doing, determined the emotion the participants felt. Even humor was augmented by the injection. Humor and fear, the same? What...? Yes! And because of this similarity, we need other cues to consciously understand what emotion we are feeling—external, environmental cues.

Secondly, what is even more fascinating is the way these findings are related to later studies on mirror neurons. Not only did Singer's and Schachter's work provide support for some physiological process that allows us to make sense of what we witness others doing and experiencing, it factored in the role of environment. Modern research shows that environmental cues aid the effectiveness of mirror neurons to provide information. Our brains and bodies process data from the outside in *and* from the inside out, and what we get in response is essential for our ability to enjoy horror.

But, how do these astounding physiological mechanisms even get their data to begin with? Through our sensory systems, of course—the somatosensory (touch), auditory (sound), gustatory (taste), visual (sight), and olfactory (smell)—and *that* is what this book is about.

That is what nightmares are made of.

Read on.

You'll see.

THE SENSE OF TOUCH

INCLUDED:

THOUGHTS ABOUT THE SENSE OF TOUCH

BY JESSICA BAYLISS, PHD

OUCH, OUR TACTILE SENSATION, is a product of the somatosensory system. Without your somatosensory system, you would have no way of knowing that a spider is crawling up your arm or that the air just got abnormally cold. We have several types of receptors within our skin. Each type is responsible for conveying information about specific stimuli to the nervous system.

Mechanoreceptors in the skin allow the spider's legs to register in your brain. You use these same receptors to keep track of the newspaper you grab to brush the spider safely to the ground. The newspaper may not work, though, and the spider might scurry from your arm to your shoulder—sending tickling sensations up and down your neck—and then to your back. When that happens, and you twist, turn, and jump around, trying to get the eight-legged invader off, additional receptors deeper within the dermis convey messages from joints, tendons, and muscles. They allow you to keep track of what each of your body parts are doing. We also have receptors in our skin for temperature (thermoreceptors) and for pain (nociceptors).

But fiction requires us to feel *along with* the characters in the story. Let me ask you a question: Did you feel anything while reading about the spider? I bet you did. (I felt something, and I'm the one who wrote it!)

This takes us back to the mirror neurons.

It was through research on the premotor cortex of monkeys that mirror neurons were first discovered. Particular brain cells lit up when the monkeys performed certain actions. That is not terribly interesting. But monkeys that were merely observing *also* showed activation of these pathways. Dr. Giacomo Rizzolatti made the discovery that what we *see* changes the parts of our brains responsible for *movement*. And, as I just described, our various mechanoreceptors allow us to feel our own movement. Since then, neuroscientists have examined a concept called mirror-touch synesthesia, which is what occurs when *I* feel somatosensory sensations while watching a spider crawl up *your* back.

This is why we can read about that same thing happening to a character in a story and get the willies.

This phenomenon does not end with creepy crawlies. Rizzolatti was also the first to make the mirror neuron-empathy link; it is this very pattern of activation in our brains that lets us understand the emotions of others. We witness their emotion, and we understand it because we feel it too, at least to a small extent.

Seeing their facial emotion is not even necessary.

We can literally tell the emotions of a person based on how they touch us, and studies have shown that our mirror neurons tell us about the emotional meaning behind a touch we merely observe. Our somatosensory system conveys information about emotion. All emotions. Including fear.

That means that fear is processed via our skin. (I told you that fear was a whole-body experience.)

No discussion of touch and horror fiction would be complete without the inclusion of pain. Have you ever cringed looking at, or reading about, a particularly gruesome injury? By now, you will not be surprised to learn that mirror neurons also respond to observations of someone else's pain. Scientists do some very interesting studies in this area. Here is how it goes: Research participants come to the lab where scientists subject them to mild pain. They are then asked to observe another person—a confederate—who is displaying very perceivable pain behavior. When compared to a control, the participants who are in pain while watching someone else in pain will rate their discomfort as more severe.

In other words, watching someone in pain will make our own pain worse.

What about adding fear to our tactile sensation? Actually, fear will dampen this sense, which is why someone in extreme terror may not even know they are injured until they calm down and experience the adrenaline crash of the fight-or-flight system turning off. The brain's fear center, the amygdala, may play a role in mediating the relationship between fear and tactile sensation, including pain. There appears to be a hyperalgesia effect—we simply feel less pain—but this is only true during short-term stressors. The amygdala can actually create the opposite—pain hyperalgesia—in cases when we have chronic pain. We may not feel that skin-searing gash while the werewolf is still at our backs, but we will feel it tomorrow. And the day after that.

And the day after *that*.

HEADING HOME

BY RAMSEY CAMPBELL

EDITOR'S NOTES: Our skin—the largest organ in the human body—gives us the ability to perceive millions of touch sensations hourly, sending to our brain a wealth of information such as pain, pleasure, pressure, and temperature, and otherwise acting as the interface between our bodies and the outside world. Or, as researchers at Johns Hopkins University explain: "Our entire skin is a sensing, guessing, logic-seeking organ of perception, a blanket with a brain in every micro-inch."

Without touch, we wouldn't sense the cold ground beneath us, wouldn't know when something sharp cut us, wouldn't feel the wood stair under our jaw when needing to gain certain leverage . . .

Author Ramsey Campbell is hailed as "Britain's most respected living horror writer," and the following masterpiece is a compelling illustration why such an assertion holds true. Timeless, wicked, gleeful, this story not only employs the sense of touch for its success, but it also 'touches the heart' in empathy for a villain.

The betrayed and wounded protagonist herein must traverse a tactually-demanding—if not notably familiar—environment or he will surely die. Or, more simply put: Can he survive, *Heading Home*?

"You raise yourself, muscles shuddering with the effort, your cheek chafing against the wood of the stair . . . "

(** Orthographic purists, please note: British spelling has been used for this story by request of its author.)

S OMEWHERE ABOVE YOU CAN HEAR your wife and the young man talking. You strain yourself upwards, your muscles trembling like water, and manage to shift your unsteady balance onto the next stair.

They must think he finished you. They haven't even bothered to close the cellar door, and it's the trickle of flickering light through the crack that you're striving towards. Anyone else but you would be dead. He must have carried you from the laboratory and thrown you down the stairs into the cellar, where you regained consciousness on the dusty stone. Your left cheek still feels like a rigid plate slipped into your flesh where it struck the floor. You rest on the stair you've reached and listen.

They're silent now. It must be night, since they've lit the hall lamp whose flame is peeking into the cellar. They can't intend to leave the house until tomorrow, if at all. You can only guess what they're doing now, thinking themselves alone in the house. Your numb lips crack again as you grin. Let them enjoy themselves while they can.

He didn't leave you many muscles you can use; it was a thorough job. No wonder they feel safe. Now you have to concentrate yourself in those muscles that still function. Swaying, you manage to raise yourself momentarily to a position from which you can grip the next higher stair. You clench on your advantage. Then, pushing with muscles you'd almost forgotten you had, you manage to lever yourself one step higher.

You manoeuvre yourself until you're sitting upright. There's less risk that way of losing your balance for a moment and rolling all the way down to the cellar floor where, hours ago, you began climbing. Then you rest. Only six more stairs.

You wonder again how they met. Of course you should have known

that it was going on, but your work was your wife
the time to watch over the woman you'd married. You
that when she went to the village she would meet people
as silent as at home. But her room might have been as far from
village is from the house; you gave little thought to the people in ex.

Not that you blame yourself. When you met her—in the town w
you attended the University—you'd thought she understood th
importance of your work. It wasn't as if you'd intended to trick her. It was
only when she tried to seduce you from your work, both for her own
gratification and because she was afraid of it, that you barred her from your
companionship by silence.

You can hear the voices again. They're on the upper floor. You don't
know whether they're celebrating or comforting each other as guilt settles
on them. It doesn't matter. So long as he didn't close the laboratory door
when he returned from the cellar. If it's closed you'll never be able to open
it. And if you can't get into the laboratory he has killed you after all. You
raise yourself, muscles shuddering with the effort, your cheek chafing
against the wood of the stair. You won't relax until you can see the
laboratory door.

You're reaching for the top stair when you slip. Your chin comes down
on it and slides back. You grip the wooden stair with your jaws, feeling
splinters lodge between your teeth. Your neck scrapes the lower stair, but it
has lost all feeling save an ache fading slowly into dullness. Only your jaws
prevent you from falling back where you started, and they're throbbing as if
nails are being driven into their hinges with measured strokes. You close
them tighter, pounding with pain, then you overbalance yourself onto the
top stair. You teeter for a moment, then you're secure.

But you don't rest yet. You edge yourself forward and sit up so that you
can peer out of the cellar. The outline of the laboratory door billows
slightly as the lamp flickers. It occurs to you that they've lit the lamp
because she's terrified of you, lying dead beyond the main staircase as she
thinks. You laugh silently. You can afford to. When the flame steadies you
can see darkness gaping for inches around the laboratory door.

You listen to their voices upstairs and rest. You know he's a butcher,
because once he helped one of the servants carry the meat from the village.

any case, you could have told his profession from what he has done to
ou. You're still astonished that she should have taken up with him. From
the little you knew of the village people you were delighted that they
avoided the house.

You remember the day the new priest visited. You could tell he'd heard
all the wildest village tales about your experiments; you were surprised he
didn't try to ward you off with a cross. When he found you could argue his
theology into a corner he left, a twitch pulling his smile awry. He'd tried to
persuade you both to attend the church, but your wife had sat silent
throughout. It had been then that you decided to trust her to go to the
village. You'd dismissed the servants, but you told yourself she would be
less likely to talk. You grin fiercely. If you'd been as inaccurate in your
experiments you would be dead.

Upstairs they're still talking. You rock forward and try to wedge
yourself between the cellar door and its frame. With your limited control
it's difficult, and you find yourself leaning in the crack without any
purchase on the wood. Your weight hasn't moved the door, which is
heavier than you have ever before had cause to realise. Eventually you
manage to wedge yourself in the crack, gripping the frame with all your
strength. The door rests on you, and you nudge your weight clumsily
against it.

It creaks away from you a little, then swings back, crushing you. It has
always hung unevenly and persisted in standing ajar; it never troubled you
before. Now the strength he left you, even focused like light through a
burning glass, seems unequal to shifting the door. Trapped in the crack,
you relax for a moment. Then, as if to take it unawares, you close your grip
on the frame and shove against the door, pushing yourself forward as it
swings away. It returns, answering the force of your shove, and you aren't
clear. But you're still falling into the hall, and as the door chops into the
frame you fall on your back, beyond the sweep of the door.

You're free of the cellar, but on your back you're helpless. The slowing
door is more mobile than you. All the muscles you've been using can only
work aimlessly and loll in the air. You're laid out on the hall floor like a
laboratory subject, beneath the steadying flame.

Then you hear the butcher call to your wife "I'll see" and start downstairs.

You begin to twitch all the muscles on your right side frantically. You roll a little towards that side, then your wild twitching rocks you back. About you the light shakes, making your shadow play the cruel trick of achieving the movement you're struggling for. He's at the halfway landing now. You work your right side again and hold your muscles still as you begin to turn that way. Suddenly you've swung over your point of equilibrium and are lying on your right side. You strain your aching muscles to inch you forward, but the laboratory is feet away, and you're by no means moving in a straight line. His footsteps resound. You hear your wife's terrified voice, entreating him to return to her. There's a long pondering silence. Then he hurries back upstairs.

You don't let yourself rest until you're inside the laboratory, although by then your ache feels like a cold stiff surface within your flesh, and your mouth tastes like a dusty hole in stone. Once beyond the door you sit still, gazing about. Moonlight is spread from the window to the door. Your gaze seeks the bench where you were working when he found you. He hasn't cleared up any of the material that was thrown to the floor by your convulsions. Glinting on the floor you see a needle, and nearby the surgical thread which you never had occasion to use. You relax to prepare for your last concerted effort, remembering.

You recall the day you perfected the solution. As soon as you'd quaffed it you felt your brain achieve a piercing alertness, become precisely and continually aware of the messages of each nerve and preside over them, making minute adjustments at the first hint of danger. You knew this was what you'd worked for, but you couldn't prove it to yourself until the day you felt the stirrings of cancer. Then your brain seemed to condense into a keen strand of energy that stretched down and burned out the cancer. That was proof. You were immortal.

Not that some of the research hadn't been unpleasant. It had taken you a great deal of furtive expenditure at the mortuaries to discover that some of the extracts you needed for the solution had to be taken from the living brain. The villagers thought the children had drowned, for their clothes were found on the river bank. Medical progress, you told yourself, has always involved suffering.

Perhaps your wife suspected something of this stage of your work, or perhaps she and the butcher had simply decided to rid themselves of you. You were working at your bench, trying to synthesise your discovery, when you heard him enter. He must have rushed at you, for before you could turn you felt a blazing slash gape at the back of your neck. Then you awoke on the cellar floor.

You edge yourself forward across the laboratory. Your greatest exertion is past, but this is the most exacting part. When you're nearly touching your prone body you have to turn round. You move yourself with your jaws and steer with your tongue. It's difficult, but less so than tonguing yourself upright on your neck to rest on the stairs. Then you fit yourself to your shoulders, groping with your perfected mind until you feel the nerves linking again.

Now you'll have to hold yourself unflinching or you'll roll apart. With your mind you can do it. Gingerly, so as not to part yourself, you stretch out your arm for the surgical needle and thread.

The Oxford Companion to English Literature *describes* **Ramsey Campbell** *as "Britain's most respected living horror writer." He has been given more awards than any other writer in the field, including the Grand Master Award of the World Horror Convention, the Lifetime Achievement Award of the Horror Writers Association, the Living Legend Award of the International Horror Guild, and the World Fantasy Lifetime Achievement Award. In 2015 he was made an Honorary Fellow of Liverpool John Moores University for outstanding services to literature. Among his novels are* The Face That Must Die, Incarnate, Midnight Sun, The Count of Eleven, Silent Children, The Darkest Part of the Woods, The Overnight, Secret Story, The Grin of the Dark, Thieving Fear, Creatures of the Pool, The Seven Days of Cain, Ghosts Know, The Kind Folk, Think Yourself Lucky *and* Thirteen Days by Sunset Beach. *He recently brought out his Brichester Mythos trilogy, consisting of* The Searching Dead, Born to the Dark *and* The Way of the Worm. Needing Ghosts, The Last Revelation of Gla'aki, The Pretence *and* The Booking *are novellas. His collections include* Waking Nightmares, Alone with the Horrors, Ghosts and Grisly Things, Told by the Dead, Just Behind You, Holes for Faces, Fearful Implications *and* By the Light of My Skull, *and his non-fiction is collected as* Ramsey Campbell, Probably. Limericks of the Alarming and Phantasmal *is a history of horror fiction in the form of fifty limericks. His novels* The Nameless *and* Pact of the Fathers *have been filmed in Spain, where a film of* The Influence *is in production. He is the President of the Society of Fantastic Films.*

Ramsey Campbell lives on Merseyside with his wife Jenny. His pleasures include classical music, good food and wine, and whatever's in that pipe. His web site is at www.ramseycampbell.com.

SOFT

BY DARRELL SCHWEITZER

EDITOR'S NOTES: This next selection is something I'd first discovered over twenty years ago, probably in early college about 1995, when I'd picked up a value edition hardback of *Best of Weird Tales*. I'd read author Darrell Schweitzer before, as he'd been writing horror fiction for the prior quarter century (and still going strong today!), but none of his works stayed in my youthful and receptive, Grateful Dead-groovin' mind quite like *Soft*.

While there's no scientific fact or condition to relate or extrapolate for this following dark fantasy tale, the boundaries of tactile sensation are nonetheless expanded in strange and penetrating ways, relating what it might feel like to ply certain things that should not be malleable.

After a monumental argument, Richard lies in bed next to his wife while contemplating divorce. He tries to remember just one "perfect" moment with her, and if only he could mold her . . .

Heartbreaking yet hopeful, weird yet insightful, and multi-layered to the sense of touch—For don't we all wish we could perhaps shape those around us, even if just a bit?

> *"His fingers left a deep, firm impression in her flesh, as if she were a clay figure and he had just ruined the sculptor's work . . . "*

R ICHARD NEVER KNEW WHY it happened, or how, but, in the end, he thought he understood what it meant. And perhaps that, at the very end, was enough.

The screaming was over. The completely inarticulate fits of obscenities they'd both descended to when they'd run out of real words were gone too, passed like a sudden summer storm.

He felt merely drained. He stood alone in the living room, listening to the ticking of the clock on the mantel, and, beyond that, to the silence of their disheveled apartment. When at last he made his way to the bedroom, he found, much to his surprise, that his wife had left the door unlocked.

He turned the handle slowly.

"Karen?"

The bedroom was dark.

"Karen?"

She muttered something he could not make out, a single word like a profound sigh.

"What?"

She did not answer.

His only thought had been to slip through the bedroom into the bathroom, then come out again and retrieve his pajamas and a blanket from the closet so he could spend what would very probably be his last night in this apartment on the sofa.

But as his eyes adjusted to the darkness he saw that she had rolled over to one side of the bed, the way she always did. When he was ready, he got into bed beside her, more out of habit than any hope or conviction.

The bedsprings creaked. If he listened very hard, he could still hear the clock over the mantel in the living room.

Karen muttered something again. She was talking in her sleep. It was just like her, it seemed to him then, just like the self-absorbed, overgrown child she had become, or perhaps had always been, to go straight to bed after the domestic war to end all wars and sleep it off like a Saturday night's drunk.

He lay still for a while beside her, staring at the ceiling, his hands joined behind his head.

It was beyond apology now, beyond groveling, beyond absurd bunches of roses with absurd cards. Everything was decided, and there was some relief in that, a release from all doubt and tension. It was *over*. They were getting divorced as soon as possible.

That was a simple fact he could cling to.

But the fact didn't seem so simple as he lay there. He spent a long, masochistic time rehearsing their early years together in his mind, not dwelling so much on *her*, but on how he had felt, the sensation, the satisfaction of being perfectly in love for just *one* perfect day. There had been one perfect day, he somehow knew, and everything had declined subtly from it. Yet he couldn't find the day in his memory, for all he was sure there had been "one, brief, shining moment," as the phrase went, and he wept softly for the loss of it.

Then he turned angrily on his side, his back to Karen, his fists tight against his chest, and he cursed himself for the sort of fool who would go back for punishment again and again and never learn.

He listened to the clock ticking, and to Karen breathing. Once again she babbled something in her sleep. It seemed to be a single word over and over. He still couldn't make it out.

Perhaps he slept briefly. He was aware of some transition, a vague disorientation, as if a few minutes had been clipped from the filmstrip of his life. Still he lay in the darkness on the bed, his back to Karen.

He couldn't hear the clock. There was only the silent darkness holding him like a fly suspended in amber.

And a word. He felt it forming on his own lips, and he had to speak it aloud just to know what it was.

"Soft," he said.

What followed was temptation. Part of his mind laughed bitterly and remembered the old Oscar Wilde gibe about the only way to deal with temptation being to give in to it. Part of his mind watched, a disinterested observer, as his body turned toward Karen, as his lips said again, almost soundlessly, "Soft."

She was wearing a sleeveless nightgown. The same compulsion that made him turn, that made him speak, now caused him to reach up, ever so gently, and touch her bare shoulder.

"Soft," he said. He squeezed, and his detached puzzlement grew as he felt that her shoulder was indeed soft, like warm, living clay. His fingers left a deep, firm impression in her flesh, as if she *were* a clay figure and he had just ruined the sculptor's work.

He ran his fingers into the grooves and out again, confirming what he felt.

Then he drew his hand back quickly and lay still, afraid, his heart racing. He stared at the dark shape of his wife on the bed beside him. He thought he could make out just a hint of the disfigurement.

It was impossible, of course, but he couldn't bring himself to *tell* himself that, to say aloud, or firmly in his own mind, *You must be dreaming. People do not turn into silly-putty, not in real life.*

Part of him wanted to believe.

The word came to him once more. The urge to reach out to her followed, like a child's uncontrollable desire to pick at a scab, to touch a sore.

"Soft," he said, kneading the whole length of her arm like dough. She didn't seem to feel any pain. Her breathing remained the same regular in-out of deep sleep.

Again she mumbled something, her breath passing through flapping lips almost as if she were trying to imitate a horse.

He touched her. He felt the warm flesh passing between his fingers, never breaking off the way clay would, but losing all shape as he squeezed again and again. He felt the hard joint of her elbow for only a second before it too became flaccid, endlessly plastic.

"Soft," he said, and with horrified fascination he stretched her arm until it reached down past her ankle, then flattened it until it was like the deflated arm of a balloon figure. That was what she was, he decided, an Inflato-Girl ordered from the back pages of a men's magazine. That was what she deserved to be, he told himself, and his anger suddenly returned. He knelt over her now, astride her, and he touched her flesh again and again, smearing her face out on the pillowcase, crushing her other shoulder, while he thought how much he hated her and could not find the words until he arrived at Poe's perfect phrase, *the thousand injuries of Fortunato*.

"Yes," he whispered as he pressed her, as her flesh flowed and changed and spread across the covers. "Yes. Fortunato. Soft, Fortunato. *Soft*."

And finally, reaching into the ruin of her chest, pushing his hands under the layers of flesh as he might under a heap of old clothes, he held her beating heart between his fingers.

Still she breathed gently, her distended, lumpy body rising and falling as if someone were making a feeble attempt to inflate the Inflato-Girl.

Then his anger passed, and once again he wept, and lay motionless on the bed, atop her, beside her, her flesh all around him, her steady breathing caressing every part of him. He felt himself becoming sexually aroused, and he was afraid and ashamed.

He listened to the silence of the apartment where he was spending his last night and wondered what precisely he should do. He laughed aloud, bitterly, at the prospect of going into the street now, at whatever late hour it was, approaching a policeman and saying, "Er, excuse me officer, but I've squeezed my wife a little too hard and—"

He imagined the expressions on the faces of the nurses at the hospital emergency room as he brought Karen in draped over himself like a poncho, her face and hands dangling down by the floor.

Her breathing caressed him, and he said again and again, "Soft. Soft. For you, my dearest Fortunato, soft forever."

Once more he wept, then laughed aloud hysterically, then hushed himself in sudden, desperate dread, terribly afraid that he might *wake* her.

He lay paralyzed, and swiftly, without the slightest effort on his part, the memory he had been searching for came to him, and he remembered that day ten years ago when they were both twenty-three, about six months before they were married, when he took her on a picnic to some scenic spot up the Hudson, near Tarrytown perhaps, where the towers of Manhattan were like gray shapes of cloud just around a bend in the river.

Nothing much happened, but he remembered lying beside her on the blanket in the warm sun, gently stroking her hair while an orange and brown butterfly flapped around their faces and neither one of them bothered to brush it away.

It was a moment of perfect harmony, perfect agreement, and their futures seemed so certain. It was a relief, a release from all doubt and tension.

She had risen on her elbow, holding her chin in her hand, and smiled down at him.

"I love you," she said. "When they made you, they broke the mold."

"You too," he said.

He awoke with a feeling like a sudden drop, as if he'd stepped off a cliff in a dream.

It was dawn. By the first gray light seeping through the Venetian blinds he could make out the dresser against the far wall and the bathroom door hanging open.

Something stirred on the bed, touching him from many directions at once, caressing him.

He closed his eyes desperately, and groped about in this self-imposed, utter darkness, weeping again, sobbing, "Soft, soft, damn it, one more time, please," as he tried to gather her flesh together, to shape it, to reassemble the ruined form into some semblance of the original.

But he was no sculptor.

By full light of day he had to, at last, open his eyes and behold his attempt.

He screamed.

She opened her eyes.

He felt her flesh closing over his hand, his fingers giving way, mingling with hers.

She spoke out of a gaping wound that might have once been a mouth.

"Soft," she said.

Darrell Schweitzer is the author of three fantasy novels, The White Isle, The Shattered Goddess, *and* The Mask of the Sorcerer, *plus about 300 short stories which have appeared in many anthologies and magazines. His most recent collection is* Awaiting Strange Gods *from Fedogan & Bremer. Others include* Tom O'Bedlam's Night Out, Transients, Nightscapes, The Emperor of the Ancient Word, *etc. He is also a critic, essayist, the author of books about H.P. Lovecraft and Lord Dunsany, and a former editor of* Weird Tales *magazine. He has been nominated for the World Fantasy Award four times and won it once.*

FEEL THE NOISE

BY LISA MORTON

EDITOR'S NOTES: As dreadful a condition as this next story relates, it's based on medical legitimacy, and something that in one form or another affects about 4.4% of the human population, although not necessarily considered adverse to those afflicted. Synesthesia is a neurological phenomenon in which two or more of the senses are united, so that the stimulation of one sense leads to automatic experience in another: Auditory-tactile synesthesia causes sounds to produce sensations of touch; lexical-gustatory synesthesia causes words to have taste; smell-color synesthesia brings colors to scents. Other anomalies cause colors to be felt, tastes to have sounds, and numbers to be flavorful.

In the following, Private Jackson Howard unfortunately suffers from a jumble of them all.

The immensely talented author and screenwriter Lisa Morton brings us into the world of Scrambleheads, where nothing is sensed as it should be, and even communication is an exercise in neurosis. Lisa has written across the genre's board from gore to ghosts to mystery to nonfiction, although nothing may be more frightening than her sketch of experiencing this affliction's symptoms in the worst way, and the magnitude of its associated confusion, when Pvt. Jackson wakes from injury to discover he can *Feel the Noise.*

> *"You spend that year screaming a lot, but what comes out feels like a slap and looks jagged and smells like death . . . "*

I WAS ON THE CLUB FLOOR waiting for the show to start, feeling the anticipation in a wave of smells like a girlfriend's body after a shower, the stage lights overhead making me taste whiskey, when a young man walked up to me. His approach brought the wary tang of mustard, and he sounded like an itch when he asked, "Private Jackson Howard?"

I'd been out of rehab at the V.A. hospital for two years, but it still took me a few extra seconds to turn his gush of sensations into words. Then I answered, "I haven't been a private for a while."

The kid—ironic, since he was probably my age, but I thought of myself as old—smiled, and asked if we could go outside to talk.

To talk . . . sure. It was still easy for him.

His name was Kevin. He worked as a blogger for a news outlet.

Here's what I told him, when he asked what being scrambled was like:

You wake up, and you're not sure where you are or what happened to you. Some part of you recognizes a hospital, but the man standing over you tastes like aspirin, and the antiseptic smells sound like a low buzz, and the feeling of the meds in your system reminds you of the scent of your grandmother's mothballs, back when you were a normal little kid playing in the attic in her big old house down in your home town. And you start to panic, you think back to your last memory—in the desert, and some bad shit had just gone down, and the sergeant was screaming and no one was paying attention as we made our way back to the Hummer, and—

Scrambler.

Suddenly you know. You were hit by a scrambler. You've got a condition now called "systemic synesthesia," and it's every soldier's second worst nightmare; you'd rather lose an arm or a leg or an eye than have your brain rewired so no two senses match up right. In fact, a lot of scrambleheads say they wish they'd just died, so maybe it's Nightmare #1. You frantically try to think back to that day in basic training when you sat in a classroom and they told you about this new weapon the other side had called scramblers, and how they're electronic bombs that were really designed to mess up communications equipment, but they messed up soldiers instead, and you curse yourself—fucking idiot—for getting bored then, for sitting there thinking, *That'll never happen to me, and when do we finish with this pussy training and get over there to mix it up?*

Mix it up. That's rich.

They kick you out of the main hospital after a week and send you to the special clinic, and over the next year you hang out with a lot of other scrambleheads like yourself while they try to teach you how to alter your thinking and reprogram your brain, and you spend that year screaming a lot, but what comes out feels like a slap and looks jagged and smells like death. And after a while you start to figure it out: Seeing red means you just ate some meat, and hearing a screeching noise means you just smelled something bad. You learn to read again by examining the tastes the letters make, and you know who's touched you by how nice the smell is. You scream a little less every day.

And then you find the one thing makes you feel something strong: Music. And if you want to feel like you're with the world's sexiest woman, and she's rubbing all over you and you think you could take on everything, then you need it fast, loud, and hard.

And that's why all the scrambleheads who used to spend their furloughs chasing pussy are chasing music now instead.

It took me another year to be able to figure out how to talk again.

And during that year, I went a little crazy (crazier?) locked up in my head, because I had to tell someone what happened. What I saw every night when I closed my eyes. What fucking Sergeant Dean Craig had done.

He'd popped off and shot a kid. The parents, too.

We'd been doing a routine patrol on the outskirts of a desert town. Searching abandoned houses, making sure the bad guys weren't still hiding out or hadn't left some presents behind.

In one of the houses we found this family, this poor family. Mother, father, young son, couldn't have been more than five years old. Sergeant Craig started screaming at 'em to put their hands on their heads and get on their knees, but they didn't speak English and they just kind of flapped their hands a lot and argued.

The kid had started to reach for something inside his shirt.

Craig shot him.

Just like that. A five-year-old with a bloody hole in his chest. No one should ever have to see that.

The parents screamed and charged, and so Craig shot them, too. Three people dead. Three people who'd wanted nothing but an abandoned house to squat in, to be left alone to scrounge whatever kind of living they could. Now they were dead, because Sergeant Dean Craig was a fucking terrible soldier who should have been back home yelling at his junior salesmen, not deep in the shit with an assault rifle.

There were three of us who saw it. Craig turned on us next, and if he didn't exactly point that rifle at us, he didn't completely lower it, either. He told us the kid had drawn a gun, right? That's what we'd all seen, *right*? And Private Quint, he was this O.G. from Detroit, he just walked out. And Craig followed him, shouting, and neither of them noticed the sensors in the sand, I guess, because the next thing I knew, I was in that hospital bed that felt like the stink of naphthalene, and I was screaming.

There, outside the house, with a five-year-old's blood splattered on me, just as a scrambler hit, was the last time I saw Craig.

Of course I told them what had happened, once I could communicate again. I saw an army shrink who said he'd ask around, find out what'd happened. He couldn't turn up anything on either the incident or Craig. Sergeant Craig had ceased to exist, as far as the feds were concerned. It was a convenient way to deal with an inconvenient problem. The war was already unpopular, and the government didn't need to have the public hearing about soldiers gunning down five-year-olds.

And then my benefits ran out, and they threw me out into the world and told me to deal with it.

So I did. I got the simplest job I could find—washing dishes in a restaurant—and a one-room apartment that was the only thing I could afford. I slept a lot, got free meals at work, washed dishes, stayed to myself.

Dreamed a lot about five-year-olds wearing bullet holes, who followed me down dark alleys and looked at me with bloodshot, sad eyes, until I woke up gasping, maybe crying.

Only the music kept me going.

When you're scrambled, you find out pretty quickly that music can still get you off, but it has to be live; recorded music is like watching porn—close but not the real thing. So you go to a lot of clubs and concerts, and you soon realize that some bands are better at it than others. But only one band really gets it and plays to scrambleheads: The Violence. They play medium-sized clubs, so all of us can stand right in front of those fucking amps and feel every guitar lick and wailed lyric right in our groins. There are always a few civvies at the sidelines, and they must be wondering what the fuck's going on—they see a bunch of guys in old army fatigues jerking around near the stage with these ecstatic looks on their faces, because they can all feel the noise. We'll be there all night, and we'll come back every night.

The music was the only thing that kept my mind off the horror of what I'd seen. My job sure didn't; there's nothing more tedious than doing the same task over and over, and your thoughts starts to wander. In my case, it always wandered right back to a desert on the other side of the world and a trigger-happy asshole who'd killed a kid. My elbows immersed in warm, sudsy water meant seeing a five-year-old take a bullet in the chest yet again. And again. And again. Of course everything meant that; I saw it while I worked, while I ate, while I rode the train from home to work, and in my dreams while I slept. I saw it while I tried to parse what the boss said, while I tried to buy the right breakfast cereal, while I tried to read or watch things on television that I couldn't completely understand.

Sometimes I thought about really trying to find Craig; find him and somehow bring him to justice. If I could locate Quint and the other two guys who'd been there, we could all testify. But then I'd remember that the dishes I washed felt like the smell of spoiled food, and I knew I'd never find Craig or any of them on my own. I was fucked, and Craig was free.

And then Kevin arrived.

When we walked outside, what it was like getting scrambled wasn't the first thing we talked about; that actually came later. No, the first thing was what Kevin showed me. He held up his smart phone, hit a button, and let me watch a video.

I didn't do well with movies—they unreeled in my head with a stream of tastes and the feeling of being prodded all over. I couldn't figure this one any better than the latest 3-D Hollywood blockbuster, and I asked Kevin what it was.

"It's video from a helmet-cam. *Your* helmet-cam, specifically."

My heart did an arpeggio in my chest. "Is it Craig? Is it . . . ?"

Kevin nodded. "Shooting a little boy. And two other people. Do you remember this?"

I thought I might cry. My face grew hot, which in turn made me smell smoke. "Remember it? Man, I've been trying to forget it for three years."

"We acquired this from a source. The government thought they'd squelched it, but they just don't pay some of their workers enough."

"I tried," I told him, and I didn't care if he saw me wipe at my eyes, "God damn it, I tried to get them to listen to me, but they wouldn't, they told me it never happened, and—you're going public with it, right?"

The heady scent of a meadow on a warm summer day nearly overpowered me just then, and I knew that meant Kevin had put a comforting hand on my shoulder. "It's okay. Yeah, soon the whole world's going to see what Craig did, and know what happened to you. We just want to know that you'll back it up."

"I will. Fuckin' A, I will."

"Good. We'll take him down, then."

"If you can find him."

I tasted something odd—Kevin was looking at me strangely. "Uh, Jackson . . . "

"Call me Jack."

"Jack . . . " He stepped back, and I think he was looking deep into my eyes, like he was trying to see if my pupils were dilated, if I was high. I get that a lot. "He won't be hard to find."

"He won't?"

Kevin made a sound like a muscle jerk. "You can't recognize him, can you?"

My stomach started to knot. "Why?"

"Because he's right inside. In the club."

I went cold, and smelled nothing at all. "He's . . ." I couldn't get out anymore. It couldn't be true. "Show me," I said, a croak.

Kevin motioned, and I followed his blur of shifting flavors back into the club.

Just as we stepped inside, the band took the stage. The opening guitar chord struck me with a shiver, and I knew it'd hit the rest of the scrambleheads the same way. There must've been fifty of them there—every fucked-up vet on the eastern seaboard had come to get laid by the music, and as the guitar player lashed into the first song, they trembled with the foreplay stroke of fingers against skin.

I had to struggle to stay focused on Kevin, as he pushed through them. The rhythm had kicked in now, and the ex-soldiers before the stage had become a seething, gyrating mass. A lot of them must have been wearing their old fatigues, because I tasted sand-blasted metal and sweat. Kevin paused just long enough to examine each face before pushing through again, pulling me after him. They ignored him; he was just a whiff of smell intruding on the beautiful noise they were feeling.

Finally Kevin stopped, and I tried to look where he was looking. He'd paused before a man who tasted the same as all the rest, whose gasps provoked the same sandpapery sensations that the others did. I must have looked perplexed, because Kevin leaned over, put his mouth up against my ear, and I felt, "Craig."

I tried to look, God *damn* it, I tried, but the confused synapses in my brain sent the same wrong message. I had to take Kevin's word for it, that this was Sergeant Dean Craig, that this flood of sour tastes that made me gag was the murderer who had haunted me for three fucking years.

And then I knew: It was Craig. It had *always* been Craig. Of course—he'd been here right next to me, every time the band had played, show after show, night after night, for at least a year, and I'd been too fucked up to know it. He'd stood by me, shouting and gasping and ejaculating into his stained army pants just like I had, and every night I'd let him walk away from the show. Every night I'd let this fucking killer go home; it was practically like I'd helped the army bury Craig's crimes.

Except they'd done it skillfully; I'd done nothing, just sat back like a useless lump of flesh and let them all go on.

No more. Not tonight.

"Can I have your phone?" I asked Kevin. My new best friend, Kevin, a man my age who would never really understand what it was like to wake up screaming and feel the sound, although later I'd try to explain it to him, and he would nod and I'd taste his nod rather than see it, but he wouldn't get it. And then he'd put Craig away while I struggled against my own senses just to wash other people's food-stained plates.

Kevin gave me his phone. It was still set up to the helmet video, the one that would show the whole world what Craig had done, and his supporters had covered up. I fingered the "play" arrow. The video started. I hoped it was at the right place; I only knew I tasted something like the bottom of a garbage pail.

Craig was bouncing around with the rest, but he slowed and then stopped when I held the video up before his face. He was being assaulted with tastes that he couldn't put together, even though he tried. He knew it was bad. Really fucking bad.

I leaned over to him, screaming to be heard over the music, hoping he was at least as good as I was at unscrambling our scrambled signals.

"Craig," I shouted, my lips an inch from his ear, "you're fucked."

He felt that, all right, because he turned and stared at me. "Who the goddamn hell are you?" he asked, his body still trying to jitter to the music.

"Private Jackson Howard, *sir.*" I saluted him—and then, while my hand was still on my forehead, I uncurled only my middle finger.

That got through, because Craig panicked and bolted.

He didn't even make it off the dance floor before I caught up to him. I grabbed a fistful of his shirt and yanked him around, and for a split second my senses unscrambled, and I saw his face, his real face, at the same time as I saw his memory face, three years ago, as he stood over a dead family.

When my fist connected with Craig's face, I smelled ozone and rank fear sweat, and he dropped to the floor as I tasted bile . . . but the image in my head of a shot-up kid wasn't tainted with any sensation but horror, it was clear as yesterday, and it drove me to squat and hit him again. The music was still going, and they were playing my favorite song, but the release I was feeling was anything but sexual. It was knowing that the nightmares might end now, and that I might be able to get through a day without feeling/smelling my gut drop out whenever I thought about the war. It was knowing that the dark alleys in my dreams might be empty at last.

Then somebody—Kevin—was pulling me back, and I stumbled to my feet, and he shouted, "You got him, Jack. It's done."

I was panting and I knew there was blood on my knuckles, but I didn't care. The music took me, then, and it was a victory dance and an orgasm and a giant jitter of joy and relief all together.

The noise had never felt so good.

Lisa Morton is a six-time winner of the Bram Stoker Award®, a screenwriter, a novelist, and a Halloween expert whose work was described by the American Library Association's Readers' Advisory Guide to Horror as "consistently dark, unsettling, and frightening." Her most recent releases are the non-fiction books Ghosts: A Cultural History and Adventures in the Scream Trade. She lives in the San Fernando Valley, and can be found online at www.lisamorton.com.

THE SENSE
OF
HEARING

THOUGHTS ABOUT THE SENSE OF HEARING

BY JESSICA BAYLISS, PHD

 SHRIEKING LAUGH in the night. Knocking from inside the walls. The elastic surface of hundreds of balloons rubbing together.

Sound is a central part of the horror experience.

Our brains are built to link sounds to fear, and to remember them. The auditory cortex, the amygdala, and the hippocampus—the part of the brain that turns new information into memory—are all located in the temporal lobe. Because these structures are clustered together, auditory stimuli are processed almost instantaneously.

When it comes to fear, not all noises are created equal. Repetitive, low intensity sounds do not seem to bother the amygdala or auditory cortex all that much. Irregular, sharp noises, on the other hand, appear to have a direct, and immediate impact on our brains. In one study, researchers examined what types of sounds trigger high levels of negative emotion. It turned out that non-linear sounds caused the most fear. This makes sense. It is this type of sharp, irregular noise that is most likely to signal danger to an organism in the wild.

Where there is danger, there is fight-or-flight. Fight-or-flight means what it sounds like; in response to a threat, we run away or make our stand. In other words, we need to respond behaviorally when the threat comes at us. One area of the auditory cortex, the inferior colliculus, seems most important for communicating with motor areas to turn on the defensive behaviors we see during fight-or-flight—namely fighting, fleeing, and freezing.

Remember when I mentioned that the auditory cortex, amygdala, and hippocampus—the structure needed to turn new experiences into long-term memory—are directly wired together? That means the human brain is particularly good at *remembering* scary sounds.

Using traditional Pavlovian conditioning, laboratory animals learn to discriminate between similar tones. This is just like the Little Albert experiment with one small difference. For poor Albert, a fluffy white object meant a frightening sound was coming, and therefore he experienced fear. In animal studies, a particular tone is linked with a similarly aversive consequence—an electric shock. Rats literally learn what tones mean a shock is coming. Now, in the Little Albert experiment, the fear generalized. Watson used a white rat for the initial conditioning, but he also repeated it with other fluffy white things. In the end Albert feared everything from white stuffed toys to a Santa mask. This is desirable—I mean, not a Santa phobia; that's just cruel. But when it comes to stimuli that actually mean something, it would do no good to only respond to one specific example—the roar of only one kind of monster or the ring of a single type of blade being drawn from a sheath.

We would not live very long if we had to literally learn to fear each similar sound individually.

From an evolutionary standpoint, generalization makes sense, but the animal studies also showed the opposite to be true. While fear will often generalize from one stimulus to similar, related stimuli, animals can be taught to distinguish between similar sounds. The way researchers test this is to condition fear using a tone of a particular pitch. Scientists then vary the tones until they are only fractionally different from one another, and the animals learn which ones signal danger and which ones are safe—even when, initially, they were unable to tell the pitches apart.

All of these studies are totally cruel—poor Albert, poor rats—but they are also very informative. Unlike tactile sensations, which fear seems to dampen, fear can make hearing sharper. From an evolutionary standpoint, discrimination makes just as much sense as does generalization. The brain's ability to make these increasingly-fine distinctions can be just as advantageous as stimulus generalization—depending on the circumstance. If a zombie horde is waiting in the backyard, it would not be wise to run screaming from the house any time footfalls echo in the hallway (generalization), but learning what a zombie shuffling outside the bedroom door sounds like (discrimination)—that might be helpful.

But we are talking about fiction here, written stories, a silent medium. We cannot hear words on paper.

Actually, we can.

Mirror neurons in the auditory cortex respond when we imagine a sound and when we are listening for a sound we expect to hear. The auditory cortex can even be stimulated during periods of silence. In one study, researchers played popular music for participants—songs the participants knew. The researchers then interspersed these tracks with periods of silence, and the participants conveyed the sense that the songs continued despite the lack of stimulus.

And their brains responded in kind, as if there was no disruption to the music.

As readers, our brains can manufacture a complete sensory experience. So, whether we are actually listening to a ghostly whisper right near our ear, waiting for it to sound again, or reading about it, the auditory system is at work.

BOO! (Consider your auditory mirror neurons stimulated.)

IN THE CAVE OF THE DELICATE SINGERS

BY LUCY TAYLOR

EDITOR'S NOTES: Another story based on synesthesia follows after Lisa Morton's *Feel the Noise*, although unlike Lisa's take, this next selection finds the condition more normalized, as limited to only one type of synesthetic crossover (yet still being incredibly rare), that of "Hearing-Touch Synesthesia," in which tactile feelings are experienced upon the reception of sound waves or, as author Lucy Taylor describes: "Aural imagism, in which sounds are heard through the skin."

While some synesthetes suffer a variety of psychological traumas from the effects of this phenomenon, there are just as many who call synesthesia "a gift," and have learned to apply it in pushing past creative and cognitive boundaries that the rest of us encounter.

I've become very much enamored with Lucy's intense and expressive way of storytelling, especially as recently reading up on several of her latest works in preparation to interview her for the mobile reading app, Great Jones Street. Lucy's characters are rich with depth, her tales filled with natural fears—as well as supernatural ones—and her prose vivid to all the senses, as in the following rescue adventure: Karyn struggles for survival in a half-mile-deep underground system that is rumored to drive people mad with its song, *In the Cave of the Delicate Singers*.

"Her vocal tones prickled the soles of my feet; it felt like dancing on tiny ball bearings . . . "

I N SPITE OF ITS DARK HISTORY, the entrance to the Brotterling Cave complex, eleven miles south of Kremming, Kentucky, appears bucolic, even inviting—a rocky, green arch, swathed in bulblet ferns, Virginia creepers, and sumacs meandering in lazy zigzags along the slope of the hill. In summer, a sumptuous veil of ironweed and lobelia spills over the lava-dark basalt, and cavers, from novice to expert, grind up the mudhole-pocked logging road in their four-wheel-drives, leave their rides in the turn-around, and trek inside like ants marching into the maw of a sleeping triceratops.

Most of the time, they come back just fine.

I've caved in the Brotterling a few times myself, but never before alone and always in thoroughly mapped parts of the cave system. And even though I'd heard all the stories, I was never afraid.

Now I'm terrified.

Just before sunrise, a little over seven hours ago, I crept through the woods alongside the dirt road and slipped inside the leafy green mouth of the cave. Only Boone knew what I wanted to do, and he didn't approve it, of course—how could he, when he's captain of Bluegrass Search and Rescue? In the heat of our argument about how to find and extract the four cavers who are currently missing, he called me "reckless and goddamn delusional" and accused me of thinking I was invulnerable because "you've got that synthetic thing going on."

I bit back a laugh that would've embarrassed us both and told him the word was synesthesia and mine is a rare form in which sounds are "heard" through the skin as vibrations. I explained to him again how my ability could help in a situation where noises inside the cave appeared to be causing a neurological event in the brains of those exposed to them. I said I would go into the cave wearing the in-ear waterproof headphones I use on occasion to get relief from life's general babble, which can prove overwhelming for someone with my sound sensitivities. He just shook his head and looked at me like I was contesting the curve of the earth. But this morning, no one was posted at the cave entrance to stop me, so I took that as his tacit blessing.

Or maybe he was so desperate to get Pree and the others back that losing me is an acceptable risk, albeit one he won't sign off on.

As any caver around here will tell you, even minus the uncanny noises, the Brotterling can kill you in any number of ways. One is by tricking you into thinking it's not a damn dangerous cave. The first two hundred feet or so are deceptively easy: after you've slithered and squeaked past a row of huge boulders crowded together like a mouthful of gray, diseased teeth, the cave opens up like a belly. A bit farther on, you stroll down a broad, pebbly incline while the natural light gradually dims. The vertical slit of the opening shrinks to the size of a peach pit. Suddenly you find yourself in a constricted, mausoleum-black oubliette. You switch on your headlamp and commence the descent, scuttling through barely shoulder-width tunnels, snaking up vertical cracks, traversing a series of amber-blue lakes, some of which you can ford without getting your knees wet, others deepening into treacherous sumps where you'll drown if you don't have a rebreather or a damn good set of lungs.

Piece of cake was my grandiose appraisal the first time Pree Yazzie guided me through the Brotterling, but I was twenty then, brand-new to caving, recently graduated from the University of Louisville with an altogether useless BA in English lit, and just out of a closet I had not fully realized I even was in. I was also in love with her and thought it was mutual, a conclusion based on nothing more solid than a couple nights of hot sex. I didn't realize then that the only thing Pree ever lusted for was adventure, which she found in equal measure in caves, beds, and underground rivers. She came, she saw, etc. We'd met at a meeting of Search and Rescue, where Boone gave a presentation on abseiling techniques. I paid scant attention; Boone Pike was just another fortysomething, hardcore cave rat with a granite-gray ponytail, a smile like a crack in an anchor bolt, and big, spade-shaped hands that looked like they'd been crushed and pinned back together a time or two. I kept sneaking glances at Pree, the only other woman in a room full of men who, as the bumper stickers boast, "do it in tight places."

A line that would make me chuckle right now, if I could expand my squeezed lungs enough to get a full breath of air. Tight places, indeed.

During that day when Pree and I explored the Brotterling, she filled me in on the cave's not-so-savory past—how every few decades, a caver fails to resurface or, worse, crawls back out physically whole but with a maimed mind and homicidal intent.

Not quite what I wanted to hear a quarter mile under the earth, but I loved the sound of her voice when she explained the cave's frightening history.

The first incident was Dr. Reginald Moore, a caver and Presbyterian minister who spent four days lost in the Brotterling in 1935. Lacking modern caving equipment and (perhaps a greater hindrance) a suitably arachnid-like frame, he was thwarted by narrow tunnels and unswimmable sumps, but eventually found his way to the surface and described the "eerie and infernal yodeling" of demons who tormented him by chanting the Psalms backward in fiendish, fist-thumping cadences.

Widely mocked by the press, Moore later hung himself after setting fire to his house with his wife, father-in-law, and two young sons tied up inside.

Twenty-seven years later, Garth Tidwell, a teenager who entered the Brotterling on a dare, killed himself, his parents, and a neighbor hours after exiting the cave, writing in his suicide note about singing that sounded like "a wild hallelujah of wind chimes and fornicating bobcats."

The lurid description was dismissed as psychotic rambling, probably exacerbated by the terror of being alone and disoriented. If Tidwell had heard anything at all, it was explained away as wind hissing through passageways or water burbling up from an underground stream.

But now we come to the Hargrave brothers—Mathew and Lionel—experienced cavers who entered the Brotterling this past Sunday. Lionel, an Iraqi War Vet whose hearing was lost to a roadside IED in Mosel, is totally deaf. A few hours after the two men entered the cave, he emerged alone, battered and bloody. He described how, half a mile below the surface, Mathew had signed to him that he could hear music "coming from distant and delicate singers" and insisted they search for the source of the sound. For a while, Lionel obliged him, but when the way proved too difficult, he suggested they turn back. In response, Mathew became enraged, bludgeoned his brother with a rock, and left him unconscious and bleeding.

When Lionel finally found his way to the surface and summoned help, three senior members of Bluegrass Search and Rescue were dispatched—obsessive, spearmint-gum-chewing Bruce Starkeweather, extreme ectomorph Issa Mamoudi, and the ever elusive Pree Yazzie.

Boone's Dream Team.

That's when things started getting weird.

At nine that night, Starkeweather contacted Boone via cave phone to report high-pitched humming or chanting. Boone told him to return to the surface. The final transmission, a few hours later, came from a distraught, incoherent Mamoudi—mangled syntax and a garble of English, French, and Farsi that degenerated into choking and wails.

No one's heard from any of them since.

Which is how I come to be half a mile under the earth, worming my way through a twist in the moist, black, and aptly named Intestinal Bypass, a wretched, rib-crushing, claustrophobia-inducing belly crawl. Nearing the end, just a minute ago, I came to a plug in the tunnel about ten feet ahead. I can see the bottoms of dirt-packed, lug-soled boots, a damp, filthy oversuit, and, if I crane my neck almost out of joint, I can make out the white dome of a mud-splattered helmet. It's not Pree, who's waif-thin and wears size six boots, but one of the men, Hargrave, Mamoudi, or Starkeweather.

I crawl closer, scraping along on my elbows and toes, but get no reaction to the light flaring out from my headlamp. My initial thought is that the caver's become wedged in the last few feet of the Bypass, where the tunnel cinches like a cruelly corseted waist. The first time I came through here with Pree, I tore a rotator cuff trying to shove myself through the passage. Now, four years later and at least fifteen pounds thinner, it's still a brutal squeeze.

My second thought, after I grab a leg and begin shaking it, is that while he may or may not be stuck, this guy's stone-cold dead.

Which means if I can't push him out, I'm fucked.

Shit. Panic pinballs around my ribs. My lungs rasp, and all the air's vanished.

Forget whatever's inside the cave. Forget Pree and the chance of finding survivors. I want out of here—NOW!

Then a soothing, calm voice that I've trained for just such situations begins speaking inside my head: *Breathe, Karyn. Just breathe. You're okay. We'll figure this out.*

It's my own voice, the voice I've heard in other bad situations above and below ground, and I heed it. I must if I want to live. Gradually, I coax a full breath past the terror constricting my throat. I'm not going to die down here. Not yet, anyway. A numb resolve settles in: I can do this.

Trying to eject a dead guy out the end of a tomb-black tunnel while you're flat on your belly feels like a sadist's idea of a stunt on some nightmarish survival TV show. I push until my biceps blaze, but it's impossible to get any traction. I might as well be trying to strongarm Atlas's Dick, a colossal stalagmite cavers use as a waypoint in one of the Brotterling's upper chambers.

I strain and curse and hyperventilate. Drink tears and cold, musky sweat. The white noise churning through the headphones under my helmet provides an incongruous soundtrack to my struggle: monster breakers shattering on a raw, rocky coastline of black sand and a harsh sun (at least, this is the image I get of it). The sound's meant to protect me from the singing, but right now—pinched like a thumb in a pair of Chinese handcuffs—the buffering noise only intensifies the terror of being stuck in a limestone tube with a corpse.

Desperate, I decide to wiggle back out and look for another way to go on, but the tunnel twists and contorts at excruciating angles. It's impossible to slither out the way I came in. All I get for my efforts are bruised elbows, torn knees, and the mother of all wedgies.

Panic claws at my throat. *I'll never get out.* I'll die here, squished inside a stone straightjacket. But the voice in my head bullies and curses me onward, so I crawl back to the body. Since I'm not strong enough to rely on brute force, I devise a slow, minimalist series of tweaks that gradually loosens this obstinate flesh-cork in its stone bottleneck: nudge, twist, rock side to side, nudge again.

The poor son of a bitch must have died two to six hours ago, because rigor's setting in, which helps me extract him. He's plank-stiff and (I discover later) both arms are arrowed out in front of him like a cliff diver, the body so rigid by the time it finally pops free, he could double as a javelin or a maypole.

I wriggle out, shaking and sweat-slick, and aim my lamp down at the dead man, groaning when it illuminates the back of Mamoudi's seamed, bloodied neck and reveals the muddy helmet to be a porridge of gray matter and hair glommed around a split, trepanned skull. I picture Mamoudi frantically trying to birth himself out those last crushing inches of squeeze, the irony of a rockfall shattering his skull just as his head poked free. It's a reasonable theory, except that I don't see any fallen rocks or broken stalactites to back it up.

Looking around, I find myself in a wide, high-domed chamber forested floor to ceiling with dripstone. Farther back, overlapping ledges of white limestone crease and crinkle like bolts of brocade. The scene is enchanting and eerie, a grand Gothic hall carved out of calcite and ornamented with aragonite blooms. At one end glimmers a deceptively shallow-looking pond where eyeless albino salamanders laze on its mineral shores. I know from the survey map this is a sump, the entrance to a flooded tunnel leading into the next chamber, but whether it's swimmable without a rebreather, I won't know until I'm underwater.

Before I can ponder this or Mamoudi's demise any further, something more compelling than mere violent death snags my attention: a rapid-fire spitting of sound energy, like a mad tattoo artist bedeviling my nervous system with rhythm rather than ink.

The energy natters against my palms and wet-kisses the space between my breasts. I get a sense of its volume and pitch, the aural equivalent of a blind person reading Braille, and I'm lashed with fear and euphoria. Although I've come down here to find Pree and the others, I also want to locate the mysterious noise. Boone must have realized that too. It's why he didn't want me to go.

Displaced air caused by something big lunging out of a passageway makes me whirl around. A frenzy of shadows spills over the chamber as my lamp illuminates a surreal sight: Bruce Starkeweather, his naked torso smeared with geometric designs painted in cave dirt and gore, brandishing three feet of a blood-streaked stalactite.

His shell-shocked stare tells me all too clearly I'm nobody he's ever seen in his life, and my death is all he desires. As the sound energy from the faraway singing swells over me, he raises his club and charges.

"You should wear headphones to block out the sounds," I'd told Boone and the others less than twenty-four hours earlier. We were in a small conference room in the Timber Hill Lodge outside Kremming. A map of the known parts of the cave system was tacked up on a board, the shaded areas indicating parts not yet surveyed. Mamoudi and Pree sat together, guzzling coffee and wolfing down bear claws, while Starkeweather, ascetic as ever, stripped foil off a stick of Wrigley's.

Boone, unshaven and haggard-looking, had just come from the hospital where Lionel Hargrave was recovering from a concussion. He told us Hargrave had described his brother's manic insistence on finding the source of the singing. In his deafness, of course, Lionel heard nothing and, probably for that reason (and because he evidently had a thick cranium), had survived to talk about it.

At my remark about the headphones, Pree laughed. Boone looked away, and Mamoudi got up to refill his and Pree's coffee mugs.

I couldn't entirely blame them. I was technically there as backup, but since I'm also the newest member of the team and never found time to get my cave diving certificate, my inclusion in the expedition was unlikely.

Pree, looking fetchingly peeved, said, "How do we communicate if we can't hear? What are we supposed to do? Use sign language? Text?"

Starkeweather mimed headbanging. "Maybe it's a death metal band down there making people go batshit. That used to drive my old man insane."

Met with such thoughtful responses, what could I say? I wanted to point out that noise isn't always benign, that whatever's down there might be the aural equivalent of lobotomy picks jabbed into the brain via the ears. But it's only a feeling I have, and this group, Pree especially, is not into feelings.

Starkeweather asked a question about the survival kits, and while

Boone was responding, I went outside and paced alongside a thin strip of forest next to the parking lot.

After a short time, Pree came up beside me and tried to slide her arm beneath mine. I swatted her off like you would a pesky mosquito. Only a few hours earlier, she'd stopped by my apartment to try to rekindle some romance. We'd smoked a joint, laughed about old times. Then she took everything off except Mamoudi's engagement ring and made love to me like I was the last woman on earth. And I let her. Figured I'd hate myself for it later.

Seemed like *later* had come sooner than I expected.

"Seriously, Karyn," she was saying, "if anything goes wrong down there, if there's a problem, Issa and Bruce and I will deal with it. We know the Brotterling, and we know what we're doing. So, don't try anything heroic." She should've stopped there, but she added, "I know it must be tempting, you with your superpowers and all."

I glared and walked faster.

"Okay, sorry. It's just that hearing sounds through your skin, that's pretty bizarre."

That's one word for it. It's also a gift, this intertwining of hearing and touch, where sounds can be physically felt as everything from a shy tap to a punishing blow. It's a door into something most people never experience. Pree's voice, for example, feels lemony, tart. It fizzes under my nails and buzzes up my spine like spikes of Kundalini flame. Intimacy enhances the effect. Pree's voice used to give me not just sensations but images, too: a fire crackling in the kiva of a house that must be from her childhood in Gallup, New Mexico, a young Pree popping figs into her mouth outside an adobe church, and a pale, bearded man who cooed to her while he lay over her body and pounded. My skin drank her life in through her voice. None of this, of course, I could tell her.

"Bizarre's not the word I'd have chosen," I said. "But when you put it that way, I feel so special."

"You are special, though, aren't you? You got written up in that magazine."

She was talking about a story that ran in *Scientific American* (June 2008), in which I was tested along with a number of other more "traditional" synesthetes. Some heard colors; others tasted or smelled numbers and words. An anomaly even among anomalies, I was the only one who could pick up tactile sensations and images via sound waves, even when I didn't understand the language. "Aural imagism," the writer of the article called it.

I sat with my eyes closed and listened to a woman recite the same passage in a foreign language over and over. Later, I learned it was Finnish. Her vocal tones prickled the soles of my feet; it felt like dancing on tiny ball bearings. The vibrations of her voice formed images like patterns in a turned kaleidoscope. I described a dark red cup, a yellow rose, a strange bird on the wing. The man doing the testing glanced at his notes and paled. The speaker had read a quatrain from the Rubaiyat of Omar Khayyam, and I'd just described the primary imagery.

Pree laid a hand on my biceps, but I flinched, holding on to my indignation like it was a winning lottery ticket.

I said sullenly, "Boone's screwing up not to send me down with you. I'd be able to feel the singing before the rest of you even heard it."

She sighed and fell into step with me.

"Look, Karyn, you've been inside plenty of caves. You know what the silence is like down there. Gigantic. A void you don't want to fall into. Then all of a sudden, you hear something so spooky and so unexpected, you just about crap in your pants. If you heard it topside, you'd know it was nothing, maybe the caver in front of you farted or dropped a carabiner, but underground, it's terrifying. Most cavers shrug that stuff off, but some people can't. They have panic attacks; they hallucinate. For all we know, what Hargrave heard was a colony of bats or maybe a few million cave cockroaches."

When I didn't answer, she snapped, "Dammit, Karyn, are you even listening?"

(More intently than you can imagine.)

"Maybe Hargrave went crazy because the singing he heard was too beautiful," I said.

"What are you talking about?"

"There's a line in the *Duino Elegies* by the German poet, Rainer Maria Rilke. It's something to the effect that beauty is the beginning of terror we can just still stand. Maybe that's the deal with the singing. It triggers a level of terror humans aren't meant to endure. It's too beautiful."

Her mouth set in a pinched line. I thought she was going to slap me. "Nothing's *too* beautiful. That isn't possible." Then before I could argue, she gave me a punch on the arm that was too hard to be play. "Don't worry, Karyn, it's gonna be fine." She looked back toward the motel as though somebody there had just called her name, although nobody had. She said, "See you on the surface, babe," and hurried away.

Right now, as the sound energy of the singing floods into me and Starkeweather charges, that surface Pree spoke of might as well be on one of Jupiter's moons.

Starkeweather halts just short of the sump. He spits out a lump of gum, bares his teeth in a cannibal grin, and takes a few warm-up swings with the club. I think he's going to pound me to mud, but to any real caver, what he does next is unimaginably worse: he starts attacking the cave itself, swinging viciously, destroying elaborate lacework and yards of dripstone that have grown at a rate of a half inch per century. Clusters of wedge-shaped helictites explode overhead; stalagmites as tall as a man shatter and crash into the sump. The destruction sickens and horrifies me.

Within seconds, something sublime and ethereal has been reduced to an empty mouth full of snaggled teeth. Starkeweather, surveying the rubble, cocks his head and does a bizarre little jig, like he's shaking off a swarm of cave spiders. He shimmies and scrapes at his face while his lips form the words, *Shut up! Make it stop!*

When his eyes refocus, his red gaze finds me again. I switch off my headlamp, and the world floods away in a torrent of black. I drop to the ground and start inching along the cave floor. The headphones are a real hindrance now; they prevent me from hearing which way Starkeweather's moving. The only sound I can feel is the singing, and that has receded to a shivery caress, a centipede skittering over my eyelashes, a salamander disturbing the roots of my hair.

A hail of stones peppers my back and pings off my helmet. Suddenly, Starkeweather's big hands paw at my legs. I kick out blindly. My boot thuds meaty groin. Then he's on top of me, spearmint breath hot in my face, mud-slick fingers fumbling for my jugular. A blacker, thicker shade of night starts shutting down synapses, accompanied by a dazzle of sizzling white stars expiring behind my retinas.

Under my hand I clutch a slab of smashed dripstone and heave it in the general direction of his head. He releases my throat but then latches on to either side of my mouth and tries to unsocket my jaw. I bite down on a finger until my teeth close on a nugget of bone, then roll away as blood fills my mouth. Next thing I know, I'm underwater. The sump's frigid and inky, and—

Starkeweather be damned—I switch my headlamp back on. I'm inside a flooded tunnel where so much silt has been stirred up, it's like swimming through horse piss. I look for an air pocket overhead but can make out only jutting mineral walls and the segmented bodies of albino worms ghosting behind swirls of particled water.

My lungs bleed for air. The sump narrows into a long, jagged throat, where beyond, water splashes over a pale, fluted ledge. Between me and the air glitters a gauntlet of stone cudgels and knives. My cave pack rips off and my oversuit's torn. Dark red snakes squiggling too close alarm me until I realize I'm batting away my own blood. My head punches the surface, and I heave myself onto a milk-white dome of flowstone, then collapse across it, teeth wildly clattering.

Eventually, I rally enough to fill my hands with rocks and wait to see if Starkeweather follows me.

A short time later, he pops to the surface floating facedown. I let him stay like that for five minutes before I grab his belt and haul him up next to me. His neck and cheeks are grotesquely ballooned. When I turn him over, jagged pebbles and mineral chips mixed with shattered enamel gush out of his mouth in a torrent of red. I want to think Starkeweather was already dangerously unstable and would have acted out sooner or later, but I don't really believe it. I know the singing has unhinged him to the point of attacking the cave with his teeth—the same sounds Mamoudi and Hargrave must have heard, and that Pree, if she's still alive, is hearing right now.

It feels stronger and a helluva lot closer than it did before I passed through the sump. Those previously faint waves of energy are now sharp and urgent, a persistent scratching at various parts of my body, like a frantic child seeking entry to a house at one door and one window after another.

But the images accompanying the sensations aren't so innocuous: a debased horde of humanity crammed into a stadium of bleeding, cruelly crushed bodies, on their knees weeping and howling. Heads thrown back, ready for the knife, keening mad invocations to an obscene deity. Their blood soaks the earth, out of which bloom stone flowers brimming with nectar and death. The vision claws at my heart and I hear my own voice telling me to get moving, to find Hargrave and Pree and get out.

It's hard to obey. I go on.

The next chamber confounds me: a sprawling catacomb dripping with soda-straw stalactites and mounded with nodular masses of calcite popcorn. Crystals of moonmilk, a carbonate material the texture of cream cheese, festoon the floor. None of it corresponds to any maps I've seen. Even worse are the braided mazes of lava tubes offering a bewildering array of possible paths deeper into the cave's interior.

But the cave, in its infernal sentience, appears to respond. The energy of the singing amplifies, the frequencies becoming imperative, like the head of a silky mallet pinging a flesh xylophone. Letting it guide me, I scramble up a succession of ledges to access a passageway midway up the wall. Its coiled path empties into an angular chamber that resembles a vandalized ossuary: stone pillars surrounding a scattering of femurs, ribs, clavicles, and fragments of skull. That the bones have lain here since long before cavers first discovered the Brotterling is made clear by the centuries-old webs of calcite deposits that veil them.

I pick my way through the boneyard as quickly as possible. Beyond it, my headlamp illuminates the area from where the sound energy seems to emanate—a lavish display of boxwork about four feet overhead, where calcite blades project at angles from the cave walls, creating a dense and elaborate honeycomb.

Between the mineral blades gleam dark seams, fistulas of ebony pulsing like fat heaps of caviar that vibrate with an avid, luminescent life. Fine, blood-red webbing threads through the black, a network of alien capillaries that carries not blood but warm, coppery sound—it seeps under my scalp and teases behind my ears, seeking to peel back and penetrate the soft, vulnerable creases of brain.

If I get out of here alive, I know what I'll tell Boone: the singing's not random or chaotic; it has distinct meters and color tones, and it pulses with dark languor underlaid with vicious intent.

I will tell him the creators of this song are not human, but not unsentient, either. And if the term *life-form* applies to them at all, it's a life in service only to the obliteration of all others.

Long stretches of spellbound time pass as I stand here, watching the tiny caviar mouths pulse and burble out a black saliva of sound that feels ripe and almost sexually decadent.

Avid and succulent and, yes—Mathew Hargrave nailed it—delicate, too.

I want to slather my hands in the mineral meat between those basalt blades, squeeze up fistfuls of its alien iridescence and lather it into my pores, let it replace all the blood in my body with its unholy wails.

I take off my helmet and hurl it away. Then I reach up to remove the headphones.

And stop. Above me, imbedded into the hivework, loom strange columns worked into the stone, skeletal formations lifting toward the obsidian sky. Sections are patterned with ovoids and creases of lighter stone, the pale areas inlaid with vertical striations of crimson. The sight wallops the breath from my chest.

One of the columns is watching me.

Basalt doesn't bleed, but burst eyeballs and lacerated skin weep red down the sides of the dripstone cloaking two human forms in their mineral shrouds. Mathew Hargrave has been almost entirely consumed. Crusts of muscle and gashed bone jut out from his stone sarcophagus. Only his upper chest, the arms tucked into his torso like folded wings, and his slack, swollen face are still recognizably human. His remains are being played like a bone flute as torturesong rasps from his mouth.

But Pree, oh Pree, is another matter. Her time inside the Brotterling has been briefer than Hargrave's; less of her has been entombed. Rigid and ashen-faced, she balances on a narrow outcrop a few feet above, tarry squiggles of hair falling over the rags of her clothing. Her mouth convulses in torment. Skeins of sound tangle in her teeth and snake from her lips. Tendrils of it adhere to her face. The frequency of the vibrations chugs to the lowest registers, rich and mellow, bassoon-like, the notes unspooling in hypnotic spirals, so that each births the next lower note on the scale, and all the while, Pree's terrified eyes tell me the truth: it's a death song and she can't help but sing it.

Black rings frame the edge of my vision as Pree's silent screams flail me. Her body spasms. A rent opens under her breast as the slender spear she's impaled on exits her chest in a gleaming red fist. Behind two snapped ribs, I glimpse a gray, pulpy thing beating feebly.

The ledge is slick and cushiony, weirdly flesh-like, when I climb up, wrap my arms around her, and try to lift her free from the stone. Crimson bubbles erupt from her mouth. She tries to form words. I put my face close to hers as she exhales. Her death-rattle breath goes into me like an intubation tube, rancid and chokingly floral. There are no last words, no blessing, just a sob that's a truncated ode to damnation as she bleeds and convulses in front of me.

And I leave her. God help me, I abandon her there and begin the torturous trek to the surface, a wet, nasty, soul-crushing ordeal, while with every step, I expect the cave to crush or consume me. Most of the way, when I'm not using my hands to climb or to crawl, I clutch at the headphones, terrified they'll fall off and the singing will overpower and annihilate me.

Yet despite hours of exhaustion and terror, somehow I prevail. The passages, in fact, seem to widen as I pass through, the skin-you-alive cold of the sump is less heart-stoppingly frigid, the waypoints more easily spotted. Even the terrifying Bypass, outside of which Mamoudi's body still sprawls, feels smooth as a tube and excretes me effortlessly.

When I finally reach the surface, blinking and bedazzled by the afternoon light, a small army of cavers, media, and National Guard are assembled, as another team of cavers prepares to go down. Boone's there among them. Seeing me alive, his eyes well, as do mine. I tear off the headphones and sweet sound rushes in, the wind whistling, a truck backfiring, the crowd erupting into ecstatic cheers to see someone come out alive.

Then they get a good look at me and my appearance—soaked, shivering, smeared with cave dirt and blood—shocks them silent. As one, they reel back. Finally the braver ones gather their wits and being firing off questions.

What happened?

What's down there?

Is anyone else still alive?

But these are not words the way I remember them. What I hear is a saw-toothed cacophony, an unwholesome chorale—discordant, repellant, impure.

I want to rush back inside the cave to get away from their cawing, but I remember that first, I have something important to do. I must warn them of the terrible danger, so I focus my mind and conjure the sounds I will need. When I know what I must say, I run toward Boone, who is already beckoning me. I scream, *Get back! Get away from the cave! Everyone inside is dead!*

But that's not what comes out.

An excruciating hitch unlocks in my chest as an arcane melody, a kind of cryptic trilling, slithers free and soars to the winds—the feral and wondrous, delicate song birthed from the mouths of monsters, from Pree's mouth into mine—into theirs.

Madness made tangible.

Contagion by sound.

It spews from my lips—a song of such deadly beauty and unholy allure that I experience only the briefest frisson of horror—an emotion something inside me instantly quells—when their mouths fall open, songstruck, enthralled, and they begin to rend their own flesh and tear each other apart.

I understand this is how it must be. I go on, unfazed by the carnage, undeterred by the din.

For I am the throat of the Delicate Singers.

In the cities, the towns, in the streets, and beyond, I know others are waiting to hear me.

Lucy Taylor *is is an award-winning author of horror and dark fantasy. She has published seven novels, including the Bram Stoker Award-winning* The Safety of Unknown Cities, *six collections, and over a hundred short stories. Her work has been translated into French, Spanish, Italian, Russian, German, and Chinese.*

Her most recent short fiction can be found in the anthologies The Beauty of Death: Death by Water *(Independent Legions Publishing),* Tales of the Lake Volume 5 *(Chrystal Lake Publishing),* Endless Apocalypse *(Flame Tree Publishing),* Edward Bryant's Sphere of Influence *(Charles Anderson Books), and* A Fist Full of Dinosaurs *(Charles Anderson Books).*

A new collection, Spree and Other Stories, *was published in February 2018 by Independent Legions Publishing. Her science fiction/horror novelette "Sweetlings" was a finalist for the 2017 Bram Stoker Awards in the category of Long Fiction.*

Her short story "Wingless Beasts" is included in Ellen Datlow's The Best of the Best Horror of the Year, *to be published in late 2018.*

Lost Eye Films, a UK-based, independent production company, has purchased the rights for a film version of "In the Cave of the Delicate Singers."

Taylor lives in the high desert outside Santa Fe, New Mexico.

SOUNDS

BY KATHRYN PTACEK

EDITOR'S NOTES: I happened to be reading J.N. Williamson's 1991 anthology, *Masques IV*, while I contemplated creating *The Five Senses of Horror.*

I thought how much time and work this new anthology project would be, and I estimated six months to read for appropriate material, and that I'd have to scour every magazine back issue and moldering paperback collection I could find to assemble a wide-ranging embodiment of senses used in different ways in short horror fiction . . . Of course, that afternoon I picked up *Masques IV* where I'd left off, and the very next story was the following by Kathryn Ptacek. If only all my selections were as easy to come by!

Following, Faye Goodwin suffers from hypersensitive hearing, a real-life condition that in several variations affects millions of people in the world. It can be something a person is born with or it can develop with age or by damage to hearing, characterized by intolerability to specific frequencies heard at loud levels.

Kathy Ptacek fills the pages with identifiable imagery, capturing the predominant symptoms of this affliction—noise triggers, quick startle reflex, and increasing irritation—while the tale unfolds in a torturous escalation of tension and . . . *Sounds.*

"Face it, we live in a noisy world, and it's not going to get any quieter . . . "

*H*AMMER, HAMMER, HAMMER.

Faye Goodwin pursed her lips, sighed, and pulled the pillow over her head. Damned roofers.

Hammer, hammer.

Even through the thickness of feathers, she could still hear the whacking of the workmen's hammers on the slate roof next door.

She opened an eye. Read the clock. 7:07. In the morning, for God's sake, on her one day off this month—a Friday to make a long and very welcome weekend—and she had to be awakened by that damned whacking.

Someone started a buzzsaw. She winced.

She glanced over at her husband, Tommy, lying serenely on his back, one arm flung over his face. He was soundly asleep, would remain soundly asleep no matter what noise followed.

She envied him. She sighed, punched up her pillow, closed her eyes. She would fall asleep again, and she would sleep until nine, maybe even ten, and then—

A drill whined.

She sat up in bed.

"W-What?" her husband mumbled, only disturbed a little from her abrupt motion. Then he was asleep again, snoring mildly.

Snoring.

There'd be no more sleep for her today.

She shook her head, pushed the covers back, and got out of bed. She went to the window in the hallway and stared out at the workmen. They went on their ways blithely, completely unaware of her baleful glare.

She knew the workmen had to get an early start or they'd be working too many hours in the 90-plus temperatures under a burning sun. *But still.* Couldn't they go about these improvements a little more silently? She grinned at the thought. She went into the bathroom, washed her face, and even over the running water she could hear the hammers rapping.

Ignore it, she told herself, not for the first time. She tried to blot out the alien sound, tried to concentrate on the rushing water, a much more serene sound. A gentle, soothing frequency, hypnotic almost, quiet and peaceful and—

Tap, tap, tap.

No good.

She stepped into the shower, turned on the water full blast, and only then under the stinging stream did the other noise fade away.

She dressed, swallowed an aspirin. It was going to be one of *those* days.

Downstairs she retrieved the newspaper off the porch steps, sat down at the table to enjoy her first cup of hot tea for the day. The dining room windows faced onto the house under renovation, and she could see the crew crawling like immense ants over the gray roof.

Before she could get more irritated, she got up and pulled the windows down. The noise dimmed a little, but didn't go away.

A few minutes later, Tommy came downstairs. "Mornin'," he said, as he bent over to kiss her. He smelled of some lemony aftershave, and she smiled.

"Sleep well?" she asked.

"As always," he said, going into the kitchen. "You?"

She shrugged.

"Woke up again, huh?"

"Yeah."

"Maybe you need some sort of sleeping pill, something over the counter."

She sloshed her tea around in the mug. "I think I've tried just about every one out there. They work for the first night or two, you know, and then after that I keep waking up. In fact, I think they keep me awake."

"Well," Tommy said, sliding into the chair opposite her and dipping his spoon into his bowl of cereal, "maybe you should go to see a—"

"A therapist?" Faye asked, her voice a slightly sarcastic.

"Let me finish, okay? I was going to say a hypnotist."

"Oh. I hadn't thought of that."

"A guy at the office went to one—I could probably get the name, if you want—and he quit smoking. He used to smoke two, three packs a day."

She nodded thoughtfully. "Get the name, if it's no bother. I think that might be good. Sure is worth a try, I guess."

"Maybe you can take a nap today."

"Not with that going on," she pointed with her chin toward the windows.

"Isn't it kind of warm in here? Do you want the windows closed, Faye?"

"I wanted to cut down on the racket."

He gave her *That Look*—the expression she always hated, and always felt held more than a little condescension. "Hon, you've really got to do something about that. Face it, we live in a noisy world, and it's not going to get any quieter." He took his bowl out to the kitchen and ran water in it.

She made a face at his back, then looked down at her mug. She didn't know why she did that, except that she always suspected that he really didn't understand how horrible it was for her. How bad the level of noise could get.

"It would be much more quiet if we lived in the country," she said.

He stopped. "Hon, don't start on that again. I told you that with the cost of property, we just can't afford it. At least right now. If one of us gets a raise, maybe we can sock the extra dough away. Until then you'll just have to put up with a boisterous town. At least it's not the city."

She said nothing.

"See you later." He kissed her again, picked up his jacket and, a few minutes later, she heard him chatting with the workmen. Then the car started up. It popped and sputtered; the engine needed tuning.

Faye gritted her teeth.

With her mug in hand, she wandered into the living room and draped herself across the easy chair and turned on the TV. She didn't normally watch television in the daytime, but she was curious to see what was on at this hour. An earnest-looking host talking about incest, and some quiz show with lots of buzzers and flashing lights, a nature show about koalas, a couple of music stations, the weather channel, CNN, others. She flipped through the stations, then flipped through them again as if expecting to find something else, then finally turned the TV off. Too much noise.

From one of the houses across the street she heard the faint beat of rock music. Something by some heavy metal group.

Swell.

A car went by on the street, the windows rolled down, a Bach concerto blasting out.

Not even the classics were sacred, she thought with a faint smile.

Enough of this. Faye stood, looked around the room. So, what was she going to do? Well, she could go to the mall, but that meant a thirty-minute drive, crowds, and that maddening piped-in elevator music that followed her everywhere. Couldn't people survive without having to listen to something every minute?

No, the mall was definitely out. The grocery store was not. Once there, she claimed a cart and started up and down the aisles.

The PA system played songs from the late '60s, all homogenized into bland music. The system crackled and a man's voice announced a special today on lean ground beef. He droned on about all the different uses for ground beef. Finally, the ad ended, and the music—the Beatles' "I Want To Hold Your Hand," one of her favorites—came on, slowed-down and in mid-tune.

That irritated her even more, but she wasn't sure which was more offensive: the lackluster renditions of the music or just the plain fact that there *was* music.

She didn't know why she hated noise so much; since her early childhood she'd been particularly noise-sensitive, at least that's what her mother had called it. Faye had always disliked loud voices and sounds, and would crawl into her parents' large walk-in closet when thunder boomed outside. She could hear the whine of air conditioning as she walked into department stores when no one else could. Once she'd begun crying as a small airplane droned, circling over their house. Her father had said it was simply a stage that she would outgrow; only she hadn't.

Instead, it had grown worse, much worse.

Most of the time she had an uneasy truce with her sensitivity. Then there were the other times . . . days like today.

Somewhere, maybe a few rows over, a young child began crying.

Faye waited for the child to stop, but it didn't; it was building to an enthusiastic crescendo. It was a wonder those small lungs didn't give out. Her hands clenched on the cart handle. She braked before the paper products and tossed in rolls of paper towels.

The wailing grew louder. The high-pitched voice rose and fell in a pathetic undulation. The mother's voice was shrill, telling her child that the child really shouldn't cry.

Faye shook her head in disgust. The mother ought to just say *no*, and then bop the kid on the butt once or twice. That would stop the whining. God knows, it had happened enough to her when she was small. Of course, she hadn't been prone to pitching temper tantrums, either. That wasn't allowed in her family,

A gentle throbbing began in her temple; her headache was returning.

Faye pushed her cart toward the end of the aisle, trying to get away from the noise. But it followed her wherever she went.

She hurried through the produce section, lobbed lettuce and radishes and spinach into the basket. She would surprise Tommy with a really big salad tonight. Somewhere else in the store another child began crying, picking up the refrain of the first. Then a third started whimpering.

When she got to the check-out stand, Faye flung her items onto the belt as quickly as possible and watched the checker ring them up one by one.

"How can you stand to work with all this noise? These kids must drive you crazy."

The checker, a woman with a big black mole on her chin, shook her head. "Don't hear it after a while. It just sort of blends together pretty soon."

"You're lucky."

"Yeah, I guess so. That's $23.50. You should have been here when they were remodeling the store." The checker shook her head. "We had hammering and drilling from morning to night. It was terrible."

Faye shuddered, then returned home. The workers were still next door; she had entertained some vague hope they might have called it quits for the day.

Right.

After she took several more aspirin, she wandered into the living room. She was going to read. Really she should do a little housework, but she knew she couldn't take the howling of the vacuum cleaner.

She read for a while and only gradually became aware of another noise, a clanging and banging. She glanced out the window and saw the garbage men. Why, she wondered, when the garbage cans were plastic now, did these guys have to make all this noise? The truck moved slowly down the street, the noise finally receding.

It was noisy at the office, too, where she worked as a staff writer. Her job was to translate computer talk into people talk, and the constant clatter of printers and phones and people talking, chairs squeaking, doors being slammed, grated. Some days she wondered how anyone—how she—could stand it. But no one complained about the noise, and she figured she was just being sensitive.

Too damned sensitive for her own good—wasn't that what her father always said?

At lunch she fixed a cheese sandwich and had a soda, and while she was sitting at the dining room table still reading, she heard a high-pitched whining. Like a buzzsaw, only she knew *that* sound very well. Even over the sound of hammering and the shouts of the workmen, she could hear the new grating noise.

She stepped out onto the front porch; the sound grew louder.

Something bright flashed along the street. The whining came from it.

It turned out to be one of those remote control cars, and she watched as a man with his young son played with the toy. Around and around it went, then up and down in front of her house. It was nice that he was with his son, but why couldn't they have found something silent, like a kite, to play with?

She found herself gritting her teeth, forced herself to relax, went back in and closed the front door and windows facing that direction.

Not good enough, but the best she could do.

She read until the kids came home from school, then, her finger marking her place in the book, she looked out the window and watched as the junior high kids cut across her lawn. They yelled to one another, and one of them held a large silver radio that blasted out some loud song with a fast beat. They cursed at each other, and pushed each other around, and shouted, even though they were standing only a few feet away from each other.

Didn't kids speak in civil tones anymore? In *hushed* tones? she wondered.

One of the kids broke away and clambered up the steps of the house next door.

Oh no...

John was home, and she knew what would come next.

A few minutes later the kid stuck a trumpet out the window facing Faye's house and began playing scales. He knew somehow that she hated the sound of that damned instrument, so he was always faithful about practicing it every afternoon when he got home from school, and every evening before he went to bed. She tried to put the brassy sound of the trumpet out of her mind, but she couldn't.

It had always been hard to deal with, this noise sensitivity. She'd tried ear plugs years before, but they really hadn't helped. She tried ignoring the sounds, but couldn't concentrate fully.

Maybe the hypnotist Tommy had mentioned that morning would help; she hoped so. All these noises were driving her crazy.

It didn't help that Tommy snored so loudly at night that she woke up and was unable to go back to sleep until she came downstairs and camped out on the sofa. Even then, she'd be able to hear the snoring faintly, but at least it no longer kept her awake.

And he always kept the television volume much too high, just like her father had. Her father had been slightly deaf, though; Tommy was still young. Maybe she would suggest that he have his hearing checked out.

She knew hers didn't need it.

At least, she thought, the boy and his father and the awful toy had gone off. Maybe the thing was broken; that'd be good news.

Her mother had been the type to slam drawers and doors. If she was mad, slam went a dresser drawer. Or the door to the oven. Or the backdoor. With each jar, Faye had jumped. She was always glad that she came from a family of three rather than thirteen.

She went back to her book.

After a while, over the blasting of trumpet, she heard the ticking of the clock in the hallway. Tommy had bought that for their last anniversary. With each swing of the brass pendulum there was a resonant echo, like the striking of a padded hammer on wood. Almost a muffled sound. But not muffled enough.

The refrigerator went on. The appliance needed work, and for years it had made cooing noises, like a dove. Sometimes at night as she lay in bed, trying to sleep, she could hear that persistent cooing.

Water dripped from the kitchen faucet. Drop by drop. She would have to remind Tommy again this weekend to get a new washer for the faucet. They were wasting too much water.

Her headache was back, and growing worse. It was centered over one eye and throbbed. She bet if she put her fingers on that spot she'd feel it pulsating. She got up and took some more aspirin, took a deep breath, and told herself to relax.

Somewhere, on the other side of the street, a phone rang, and a loud voice answered, and she listened to a conversation she didn't want to hear.

A car, gunning its engine, sped by.

Kids squealed as they played in their front yards.

Blue jays squawked in the mulberry tree outside her window.

A lawn mower growled two houses down.

Tommy really was pretty good about all of this, she told herself. She tried not to complain about the noise, because he didn't understand. No one—not even her closest friends—did, because none of them could hear as well as she could. They all complained about varying hearing loss, and she always thought that they were the lucky ones, that she was the cursed one.

Someone with a weed wacker worked in the yard where the lawn mower still roared.

A jet shrieked overhead.

You're too sensitive, her father always grumbled, as if it were really something she could control.

The neighbor next door, father to the trumpet player, began working on the sports car he never drove. She heard the racing engine, a grinding of gears, the beeping of the horn.

Another phone shrilled.

It was just that she never could seem to get away from the noise. It was always badgering her, assaulting her. She hated it.

A television blared.

Somewhere a woman giggled, a high-pitched irritating noise.

Too sensitive.

A piano—someone playing "Heart and Soul" over and over—blended with the trumpet.

The pulsating pain returned.

Another jet shrieked overhead.

An ambulance, or perhaps it was a police car, raced down the next block, the wailing siren rising and falling, rising and falling.

Another lawn mower roared into life, while the kid and his father returned with the remote control car.

Too damned sensitive . . .

The refrigerator hummed again, while the furnace rumbled on.

Her phone rang. And rang, and rang, and rang, and still she sat on the couch, and listened to all the noises of the house and her neighborhood.

Tommy parked the car in the driveway, waved to old Mr. Miller who was just finishing clipping his hedges two doors down. He went into the house.

"Faye, hi, I'm home."

He heard nothing but the ticking of the grandfather clock in the hallway. He listened for running water, thinking she might be taking a bath, but he didn't hear it. Maybe she was out back.

"Faye?" This time louder.

Still no answer.

He heard something from the kitchen, and he realized she was in there, probably making dinner.

He stopped on the threshold of the kitchen. "Hi, hon, how are you?"

She stood at the counter with her back to him. She was cutting up vegetables for a salad.

"Hon?" Was this a game, he thought with a sly smile? Then: was she mad at him for some reason and ignoring him?

He stepped closer.

On the counter, not far from the salad bowl, he saw an ice pick, and a smear of something red on the countertop.

"Honey, I got the name of the hypnotist; it's some guy who just—" he began, then stopped when Faye turned around and he saw the blood trickling from her ears.

Kathryn Ptacek has published short stories, novels, articles, poetry, interviews, and various whatnots in a number of genres over the years. She edited the landmark anthologies Women of Darkness *and* Women of Darkness II *(both from Tor). She edits the monthly newsletter of the Horror Writers Association from her old Victorian house [complete with spirits] located in scenic northwest New Jersey.*

MALLEUS, INCUS, STAPES

BY SARAH TOTTON

EDITOR'S NOTES: *Malleus, Incus, Stapes* by Canadian author Sarah Totton proves to be—besides a gracefully-wrought piece of family ghosts and dark fantasy—a bit of study of the actual physiology of the middle ear and of hearing. The title, in fact, may even remind one of a certain anatomy lesson in high school biology, which is fitting as Sarah is a veterinarian by way of her day job.

Sounds and echoes and means for audio storage: Can the phantoms of voices linger, can we experience the past through hearing?

Beautiful and emotionally resonant, the following selection invokes young love and family obligation, when a boy discovers a trunk containing relics from his dead father, including an object that allows him to listen to the past as heard through his father's ear.

> *"Sound virtually exploded out of the conch: the sound of breaking brush, twigs snapping, leaves rustling . . ."*

THAT NIGHT IN HIS FATHER'S yellow brick house, up the first floor staircase, wide and wooden, up the second, narrow and steep, through a low doorway in the attic bedroom with wooden walls and floor and a sloping roof, Jack lay awake and fretted about his girl. Rain battered the roof like waves striking a ship's hull. Rain that seeped through the wooden roof and pinged in the metal wastebasket beside the bed. Jack stretched out his hand and caught the cold drops on his palm.

Lillian. Lillian by the lake in the park. Her hair like sea froth on the back of his hand. He felt like he would burst with feelings for her, that his bones would split like trees in the cold.

The wind pressed the window in his bedroom, bowing the glass, and the crumpled balls of paper on the desk rustled in the draft. Jack had been writing poems for Lillian, but they'd all come out tangled, embarrassing messes. What were words to her anyway? If he gave her something she could touch, something special that meant something to him, then things would be different.

He sat up in bed, pulled the light cord and scanned the room. His aunt had scoured the house of all his father's personal effects. The attic bedroom was virtually empty, but in the shadowy corner deep in the angle of the roof he found another, lower door that opened into the attic proper. He had always been small for his age, and he squeezed through easily. In the darkness and dust at the very back of the attic, he found a crate balanced across the joists. The damp wood bristled with slivers. Between the slats, his fingers encountered damp wood and paper, and then found something hard and curled and smooth. Above him, the rain rattled louder as though the skin of the roof was thinner here.

The crate was too heavy and awkward to lift so he dragged it along the joists, careful to do so slowly and quietly so as not to alert his sleeping aunt below. He had some trouble pulling it through the door into his bedroom as the dimensions of the crate were nearly those of the door and the difference didn't allow for the skin on his knuckles.

He knelt on the floor and picked through the contents of the crate with his bleeding hands. He pulled out balls of brittle paper: newspaper printed in a language he didn't recognize. Underneath the balls of newspaper he found an envelope bearing the name "Simon." Simon had been his father's name.

Jack took the envelope to his desk and snapped on the reading lamp. The envelope's flap had been unsealed long ago. Inside was a piece of stiff, expensive writing paper. The message was written in fountain pen, and the handwriting was almost illegible. Jack had to read it a few times to make sense of it:

> *Simon,*
>
> *I am leaving these pieces to you as you are the only one who will understand what they are and what to do with them. Remember what I taught you. You have a responsibility to acknowledge what you have learned and to use it and pass it on.*
>
> Your loving uncle,
Wally

Jack returned the card to the envelope. His hands were shaking. He frowned at them. It wasn't as though his father had written this—just some great-uncle, most likely dead too. It wasn't even as though they were his father's things—just things that had been left to him. Yet Jack found himself on his knees again, digging into the crate.

Amidst the crumpled paper, he found something fist-sized and spotted. It was a conch shell. Jack felt disappointed; he had one much like it, bought on a trip to Florida years ago. Though the outside had an attractive pattern, Lillian could hardly be expected to appreciate it. He set it on his desk and turned back to the crate. He found a leather-bound book embossed with what looked like ivory. Unfortunately, the book was written in a language that Jack guessed, based on the science he'd taken at school, was Latin. He set the book aside; even if the words had been in English, Lillian couldn't read them.

He put his hand back into the crate, and his torn knuckles grazed a hard surface. Clearing the remaining paper away he found the curved piece of wood he must have felt in the darkness of the attic. It was part of a larger object. He pulled this out with difficulty—it was heavier than it looked and rattled as he lifted it—and set it on his desk.

It was a wooden boat. After a little manipulation and a gentle shake, Jack discovered that the top of it was loose. He lifted it off and a sweet, diseased smell, like a grub-pocked apple, emanated from inside.

The boat's interior was divided into compartments. Each compartment housed a pair of white objects. Jack picked out one from the compartment in the bow. It was a carving of a four-legged animal with a wedge-shaped head, pointed ears, and green-glinting eyes. The piece was heavy, minutely carved, and it filled his palm. *Ivory*, he thought. The piece lying next to this one turned out to be its twin. On the underside of each piece the letters "W.W." had been carved. Jack set them on the desk and pulled out another pair. These were squatting monkeys, staring blankly, their tusks protruding. Jack smiled. This was a gift Lillian could appreciate.

He lined up the pairs of animals on his desk like an army. He trained the desk lamp directly at them so that their eyes shone back at him.

"You will help me win her heart," he whispered to them.

Then he picked them up and stowed them back in the boat. As he put them away, he felt an unpleasant tingling in his hands. His palms were studded with slivers from handling the crate, and his knuckles still bled from their trip through the low doorway. No wonder.

Getting caught would be worse than missing even more sleep, so he dragged the crate back through the low door into the attic and stowed the boat under his bed. Afterward, sleep wouldn't happen, so he got up and spent the remainder of the night polishing the boat with the edge of his blanket, for Lillian. She was all he had, really. Jack's father had died when he was only nine years old. He'd never known his mother. Some girl at school had once remarked that she'd taken one look at him when he was born and run away screaming. Well, Lillian didn't care about his looks.

The next morning, bleary-eyed, Jack staggered downstairs with his backpack on, the boat concealed inside. He let himself out the front door, avoiding his aunt in the kitchen, got onto his bicycle, which had been his father's, and pedaled off to the park. The bicycle wobbled a little as the weight of the boat in his pack threw his balance.

The rain puddles were drying up, but in the park the ground was muddy, especially by the edge of the lake. He sat on the park bench by the shore and waited, watching his watch, his backpack a comforting weight on his lap.

He was so eager to give her the boat that he took it out to look at it again. After all, he didn't have to worry she'd see it and spoil the surprise.

In daylight, the wood looked different, almost like plastic. He held it up and turned it this way and that, then ran his thumbnail along the bow. The brown color lay in uneven streaks, and underneath the boat was a yellow-white color. Was it ivory like the figures inside? Or was it simply heavy plastic? It seemed also to be made up of different sizes and shapes of pieces, fitted together, giving it a jigsaw appearance.

Some hours later, Jack lay in quiet bliss beside Lillian in the shade of the willow by the lake. They were made for each other, he thought. While she slept in the cool of the evening, her arms folded over the boat, the iris of her half-open eye seemed like a ship in a milky bottle, self-contained and full of blue hope. Where her other eye should be was only a closed lid. He put his thumb on it and tried to lift it, to look behind it, but it was stuck fast, like a newborn kitten's eye. He wondered what she saw with that closed eye—what other world. He looked up into the less welcoming blue eyes of her guide dog. A low growl bubbled in the dog's throat. Jack withdrew his hand. After a moment, the dog stood and moved toward the boat in Lillian's arms. Jack could hear the dog's rapid breathing as it sniffed the boat. The dog's ears flattened tight against its head, and its body tensed.

"Leave it alone!" said Jack.

And then Lillian woke, which spoiled the moment.

That night, Jack lay dozing in his bed. He was still wrought up from the events of the day, but coming on the heels of a sleepless night, he felt exhausted too. He summoned up the memory of Lillian's joyous reaction to his gift ... yet he felt like a fraud; the boat wasn't really his—someone else had made it, and he hadn't even bought it for her, just found it. If he really loved her, he thought, he would have made something for her—if he wasn't so pathetic and useless at that kind of thing.

His eyelids snapped open and he blinked; he'd dozed off. He felt a change in the house as though it had settled on its foundation. That, or the noise shaking the room must have woken him. He got out of bed and drew back the curtain to make sure that it wasn't the sea making that sound. It sounded so much like crashing waves.

The night was calm and clear, the sky a deep indigo, and the tree outside his window wasn't so much as twitching to betray a wind. He dropped the curtain. The sound was coming from below the window. He switched on the lamp.

On his desk, the conch shell he'd found in the crate was vibrating. He picked up the shell. The quality of the sound changed from a rushing of the sea to a hiss, like an ice cube fragmenting in water. He thought for a moment there must be an animal inside the shell, but there was no smell and no flesh or claw protruded from the opening. Cautiously, Jack held the shell to his ear.

He heard the sea at first. Then there was a voice—an old man's voice. "One day, when you're old enough," it said, "you'll learn how to do these things."

Then, a younger voice, a child's voice spoke, soft and meek, "But Uncle Wally, it isn't right."

"You're frightened now, but you'll get over that. Death isn't frightening when you never have to say good-bye to people. Take the bird by the wing, Simon. It won't hurt you. It's already dead. I'll show you what to do."

Jack heard a muffled sobbing, then it stopped, and there was silence.

Though he had never heard the second voice speaking as a child before, Jack knew whose it was. "Dad!" he cried. The shell was silent. He shook the conch. There was no sound. He brought it to the bedside lamp and looked inside. That was when he saw the words engraved in the polished opalescent lip of the shell: *Malleus, Incus, Stapes.* Like an incantation. Latin again. The words seemed familiar. He curled his fingers inside the shell and felt nothing but smooth hardness.

"Dad?" said Jack. He held the conch to his ear and heard nothing but silence.

After an eternity of futile waiting, he went back to bed, putting the conch on the pillow beside him.

It didn't make a sound that night, nor did it all the next day, each time he pulled it surreptitiously from his backpack to listen.

Four days later he was at Lillian's house, the first time he had ever been there. Her parents were out for the day. Jack and Lillian went up to her bedroom, and after a time they fell asleep.

Sometime later, Jack was woken abruptly with the impression of a sudden dislocation. He clambered out of bed and staggered as the blood rushed from his head.

The bedroom's bay window was dark with early evening. The little white sculptures stood along the windowsill where he and Lillian had placed them earlier. More of the sculptures and the boat itself stood on her bedside table.

He heard a quiet, drawn-out sound. Lillian lay on her back, her white hand curled by her cheek. She breathed quietly. The sound Jack heard was coming from his backpack, beside the bed. He scrambled to open it and took out the conch.

"Dad . . . " he whispered. He pressed the conch tightly to his ear.

What he first heard, the first sound he could make out amongst the sharp rustling, was a songbird. Jack was well acquainted with birdsong, having learned a little on school field trips, and he knew within a few notes that this was not a Canadian bird. As the moments passed, the song changed from melodic to screeching. Some sort of parrot or parakeet. He could make out other birds in the background, other birds he could not identify. Then silence.

"Dad?" he whispered. "It's Jack. Can you hear me?"

More silence from the conch. In the bedroom, he heard Lillian's breathing rasp. He got up to go out into the hallway where it was quieter. As he passed the window he heard a sharp sound from the conch. He froze.

"Not here!" said a voice—the same old man's voice Jack had heard the first time. "Further in. Go on."

Then he heard another voice, a teenager's voice, not much younger than Jack. Jack could tell from the tone that the guy was upset, but he couldn't understand what he was saying. It took Jack a moment to realize he was speaking a foreign language.

Jack stepped toward the hallway so that he could listen out of earshot of Lillian, but as soon as he took that step, the conch went silent. Jack stepped backward and the sound rushed in again. In fact, as he moved the conch this way and that, it became louder the nearer he got to Lillian.

Jack leaned over her. Beside him on the bedside table, he caught sight of the carving of the monkey with its bared teeth and green, shining eyes. Sound virtually exploded out of the conch: the sound of breaking brush, twigs snapping, leaves rustling, harsh breathing, that young guy's voice. His voice was now pleading, anguished, in words that almost sounded like English but weren't. Then the boy screamed. It was not a scream of shock or fright—it was a scream of pain. Jack dropped the conch.

"Jack?" said Lillian. She reached across the bed to where he'd been lying, and her palm flattened on the emptiness there. "Where are you?"

"It's okay," said Jack. He didn't move. The conch had broken at his feet. Quietly, he picked up the pieces. Under the two largest shards, he found three tiny oddly shaped yellow objects not more than few millimeters long. It was when he saw them that his memory of the words on the conch returned and he made the connection. He straightened.

"What are you doing?" said Lillian.

"I just . . . dropped something," he said.

"Come back to bed, love." She stretched out her hand toward him.

He went back to the bed and put the pieces of the conch into his backpack. Then he made an excuse to leave. Lied to her, basically. Because if he told her the truth, she'd think he was crazy. Maybe he *was*.

The next morning, Jack cut class and went to the library as soon as it opened. He found the book he needed and signed it out. He didn't want to be seen reading it in public, and there was something at the house he needed to look at.

Back home, he hid his bike behind the garage and snuck upstairs. He found the crate in the attic room where he'd left it and rooted out the heavy, leather-bound book. His eyes felt dry, and his vision felt weak and faded, so although it was daylight, he snapped on the desk lamp and opened the book. It too smelled like rotten apples. The foxed paper was slick under his fingers.

Jack opened the Latin-English dictionary he'd gotten from the library. He pulled out the pieces of conch from his backpack and fitted the two largest pieces back together until he could read the words properly. The dictionary revealed that the words were, indeed, Latin.

Malleus, Incus, Stapes.

Hammer, Anvil, Stirrup.

Why did that sound familiar? Blacksmithing terms? Which had what, exactly, to do with seashells?

He pulled the conch apart and examined the inside of it, looking for a miniature tape player, something to explain what he'd heard. He sifted through the tiny pieces of shell, turning them over in his hand. One of them had been carved into the shape of a stirrup. He turned the little piece over and over in his hand as he paged through the leather-bound book. All those words—it would take him forever to translate.

Jack turned the page and stopped. In the middle of the text were three pen-and-ink line drawings. In the first, a man lay on his back while another man cut him open with a knife. In the second drawing, the man with the knife was holding a curved white thing up over his head. In the third drawing, the man with the knife was gone, and a woman lay on her back next to man who'd been cut.

He shut the book and tapped its ivory-embossed cover while he thought about what he'd seen. Stopped tapping. Looked at the ivory that didn't feel or look quite like ivory. It was a little too gray. It had been engraved the same way the conch had: *W.W., Osteomancer.*

It wasn't ivory, nor was the little stirrup-shaped thing in his hand. Nor had it been carved. The stirrup was its natural shape. He remembered now, in Biology, how they'd learned the parts of the human body, and more specifically, the three bones in the middle ear of the human skull. The smallest bones in the body, named for the objects they resembled: hammer, anvil, stirrup. He knew whose bones had been in that conch. He had been hearing sounds from a dead man's ear.

Jack stood barefoot on the shore of the lake with the boat in his hands and Lillian's reproachful sobs in his memory. You didn't take back a gift; it was cruel. Jack knew, though she'd never told him, that this was the only gift she'd ever received from a man who wasn't a blood relative. He couldn't tell her why he'd taken it, either, and that was the worst part. She probably thought he didn't love her any more.

He'd been reading the leather-bound book with the dictionary at his elbow, and he knew now that water had some sort of cleansing power. Not tamed water, as in a bathtub or a sink or from a hose, but wild water. Jack waded into the lake. He intended only to go out to his knees, but the bottom dropped off unexpectedly, and he found himself soaked up to his belly.

He lowered the boat into the water. Immediately, the boat capsized, its cargo salting the water. They bobbed to the surface like grotesque white bubbles. He tried to snatch them up, but then they sank. Within moments, he was staring in vain into murky brown water. Maybe it was for the best.

He waded out of the lake. When he reached the shore, he turned back, expecting . . . he didn't know what. Some telltale sign on the water's surface? A white hand emerging from the water?

But the boat and all traces of its contents were gone.

The conch, he buried in the back yard. They weren't his father's bones, but still, a part of him was in there, in his great-uncle's memory. Jack flattened the earth over it and then pushed a handful of apple seeds into the dirt. Maybe one of them would grow.

Then, for the first time since he'd lost his dad, Jack cried.

Jack spent many nights afterward teaching himself Latin and reading the book. Jack concluded that bone magic was not an innately evil art—it depended on how it was practiced.

Lillian refused to speak to him and had her parents turn him away at their door. Jack took to spending his afternoons in the park by the lake, waiting on the off-chance that she might come back. And a month later, she did.

He sat quietly on the bench until she sat down on the other side of it.

There was a slight breeze—perhaps that gave him away, but Lillian suddenly turned her head toward him.

Jack reached over and put the shell into her hands. It was the conch that he'd picked up in Florida years ago. Not as pretty as the conch in his father's crate, but in a way, that was the point. Along the conch's lip he had glued tiny beads in Braille code. He watched her fingers find them, move along them. Realize what they said.

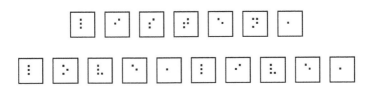

Listen. Love. Live.

Her groping hand found his face, traced his cheek and then stopped when it reached the bandage over his ear.

Bone magic, like love, demanded certain sacrifices.

Sarah Totton's short fiction has appeared in Black Static Magazine, Fantasy Magazine, The Year's Best Dark Fantasy & Horror 2011 *(Prime Books), and* Worlds of Science Fiction, Fantasy & Horror Volume 1 *(2016). Her debut short story collection,* Animythical Tales, *was published in 2010 by Fantastic Books. She is a licensed veterinarian and a zoologist and has taken more comparative anatomy courses than is probably healthy.*

THE SENSE OF TASTE

THOUGHTS ABOUT THE SENSE OF TASTE

BY JESSICA BAYLISS, PhD

MANY CREATURES, INCLUDING HUMANS, naturally avoid certain tastes.

Bitter, for example, can signify the presence of toxic ingredients, so many animals naturally skip over the bitter berries. Humans, too, are not the biggest fan of this particular gustatory experience, and we are wired to detect it. Researchers examined humans' ability to taste glucosinolates, a bitter and potentially toxic compound found in many plant-based foods such as watercress, broccoli, and turnip. The researchers concluded that there may be a gene that helps us avoid consuming too much of these foods.

Our sense of taste is immensely sensitive, but how does this relate to fear and horror?

First, let us look at the question of whether we can be afraid of a taste.

Have you ever consumed a food or drink and then become very ill afterward? So ill that you vomited? If so, you may have avoided that food for a long time after, maybe forever. Go ahead and think about that flavor for a moment . . . Not pleasant, huh? Just conjuring up the memories can trigger nausea.

What you are feeling right now is what scientists call *conditioned taste aversion*. When nausea or vomiting are paired with a taste, the body learns this, and next time the person encounters that same taste—or even the thought of the flavor—quick onset of nausea will prevent or quickly stop them from eating it again.

It is hypothesized that conditioned aversion developed to help us avoid eating foods that can make us sick. No one wants to be poisoned.

This process is another version of Pavlovian conditioning. Watson's Little Albert experiment caused conditioning of the fight-or-flight fear response by pairing the white rat with a frightening noise, but we can condition any automatic process to respond to an external stimulus—pupil contraction/dilation, skin conductivity, heart rate. Nausea is no different. The most interesting thing about conditioned taste aversion is that it usually only takes one presentation of the sickening flavor, whereas Watson had to freak out Albert many times before the association was formed. Again, no one likes to be poisoned, so fast learning is essential.

A similar but different process occurs when an aversive stimulus other than nausea/vomiting is presented following a certain gustatory sensation. This is called *taste avoidance*. This is the exact same process as we saw with Little Albert. In fact, Watson could have conditioned Albert to fear the taste of chocolate or Brussels sprouts using the exact same method of conditioning—present the chocolate, make a terrifying noise, repeat. In that case, Watson would have used sound to condition *taste avoidance*, otherwise known as a taste phobia.

Researchers believe that taste avoidance is different than taste aversion, although both arise by the same mechanism—classical conditioning. In the case of taste *aversion*, nausea and vomiting are the aversive stimulus (instead of the loud noise made by Watson, our bodies naturally create the terrifying situation for us by making us ill). In taste *avoidance*, there is no nausea or vomiting. The feared stimulus is external (e.g., a loud noise), thereby making taste avoidance a pure anxiety situation. So, if I were on an arc housing the corpse of an ancient demon, and dinner consisted of pizza every night, I might come to associate the taste of pizza with the terror of being on a haunted ship and never want to eat pizza again—assuming the demon doesn't get me.

Disgust is one of the most basic of human emotions. It is literally the reaction we have when we encounter tastes (or smells, which are highly linked to taste) that are noxious, such as bitter or rotten foods or a food for which we have an aversion. As you know already, mirror neurons allow us to *feel with* other people. We can literally experience the ghost of a touch just by watching someone else being touched, and we can experience vicarious disgust by watching—or reading about—someone encountering a disgusting taste experience. Of course it works the other way, too. Whenever I read books with scenes involving food, I always crave whatever the characters are eating, which is its own form of diabolical torture. But, for this same reason, when the protagonist gets sprayed in the face with the bloody goo, we are there, shuddering—maybe even gagging—right along with them.

HIS MOUTH WILL TASTE OF WORMWOOD

BY POPPY Z. BRITE

EDITOR'S NOTES: Many of the stories I selected have distinct usage or emphasis in more than one of the five senses, and the following inclusion is a fine example of this, in which the narrative itself revolves around pushing the boundaries of sensation. However it is Taste (title prompt aside!) that seems to linger on the palette perhaps a bit longer than the other senses.

Few can write to the atmospheric astuteness of Poppy Z. Brite, who seems to always and effortlessly capture each of the senses when penning gothic horror tales such as this. And even besides being a selection that is deep and resonant to all the senses, *His Mouth Will Taste of Wormwood* just happens to also be one of my favorite stories since childhood, and a personal thrill to include.

College friends Louis and Howard have grown drearily apathetic to what life has to offer. Their relentless search for experiences that will give thrill or impression to their empty lives knows no taboos, even when grave robbing from the wrong tomb.

> *"He soon produced his hashish pipe to sweeten the taste of the wine, and we spoke no more of grave robbing that night . . . "*

T O THE TREASURES AND THE PLEASURES of the grave," said my friend, Louis, and raised his goblet of absinthe to me in drunken benediction.

"To the funeral lilies," I replied, "and to the calm pale bones." I drank deeply from my own glass. The absinthe cauterized my throat with its flavor, part pepper, part licorice, part rot. It had been one of our greatest finds: more than fifty bottles of the now-outlawed liqueur, sealed up in a New Orleans family tomb. Transporting them was a nuisance, but once we had learned to enjoy the taste of wormwood, our continued drunkenness was ensured for a long, long time. We'd taken the skull of the crypt's patriarch, too, and it now resided in a velvet-lined enclave in our museum.

Louis and I, you see, were dreamers of a dark and restless sort. We met in our second year of college and quickly found that we shared one vital trait: both of us were dissatisfied with everything. We drank straight whiskey and declared it too weak. We took strange drugs, but the visions they brought us were of emptiness, mindlessness, slow decay. The books we read were dull; the artists who sold their colorful drawings on the street were mere hacks in our eyes; the music we heard was never loud enough, never harsh enough to stir us. We were truly jaded, we told one another. For all the impression the world made upon us, our eyes might have been dead black holes in our heads.

For a time we thought our salvation lay in the sorcery wrought by music. We studied recordings of weird nameless dissonances, attended performances of obscure bands at ill-lit filthy clubs. But music did not save us. For a time we distracted ourselves with carnality. We explored the damp alien territory between the legs of any girl who would have us, sometimes separately, sometimes both of us in bed together with one girl or more. We bound their wrists and ankles with black lace, we lubricated and penetrated their every orifice, we shamed them with their own pleasures. I recall a mauve-haired beauty, Felicia, who was brought to wild sobbing orgasm by the rough tongue of a stray dog we trapped. We watched her from across the room, drug-dazed and unstirred.

When we exhausted the possibilities of women, we sought those of our own sex, craving the androgynous curve of a boy's cheekbone, the molten flood of ejaculation invading our mouths. Eventually we turned to one another, seeking the thresholds of pain and ecstasy no one else had been able to help us attain. Louis asked me to grow my nails long and file them into needle-sharp points. When I raked them down his back, tiny beads of blood welled up in the angry tracks they left. He loved to lie still, pretending to submit to me, as I licked the salty blood away. Afterward he would push me down and attack me with his mouth, his tongue seeming to sear a trail of liquid fire into my skin.

But sex did not save us either. We shut ourselves in our room and saw no one for days on end. At last we withdrew to the seclusion of Louis's ancestral home near Baton Rouge. Both his parents were dead—a suicide pact, Louis hinted, or perhaps a suicide and a murder. Louis, the only child, retained the family home and fortune. Built on the edge of a vast swamp, the plantation house loomed sepulchrally out of the gloom that surrounded it always, even in the middle of a summer afternoon. Oaks of primordial hugeness grew in a canopy over the house, their branches like black arms fraught with Spanish moss. The moss was everywhere, reminding me of brittle gray hair, stirring wraithlike in the dank breeze from the swamp. I had the impression that, left too long unchecked, the moss might begin to grow from the ornate window frames and fluted columns of the house itself.

The place was deserted save for us. The air was heady with the luminous scent of magnolias and the fetor of swamp gas. At night we sat on the veranda and sipped bottles of wine from the family cellar, gazing through an increasingly alcoholic mist at the will-o'-the-wisps that beckoned far off in the swamp. Obsessively we talked of new thrills and how we might get them. Louis's wit sparkled liveliest when he was bored, and on the night he first mentioned grave robbing, I laughed. I could not imagine that he was serious.

"What would we do with a bunch of dried-up old remains? Grind them to make a voodoo potion? I preferred your idea of increasing our tolerance to various poisons."

Louis's sharp face snapped toward me. His eyes were painfully sensitive to light, so that even in this gloaming he wore tinted glasses and it was impossible to see his expression. He kept his fair hair clipped very short, so that it stood up in crazy tufts when he raked a nervous hand through it. "No, Howard. Think of it: our own collection of death. A catalogue of pain, of human frailty—all for us. Set against a backdrop of tranquil loveliness. Think what it would be to walk through such a place, meditating, reflecting upon your own ephemeral essence. Think of making love in a charnel house! We have only to assemble the parts—they will create a whole into which we may fall."

(Louis enjoyed speaking in cryptic puns; anagrams and palindromes, too, and any sort of puzzle appealed to him. I wonder whether that was not the root of his determination to look into the fathomless eye of death and master it. Perhaps he saw the mortality of the flesh as a gigantic jigsaw or crossword which, if he fitted all the parts into place, he might solve and thus defeat. Louis would have loved to live forever, though he would never have known what to do with all his time.)

He soon produced his hashish pipe to sweeten the taste of the wine, and we spoke no more of grave robbing that night. But the thought preyed upon me in the languorous weeks to come. The smell of a freshly opened grave, I thought, must in its way be as intoxicating as the perfume of the swamp or a girl's most intimate sweat. Could we truly assemble a collection of the grave's treasures that would be lovely to look upon, that would soothe our fevered souls?

The caresses of Louis's tongue grew languid. Sometimes, instead of nestling with me between the black satin sheets of our bed, he would sleep on a torn blanket in one of the underground rooms. These had originally been built for indeterminate but always intriguing purposes—abolitionist meetings had taken place there, Louis told me, and a weekend of free love, and an earnest but wildly incompetent Black Mass replete with a vestal virgin and phallic candles.

These rooms were where our museum would be set up. At last I came to agree with Louis that only the plundering of graves might cure us of the most stifling ennui we had yet suffered. I could not bear to watch his tormented sleep, the pallor of his hollow cheeks, the delicate bruise-like darkening of the skin beneath his flickering eyes. Besides, the notion of grave robbing had begun to entice me. In ultimate corruption, might we not find the path to ultimate salvation?

Our first grisly prize was the head of Louis's mother, rotten as a pumpkin forgotten on the vine, half-shattered by two bullets from an antique Civil War revolver. We took it from the family crypt by the light of a full moon. The will-o'-the-wisps glowed weakly, like dying beacons on some unattainable shore, as we crept back to the manse. I dragged pick and shovel behind me; Louis carried the putrescent trophy tucked beneath his arm. After we descended into the museum, I lit three candles scented with the russet spices of autumn (the season when Louis's parents had died) while Louis placed the head in the alcove we had prepared for it. I thought I detected a certain tenderness in his manner. "May she give us the family blessing," he murmured, absently wiping on the lapel of his jacket a few shreds of pulpy flesh that had adhered to his fingers.

We spent a happy time refurbishing the museum, polishing the inlaid precious metals of the wall fixtures, brushing away the dust that frosted the velvet designs of the wallpaper, alternately burning incense and charring bits of cloth we had saturated with our blood, in order to give the rooms the odor we desired—a charnel perfume strong enough to drive us to frenzy. We travelled far in our collections, but always we returned home with crates full of things no man had ever been meant to possess. We heard of a girl with violet eyes who had died in some distant town; not seven days later we had those eyes in an ornate cut-glass jar, pickled in formaldehyde. We scraped bone dust and nitre from the bottoms of ancient coffins; we stole the barely withered heads and hands of children fresh in their graves, with their soft little fingers and their lips like flower petals. We had baubles and precious heirlooms, vermiculated prayer books and shrouds encrusted with mold. I had not taken seriously Louis's talk of making love in a charnel-house—but neither had I reckoned on the pleasure he could inflict with a femur dipped in rose-scented oil.

Upon the night I speak of—the night we drank our toast to the grave and its riches—we had just acquired our finest prize yet. Later in the evening we planned a celebratory debauch at a nightclub in the city. We had returned from our most recent travels not with the usual assortment of sacks and crates, but with only one small box carefully wrapped and tucked into Louis's breast pocket. The box contained an object whose existence we had only speculated upon previously. From certain half-articulate mutterings of an old blind man plied with cheap liquor in a French Quarter bar, we traced rumors of a certain fetish or charm to a Negro graveyard in the southern bayou country. The fetish was said to be a thing of eerie beauty, capable of luring any lover to one's bed, hexing any enemy to a sick and painful death, and (this, I think, was what intrigued Louis the most) turning back tenfold on anyone who used it with less than the touch of a master.

A heavy mist hung low over the graveyard when we arrived there, lapping at our ankles, pooling around the markers of wood and stone, abruptly melting away in patches to reveal a gnarled root or a patch of blackened grass, then closing back in. By the light of a waning moon we made our way along a path overgrown with rioting weeds. The graves were decorated with elaborate mosaics of broken glass, coins, bottle caps, oyster shells lacquered silver and gold. Some mounds were outlined by empty bottles shoved neck-downward into the earth. I saw a lone plaster saint whose features had been worn away by years of wind and rain. I kicked half-buried rusty cans that had once held flowers; now they held only bare brittle stems and pestilent rainwater, or nothing at all. Only the scent of wild spider lilies pervaded the night.

The earth in one corner of the graveyard seemed blacker than the rest. The grave we sought was marked only by a crude cross of charred and twisted wood. We were skilled at the art of violating the dead; soon we had the coffin uncovered. The boards were warped by years of burial in wet, foul earth. Louis pried up the lid with his spade and, by the moon's meager and watery light, we gazed upon what lay within.

Of the inhabitant we knew almost nothing. Some said a hideously disfigured old conjure woman lay buried here. Some said she was a young girl with a face as lovely and cold as moonlight on water, and a soul crueler than Fate itself. Some claimed the body was not a woman's at all, but that of a white voodoo priest who had ruled the bayou. He had features of a cool, unearthly beauty, they said, and a stock of fetishes and potions which he would hand out with the kindest blessing... or the direst curse. This was the story Louis and I liked best; the sorcerer's capriciousness appealed to us, and the fact that he was beautiful.

No trace of beauty remained to the thing in the coffin—at least not the sort of beauty that a healthy eye might cherish. Louis and I loved the translucent parchment skin stretched tight over long bones that seemed to have been carved from ivory. The delicate brittle hands folded across the sunken chest, the soft black caverns of the eyes, the colorless strands of hair that still clung to the fine white dome of the skull—to us these things were the poetry of death.

Louis played his flashlight over the withered cords of the neck. There, on a silver chain gone black with age, was the object we had come seeking. No crude wax doll or bit of dried root was this. Louis and I gazed at each other, moved by the beauty of the thing; then, as if in a dream, he reached to grasp it. This was our rightful night's prize, our plunder from a sorcerer's grave.

"How does it look?" Louis asked as we were dressing.

I never had to think about my clothes. On an evening such as this, when we were dressing to go out, I would choose the same garments I might wear for a night's digging in the graveyard—black, unornamented black, with only the whiteness of my face and hands showing against the backdrop of night. On a particularly festive occasion, such as this, I might smudge a bit of kohl round my eyes. The absence of color made me nearly invisible: if I walked with my shoulders hunched and my chin tucked down, no one except Louis would see me.

"Don't slouch so, Howard," said Louis irritably as I ducked past the mirror. "Turn around and look at me. Aren't I fine in my sorcerer's jewelry?"

Even when Louis wore black, he did it to be noticed. Tonight he was resplendent in narrow-legged trousers of purple paisley silk and a silvery jacket that seemed to turn all light iridescent. He had taken our prize out of its box and fastened it around his throat. As I came closer to look at it, I caught Louis's scent: rich and rather meaty, like blood kept too long in a stoppered bottle.

Against the sculpted hollow of Louis's throat, the thing on its chain seemed more strangely beautiful than ever. Have I neglected to describe the magical object, the voodoo fetish from the churned earth of the grave? I will never forget it. A polished sliver of bone (or a tooth, but what fang could have been so long, so sleekly honed, and still have somehow retained the look of a *human tooth*?) bound by a strip of copper. Set into the metal, a single ruby sparkled like the drop of gore against the verdigris. Etched in exquisite miniature upon the sliver of bone, and darkened by the rubbing in of some black-red substance, was an elaborate veve—one of the symbols used by voodooists to invoke their pantheon of terrible gods. Whoever was buried in that lonely bayou grave, he had been no mere dabbler in swamp magic. Every cross and swirl of the veve was reproduced to perfection. I thought the thing still retained a trace of the grave's scent—a dark odor like potatoes long spoiled. Each grave has its own peculiar scent, just as each living body does.

"Are you certain you should wear it?" I asked.

"It will go into the museum tomorrow," he said, "with a scarlet candle burning eternally before it. Tonight its powers are mine."

The nightclub was in a part of the city that looked as if it had been gutted from the inside out by a righteous tongue of fire. The street was lit only by occasional scribbles of neon high overhead, advertisements for cheap hotels and all-night bars. Dark eyes stared at us from the crevices and pathways between buildings, disappearing only when Louis's hand crept toward the inner pocket of his jacket. He carried a small stiletto there, and knew how to use it for more than pleasure.

We slipped through a door at the end of an alley and descended the narrow staircase into the club. The lurid glow of a blue bulb flooded the stairs, making Louis's face look sunken and dead behind his tinted glasses. Feedback blasted us as we came in, and above it, a screaming battle of guitars. The inside of the club was a patchwork of flickering light and darkness. Graffiti covered the walls and the ceiling like a tangle of barbed wire come alive. I saw bands' insignia and jeering death's-heads, crucifixes bejeweled with broken glass and black obscenities writhing in the stroboscopic light.

Louis brought me a drink from the bar. I sipped it slowly, still drunk on absinthe. Since the music was too loud for conversation, I studied the clubgoers around us. A quiet bunch they were, staring fixedly at the stage as if they'd been drugged (and no doubt many of them had—I remembered visiting a club one night on a dose of hallucinogenic mushrooms, watching in fascination as the guitar strings seemed to drip soft viscera onto the stage). Younger than Louis and myself, most of them were, and queerly beautiful in their thrift shop rags, their leather and fishnet and cheap costume jewelry, their pale faces and painted hair. Perhaps we would take one of them home with us tonight. We had done so before. "The delicious guttersnipes," Louis called them. A particularly beautiful face, starkly boned and androgynous, flickered at the edge of my vision. When I looked, it was gone.

I went into the restroom. A pair of boys stood at a single urinal, talking animatedly. I stood at the sink rinsing my hands, watching the boys in the mirror and trying to overhear their conversation. A hairline fracture in the glass seemed to pull the taller boy's eyes askew. "Caspar and Alyssa found her tonight," he said. "In some old warehouse by the river. I heard her skin was *gray*, man. And sort of withered, like something had sucked out most of the meat."

"Far out," said the other boy. His black-rimmed lips barely moved. "She was only fifteen, you know?" said the tall boy as he zipped his ragged trousers.

"She was a cunt anyway."

They turned from the urinal and started talking about the band—Ritual Sacrifice, I gathered, whose name was scrawled on the walls of the club. As they went out, the boys glanced at the mirror and the tall one's eyes met mine for an instant: nose like a haughty Indian chief's, eyelids smudged with black and silver. Louis would approve, I thought—but the night was young, and there were many drinks left to be had.

When the band took a break we visited the bar again. Louis edged in beside a thin dark-haired boy who was bare-chested except for a piece of torn lace tied about his throat. When he turned, I knew his was the androgynous and striking face I had glimpsed before. His beauty was almost feral, but overlaid with a cool elegance like a veneer of sanity hiding madness. His ivory skin stretched over cheekbones like razors; his eyes were hectic pools of darkness.

"I like your amulet," he said to Louis. "It's very unusual."

"I have another one like it at home," Louis told him.

"Really? I'd like to see them both together." The boy paused to let Louis order our vodka gimlets, then said, "I thought there was only one."

Louis's back straightened like a string of beads being pulled taut. Behind his glasses, I knew, his pupils would have shrunk to pinpoints: the light pained him more when he was nervous. But no tremor in his voice betrayed him when he said, "What do you know about it?"

The boy shrugged. On his bony shoulders, the movement was insouciant and drop-dead graceful. "It's voodoo," he said. "I know what voodoo is. Do you?"

The implication stung, but Louis only bared his teeth the slightest bit; it might have been a smile. "I am *conversant* in all types of magic," he said, "at least."

The boy moved closer to Louis, so that their hips were almost touching, and lifted the amulet between thumb and forefinger. I thought I saw one long nail brush Louis's throat, but I could not be sure. "I could tell you the meaning of this veve," he said, "if you were certain you wished to know."

"It symbolizes power," Louis said. "All the power of my soul." His voice was cold, but I saw his tongue dart out to moisten his lips. He was beginning to dislike this boy, and also to desire him.

"No," said the boy so softly that I barely caught his words. He sounded almost sad. "This cross in the center is inverted, you see, and the line encircling it represents a serpent. A thing like this can trap your soul. Instead of being rewarded with eternal life ... you might be doomed to it."

"Doomed to eternal life?" Louis permitted himself a small cold smile. "Whatever do you mean?"

"The band is starting again. Find me after the show and I'll tell you. We can have a drink ... and you can tell me all you know about voodoo." The boy threw back his head and laughed. Only then did I notice that one of his upper canine teeth was missing.

The next part of the evening remains a blur of moonlight and neon, ice cubes and blue swirling smoke and sweet drunkenness. The boy drank glass after glass of absinthe with us, seeming to relish the bitter taste. None of our other guests had liked the liqueur. "Where did you get it?" he asked. Louis was silent for a long moment before he said, "It was sent over from France." Except for its single black gap, the boy's smile would have been as perfect as the sharp-edged crescent moon.

"Another drink?" said Louis, refilling both our glasses.

When I next came to clarity, I was in the boy's arms. I could not make out the words he was whispering; they might have been an incantation, if magic may be sung to pleasure's music. A pair of hands cupped my face, guiding my lips over the boy's pale parchment skin. They might have been Louis's hands. I knew nothing except this boy, the fragile movement of the bones beneath the skin, the taste of his spit bitter with wormwood.

I do not remember when he finally turned away from me and began lavishing his love upon Louis. I wish I could have watched, could have seen the lust bleeding into Louis's eyes, the pleasure wracking his body. For, as it turned out, the boy loved Louis so much more thoroughly than ever he loved me.

When I awoke, the bass thump of my pulse echoing through my skull blotted out all other sensations. Gradually, though, I became aware of tangled silk sheets, of hot sunlight on my face. Not until I came fully awake did I see the thing I had cradled like a lover all through the night.

For an instant two realities shifted in uneasy juxtaposition and almost merged. I was in Louis's bed; I recognized the feel of the sheets, their odor of silk and sweat. But this thing I held—this was surely one of the fragile mummies we had dragged out of their graves, the things we dissected for our museum. It took me only a moment, though, to recognize the familiar ruined features—the sharp chin, the high elegant brow. Something had desiccated Louis, had drained him of every drop of his moisture, his vitality. His skin crackled and flaked away beneath my fingers. His hair stuck to my lips, dry and colorless. The amulet, which had still been around his throat in bed last night, was gone.

The boy had left no trace—or so I thought until I saw a nearly transparent thing at the foot of the bed. It was like a quantity of spiderweb, or a damp and insubstantial veil. I picked it up and shook it out, but could not see its features until I held it up to the window. The thing was vaguely human-shaped, with empty limbs trailing off into nearly invisible tatters. As the thing wafted and billowed, I saw part of a face in it—the sharp curve left by a cheekbone, the hole where an eye had been—as if a face were imprinted upon gauze.

I carried Louis's brittle shell of a corpse down into the museum. Laying him before his mother's niche, I left a stick of incense burning in his folded hands and a pillow of black silk cradling the papery dry bulb of his skull. He would have wished it thus.

The boy has not come to me again, though I leave the window open every night. I have been back to the club, where I stand sipping vodka and watching the crowd. I have seen many beauties, many strange wasted faces, but not the one I seek. I think I know where I will find him. Perhaps he still desires me—I must know.

I will go again to the lonely graveyard in the bayou. Once more—alone, this time—I will find the unmarked grave and plant my spade in its black earth. When I open the coffin—I know it, I am sure of it!—I will find not the moldering thing we beheld before, but the calm beauty of replenished youth. The youth he drank from Louis. His face will be a scrimshaw mask of tranquility. The amulet—I know it; I am sure of it—will be around his neck.

Dying: the final shock of pain or nothingness that is the price we pay for everything. Could it not be the sweetest thrill, the only salvation we can attain ... the only true moment of self-knowledge? The dark pools of his eyes will open, still and deep enough to drown in. He will hold out his arms to me, inviting me to lie down with him in his rich wormy bed.

With the first kiss his mouth will taste of wormwood. After that it will taste only of me—of my blood, my life, siphoning out of my body and into his. I will feel the sensations Louis felt: the shriveling of my tissues, the drying-up of all my vital juices. I care not. The treasures and the pleasures of the grave? They are his hands, his lips, his tongue.

Poppy Z. Brite *is the pen name of Billy Martin. He is the author of* Lost Souls, Exquisite Corpse, *and many other novels and short story collections. He lives in New Orleans.*

CASSILAGO'S WIFE

BY SARAH SINGLETON

EDITOR'S NOTES: The following is another story resonant in more than one sense, yet at its heart it is a tale not only of the lonely traveler run afoul, but an anecdote about ingestion, which by its process of consumption causes the sense of taste to be the most intimate and invasive of our five senses; whatever enters our body through the mouth becomes part of us.

Interestingly, Taste is perhaps the most underused sense in fiction writing, generally engaged only when a character is actively eating or drinking, or in scenes of physical affection and sexual encounter, of which both usages are employed in this selection.

Though author Sarah Singleton's acclaim comes more oft for her novels (*The Crow Maiden* and *Century*, amongst others), it is her short fiction I most adore, notably, "Our Lady of Ruins," "They Left the City at Night," and this next story, in which a lonely traveler finds hospitality at the home of an herbalist and his much younger wife. Be wary should you ever find yourself backpacking in the lush pastoral lands and happen upon the alluring reception of *Cassilago's Wife*.

> *"Then he was kissing her, and her lips tasted of vanilla, burning his skin . . ."*

TENDRILS SLIDE THROUGH HIS BELLY. Root-tips, sharp as quills, burrow in muscle and viscera.

In the slow tide of the day, the half-light rises and recedes. The cave holds a breath stale with stone and soil.

His fingers trace rivulets of moisture creeping across the rock, and he presses his hand to his mouth, his tongue like a dry sponge, sucking the water away. He cannot close his lips. The fierce growth pries him open. Succulent blue-green leaves, semi-opaque in the twilight, erupt from the pit of his throat. Deep in his stomach a black root nestles, drawing sustenance, shaped by the contours of his mutable, elastic tissue. A network of filaments spreads between skull and skin, and fibrils press into eye sockets. Sight is fading, and slowly the flesh surrenders. He feels no pain. He thinks of insects, caterpillars, playing host to larvae, the slow consumption, the breaking down of one life into another. *Transformation.*

Bryony lifted a bucket from the well and watered the beds of herbs. The house blushed momentarily, as the last red spears of sunlight pierced the trees and stained the gray walls. Inside, a window flared white, and gold, as Cassilago lit a lamp in his study and continued his work. The air was still. From the dusky trees a solitary robin began to sing, and Bryony stopped to listen, leaning upon the well, warm and absent, lost in a dream of rose and mauve.

Then—sharp footsteps and a rattle at the gate. Bryony came to herself in a cold shock.

"Hello?" A brisk, young voice. A man.

Bryony didn't move. She turned her head. She said nothing.

"Hello?" The stupid repetition. Bryony stepped forward, onto the garden path. The young man was standing on the threshold of the garden, the gate now open. She stared at him. He was tall and blonde, his hair hanging across his forehead. His face was tanned and his body exuded an aura of health, though he looked tired. He shrugged a heavy backpack from his shoulders. His shirt was stained with sweat. He clutched a map in his hand.

"Hello," he said again. "Sorry to bother you. I'm on a walk, you see. I wanted to set up camp. Is it alright to put my tent up here?" He gestured to the meadow in front of the chestnut trees. Bryony didn't reply. She shook her head, as though the words made no sense. She stared at the young man, not knowing how she should answer. He shuffled uneasily in the silence, wiping his face with his hand. Then Cassilago came hurrying out of the house. He stood beside Bryony.

"What does he want?" he said. Bryony frowned.

"To stay in the meadow. To put up his tent." She spoke softly.

Cassilago scrutinized the young man. Then he smiled.

"Of course," he said. "Of course. Put up your tent. Then you can eat with us."

The newcomer stepped into the garden. He held out his hand.

"Thank you very much," he said. "I don't want to put you to any trouble. My name's Will. Will Ambroise."

Bryony looked into his face. Will Ambroise had blue eyes. The lilac blue of a hyacinth. As he leaned forward, she caught his scent. Despite the sweat upon his face and shirt he smelt clean, and young.

"It's no trouble," Cassilago said cordially, shaking his hand. "We lead a quiet life, and I like to have visitors."

Will chose a level site in the field. He discarded his pack, and dropped into the long grass, flat on his back, relieved to be resting. The light was fading. He lay for a moment or two, letting his body cool, then he erected the little tent and pegged it to the ground. He climbed inside. He heard crickets in the trees. The bluey darkness settled like a net above the house, the meadows, and the forest, where the last light flamed carmine beyond the trees. But a hot yellow light emerged from the house, disembodied. It bobbed toward the tent. Cassilago, with a lantern, called out:

"Come to the house. Bryony's heated some water for you."

Will found a clean tee-shirt and a bright stripey jumper, and followed

Cassilago. The house was warm and welcoming. Flagstones covered the floor. Pretty plates and dried flowers decked a deal dresser in the kitchen, and a large fire burned in a range. A lamp hanging from the ceiling burned with a soft honey light. The girl, Bryony, turned and smiled, not meeting his eyes, and she tipped a pot full of hot water into a large basin. She placed it behind a wooden screen, with a white towel, and left Will to wash himself.

He watched her leave. She was tall, very slim, and curiously unfinished—her attitude uneasy, even gawky. Was she Cassilago's daughter? Granddaughter? She could be fifteen. Maybe a backward twenty. But she drew his eyes, with her hair in a long plait, buttery gold, and the bare skin of her arms white as cream, perfectly smooth.

The house puzzled him. No electricity. And a well in the garden, though he noticed a single tap above the huge kitchen sink. Were they religious people, craving simplicity, spurning modern comforts? Like characters from a painting, a Victorian rural idyll: Cassilago, the old man, in his long black coat, and Bryony in her full blue skirts. Eccentrics perhaps, or foreigners. But he liked the house, and the quavering light, the plain white walls. He splashed himself with water, and washed his face. The towel was warm, scented with lavender.

Bryony carried in a roast chicken on a blue oval dish. The bird was stuffed with breadcrumbs, thyme, and dried apricots. She dished up potatoes, baked in garlic and rosemary, and mountains of shining broccoli, plump white leeks, and a rich gravy, steaming in the candlelight. She glanced quickly at Will, sitting at the far end of the table. She watched him devour the dinner, and then eat a second helping with equal relish. Then he leaned back in his chair, sleek, like a young animal, flushed with bodily content.

"That was amazing," he said. "The best food I've eaten in weeks. Thanks."

Bryony looked down at the table, with a quick nod. Cassilago picked at his meal, fastidious and lacking appetite. He refused the apple pie, flavored with cinnamon and fresh cream, but he gestured to Will, who consumed a generous portion and then went on to a plate of stilton and oatmeal biscuits. She observed him cautiously, his hunger, and the pleasure he took in its satisfaction. His eyelashes glinted gold, and the fine hair on his forearms. Cassilago had removed his coat, revealing a velvet waistcoat. Will wore a thin shirt with the words *Dead Kennedys* emblazoned across his chest. And whereas Cassilago's narrow, bony frame was disguised by his apparel, the young man's clothes clung to his body, displaying the strong curve of his shoulders and back, the ripple of muscle and sinew.

"Bring us some coffee," Cassilago said. His cold, quick voice broke into Bryony's dreams. She stood up quickly, cleared the plates. Will rose to his feet and clumsily began to help her.

"Don't worry," she said. "I'll do it."

"No, no," Will persisted. "Least I can do. Let me wash up. You sit down." He grabbed a plate, and his long, tawny hand brushed against her arm.

"Leave it, Will," Cassilago ordered. His nostrils flared. "You're my guest. You sit down."

Chastened, like a schoolboy, Will dropped into his seat. Bryony headed into the kitchen. She placed the pile of plates on the table. Then she sat, her head in her hands. She felt a curious tightness in her throat. She was shaking.

Will stood up, preparing to leave, but Cassilago poured a musky blue liquor into two tiny glasses. He suggested they retire to his study. Will protested his weariness, his plans for an early start the next morning, but Cassilago insisted. He led them to a dark room, overlooking the garden, and turned up the large, brass lamp burning dully on a desk by the window.

"So, Will, where are you from?" The waistcoat, poppy-red, winked golden buttons. Cassilago sat in a leather chair. Will stood, shifting uneasily, looking round the room, at shelves of leather-bound books, piles of paper, bundles of herbs poking from pots and hanging from a little wooden rack on the desk.

"Uh ... Leicestershire," he said, vaguely. "A village." He stepped across the room to a fat glass jar perched on the window ledge. Inside, suspended in a clear liquid, sepia membranes swirled around a tiny floating figure.

"What's this?" He picked up the jar, and the creature bobbed, brown and shriveled like a dried fig. Cassilago smiled.

"A fairy," he said. He dipped his face, deep shadow filling the sockets of his eyes, and the lines across his forehead. The lamplight picked out threads of white in his black hair, brushed from his face, hanging limp to his shoulders.

"I found it in the Black Hellebore last winter, lying in the flowers. Already dead—probably killed by the cold. The peasants call the hellebore the Christmas Rose. They think it protects their cattle from evil spells, and they dig it up with mystic rights. It's poisonous—but the species in the garden I sell to the homeopaths."

Will peered at the jar. He didn't know how to react. He returned the vessel to the windowsill.

"I've seen this kind of thing before," Will said. "Fairy Folk in a Jar. I bought one for my sister. Cuter than this one." He turned from the window and drew up a chair. He sat down, stretching out his long legs. He lifted the cold blue liquor to his lips. The drink stung his mouth, burning sweet on his tongue, leaving behind a bitter flowery taste.

"You don't like it?" Cassilago said. "It's one of my own."

Will took another, softer sip.

"This is what you do then," he said, gesturing the room. "You're a botanist?"

Cassilago nodded.

"I'm very lucky," he said. "I have this place and a couple of small fields growing lavender. I cultivate and collect herbs. I sell plants to herbalists and homeopaths, and seeds to the growers and the catalogue people. Bryony makes her homemade herbal soaps and papers, mostly for mail order customers."

Will couldn't help but smile. So modern commerce underpinned the retro lifestyle after all. Perhaps a mobile phone was stowed in an oak drawer, or behind an embroidered screen he'd find an Apple Mac bulging with accounts and mailing lists. He relaxed. He breathed easily, getting to grips with the situation, feeling he had the measure of these people after all. He chanced the question that had danced in his mind all evening. Still he couched it carefully.

"And Bryony? She's your assistant?"

"She's my wife." Cassilago took another sip. "The disparity in age is not as great as you might imagine," he said, perceiving Will's embarrassment. "We were drawn together by a shared interest—a mutual passion. She was a customer. We began a correspondence. Two years later we were married."

Cassilago topped up Will's glass. Will felt a vague sense of disappointment. Mechanically he responded to Cassilago's questions, concerning his walk, his route, his destination. But the drink was clouding his thoughts, and he grew very weary. When the glass was empty, he rose to his feet, thanking his host profusely. He said he had to sleep.

Cassilago led him to the front door, to a garden glistening silver in the darkness. Will put his hand to his eyes. His head ached. The moon seemed to burn his brain. He made his way down the path and stumbled heavily into his tent.

Bryony tipped cup after cup of cool amber water over her hair. The water was infused with Golden Rod, and in a mindless ritual she mused upon its properties: solitary stout stem and stalkless sulfur-yellow flowers on a long spike. Called Hag's Taper, and Great Mullein. Sedative. Narcotic. Good for bleeding lungs and bowels—in homeopathy, for migraine. And to dye hair yellow . . . Someone entered the room. She stopped rinsing and stood up. She was naked, except for a towel which she wound about her wet hair. Cassilago stared without expression, lost in thought.

"Have you filled the tub?" he said at last. Bryony nodded. Cassilago disappeared for a few moments, returning with a blue glass bottle, a small wooden box, and a handful of dried lavender. The little bath steamed by the range. He crunched the lavender and scattered it over the water. He tipped in soapy, viscous drops from the blue bottle, and sprinkled the fine ashy contents of the box. Bryony could smell mold and marigolds. She took Cassilago's hand, and stepped daintily into the water.

As she soaked, Cassilago stripped off his own clothes and began to wash at the sink. His body was gaunt and gray. A pot belly protruded below his thin chest, and fat blue veins laced around his legs. When he finished, he turned to his wife.

"Are you ready?" he asked, strangely tender. Bryony looked away, rubbing her hands together compulsively.

"I know you want to," he said. "I could smell it on you. And him. You want it."

Bryony shook her head.

"I want you," she said. She kissed him. She reached out her hand and grasped his cock, small and shrinking, slippery in her wet hand, a soft, putty-colored morsel. She stroked it gently, willing a response.

"Don't torment me," Cassilago said, drawing away. "You know what we have to do."

Bryony dried herself, and Cassilago pulled on a pair of surgical rubber gloves. He lifted a tiny china pot from the top shelf. Bryony shivered.

"Are you afraid?" he asked. She took a deep breath.

"Of the ointment? No."

"Of the act, then?"

"He's a young man. Do we have the right?"

"Have you changed your mind?"

Bryony didn't reply, so Cassilago opened the pot. His careful, patient fingers, anointed her, head to foot, covering every inch of her skin. Hands and breasts, belly and thighs, the crease of her elbows, the hollows of her feet, smoothing her face, and pressing into her intimate parts. Bryony stood perfectly still. She cleared her mind, as the new skin dried upon her, sinking into the pores.

"You are very pale," Cassilago said, peeling off the gloves. "Death the Bride, yes? Are you cold?"

Bryony nodded. Her body was stiff and numb.

"Not long. Wait a few minutes more." The clock ticked. Cassilago tidied up the kitchen. He tipped the water away. Then he gestured Bryony to the front door. She ached when she moved. She felt bruised.

"He'll be waiting," he said. Bryony stepped over the threshold, but hesitated. She looked at her husband, seeing him frail, and wounded. She reached out, but she couldn't touch him.

Slowly she walked away, feeling the rough path beneath her feet. When she looked back, Cassilago was a dark shadow in the doorway.

Will lay heavy as a stone, but his dreams were quick and volatile. His thoughts flickered in a blue haze, sweet upon his senses. Then brightness, and Bryony moving toward him, a shy, thin smile upon her curious face. Could it happen? Then he was kissing her, and her lips tasted of vanilla, burning his skin, and she turned away from him, offering the smooth, white curves of her bottom, with the soft, raspberry cleft, and he was pushing in, pushing in . . .

But he woke with a jolt, alone, in the dark confines of his tent, aching with regret. His cock pressed hot against his jeans, and quickly he pulled off his clothes and slipped into the sleeping bag, searching for sleep. But lust still prickled, and he turned and twitched, finding no relief. Was it possible? No, no, she was lying with her husband, the old man, and maybe they were doing it right now, just yards away. So Will reached for his torch and dug his book, *The Acid House*, from his rucksack. He tried to read, but the words slid away, and inevitably his thoughts returned to Bryony. He climbed from the tent, his feet wet by the dew on the grass, and he stared at the house, where a light burned still. Then—a whisper beside him. A shock—a moment of alarm.

"Will. It's me."

Will caught his breath. Perspiration broke out on his body.

"Bryony," he said. His voice was choked. "Where are you?"

She stepped closer, and he smelt soap and summer flowers. She grasped his arm with an icy hand.

"Hold me," she said. "I'm cold." She embraced him, pressing her face against his shoulder, and Will felt her bare body leaning on his own, the smooth, impossible thrill of her uncovered flesh close to his. Would he wake again? How long could he sleep, and dream?

She pulled him down to lie in the soft grass, a dim shape in the darkness. Will touched her face with his fingers, recreating her image in his mind. He searched out the contours of her body with his lips, and her skin tasted bitter. When he lay between her thighs, her body resisted him briefly. Then he slipped in, enclosed and swallowed up, and the fluids of her sex, corrosive like acid, stung the delicate membranes of his cock as he moved.

When he woke, the sky was gray and pale. Bryony lay next to him, curled like a child. Will regarded her face, the thin lines around her eyes, at the edges of her mouth. He remembered Cassilago's words, understanding that Bryony was older than he thought. She woke, as he watched her, and she stood up, not meeting his eyes, already retreating.

"I'm sorry," she said. "Thank you. I'm sorry." She hurried away, to the house. Will returned to the tent and huddled in his sleeping bag. His skin was red and hot.

Bryony closed the front door. In the kitchen, a fresh bath had been prepared. The water was cool and cloudy. She washed the film of blood and semen from her thighs. She soaked for an hour or more, till the water was quite cold, and she cleansed herself, every inch, every pore.

Afterward, she slept alone in her husband's great wooden bed. Cassilago was absent. Perhaps he had spent the night walking. Perhaps he was preparing the cave.

Will woke a few hours later. His body itched and ached. He sat up. Countless scarlet lesions patterned his skin. He crawled from his tent in a fever. When he rose to his feet the earth seemed to fall away from him. The sunlight scalded his eyes. He pulled on his jeans and struggled to the house. He hammered on the front door. Nobody came. He pushed his way inside, found Cassilago's study, and searched through the drawers. The mobile phone—here, somewhere. What had they done to him, the unwary traveler? A mutual passion, yes—Bryony, the witch, with her false youth, her seduction. And Cassilago, the sorcerer . . . had they corrupted his body with their potions and poisons? No, no. He was sick and delirious—conjuring fantasies. If only he could find the phone . . . The room reeled. He reached out for the desk, but his strength seeped away. He curled on the floor, in a daze.

Later, Cassilago loomed over him, talking, though Will couldn't hear what he said. Then Bryony appeared. They lifted him from the floor. Cassilago wore gloves. In a distant dream, Will was carried to a locked barn at the back of the house, and dropped in the back of a cherry red Fiat Punto.

From the ruins of his flesh, below his ribs, a coarse, fibrous stalk has risen. At its summit, a single bud swells, glaucous, slick with mucous. The moments of consciousness are few, and fleeting. Bryony touches his brow, murmuring quietly, and he takes comfort. Primed on cells scraped from her skin, from her mouth, the spores disregard her. She is immune. The seed is sown. He watches her, with longing.

The bud twitches. The petals unfurl, purple and glistening. Cassilago—herbalist, mage—awaits the harvest. Then he will grind and pulverize, extracting a potent essence. Renewal. Consummation.

Sarah Singleton is the author of the contemporary fantasy novel, The Crow Maiden, *and eight novels for young adults, including* Century *(Booktrust Teen Award 2005),* Heretic, *and* The Amethyst Child, *all published by Simon & Schuster UK. She has published many stories in magazines and anthologies, including* Interzone, Black Static, *and* The Dark. *Sarah has worked as a journalist and a secondary school teacher of English. She lives in Wiltshire, England, county of long barrows, stone circles, and white horses.*

SWEET SUBTLETIES

by Lisa L. Hannett

EDITOR'S NOTES: Is it true, we are what we eat, or is it that we'd rather eat what we wish to be? *Sweet Subtleties* is a glorious, rich tale of dark fantasy, sampling the tastes of connoisseurs and the lengths they may go to savor the flavor of what they desire-made-edible.

South Australian author Lisa L. Hannett arouses the sense of taste in this next selection by pushing through conventional dining boundaries. Sharp, witty, passionate, her writing just drips with the juices of eloquence, words made succulent to the page. And besides authoring unsettling speculative fiction, Lisa is a university lecturer, holding a PhD in medieval Icelandic literature, which, amongst other accomplishments, just goes to show that pursuing higher academia doesn't kill the creative spirit at all, as found in this following tale.

Una Belle is French confectioner Javier's greatest creation, a culinary fantasy to be dined upon by whatever the audience wishes her to be, although she finds the hardest tastes to satisfy are those of disappointed family.

> *"Butter-dipped petals crumbled on plates, lips that have failed to hold a pucker. Butterscotch ears, taffy lashes, glacé cherry nipples . . ."*

JAVIER CALLS ME UNA, though I'm not the first. There are leftovers all around his studio. Evidence of other, more perishable versions. Two white chocolate legs on a Grecian plinth in the corner, drained of their caramel filling. A banquet of fondant hands, some of which I've worn, amputated on trays next to the stove. Butter-dipped petals crumbled on plates, lips that have failed to hold a pucker. Butterscotch ears, taffy lashes, glacé cherry nipples. Nougat breasts, pre-used, fondled shapeless. Beside them, tools are scattered on wooden tables. Mixing bowls, whisks, chisels, flame-bottles. Needles, toothpicks, sickle probes, pliers. Pastry brushes hardening in dishes of glycerin. In alphabetical rows on the baker's rack, there are macadamias, marshmallows, mignardises. Shards of rock candies, brown, yellow, and green, that Javier uses to tint our irises. Gumdrop kidneys, red-hot livers, gelatin lungs. So many treats crammed into clear jars, ready to be pressed into cavities, tissue-wrapped and stuffed into limbs. Swallowed by throats that aren't always mine.

"Delicious," I say as Javier jams grenadine capsules into my sinuses, a surprise for clients with a taste for fizz. "Delicious." The word bubbles, vowels thick and popping in all the wrong places. Gently frowning, Javier crushes my larynx with his thumbs. He fiddles with the broken musk-sticks, tweaking and poking, then binds the voice box anew with licorice cords. I try again.

"Delicious."

Still not right. The tone is off. The timbre. It's phlegmatic, not alluring. Hoary, not whorish. It will put people off their meals, not whet appetites. It doesn't sound like me.

Javier's palm on my half-open mouth is salty. His long fingers gully my cheeks. I wait in silence as he breaks and rebuilds, breaks and rebuilds. Concentrating on my lungs, my throat. Clearing them. Making sure they are dry. I don't mind being hushed. Not really. Not at the moment. If anything goes wrong, if I collapse this instant, if I crack or dissolve, at least my last words will have been pleasant. Something sweet to remember me by.

It won't be like before, he said. There will be no weeping. No throttling chest-rattle. No thick, unbreathable air.

On Monday, I made my latest debut—I make so many. Served after the soup but before the viande at the *Salon Indien du Grand Café*. My striptease was an enormous success. Fresh and unmarked, clad in edible cellophane, my marzipan dusted with peach velvet. Even the stuffiest top-hat couldn't resist. Javier had contrived a device to drop sugared cherries onto every tongue that probed between my legs. Dozens of gentlemen laughed and slurped, delighted I was a virgin for each of them.

"Marvelous," they shouted, licking slick chops. "Belle Una, tonight you're more divine than ever!"

"Marvelous," I say, calm and mostly clear. Mostly. Close enough.

Sugar-spun wigs line a window ledge above Javier's workbench. Faceless heads, all of them. Now visible, now obscured, as he bobs over me, intent on his work. The hairdos are exquisite. Some pinned up in elaborate curls, some plaited, some styled after Godiva. Glinting honey strands. Carmine. Deep ganache. Exquisite, all of them, despite showing signs of wear.

Between soot-streaked portraits on the walls, wooden shelves support a horde of glass molds. As one, they gape at me from across the room. Their faces as like to each other as I am to them. High brows and cheekbones, pert mouths, strong jaws, noses so straight we'd be ugly if it weren't for our delicate nostrils. Javier insists we are identical, indistinguishable, impeccable casts of the original. We must be the same, he tells us. We must be. We *must*.

Once people have well and truly fallen in love, he said, *they do not want variety*. They want the same Una they enjoyed yesterday, last week, last month. They want the same Una, now and always. The same Una that Javier, confectioner gourmand, is forever recreating.

For the *hauts bohème* on Wednesday evening, I played the role of limonadière. Stationed behind the bar counter, I wept pomegranate jewels while spouting absinthe verses. Odes to beauty, freedom, love. Javier encouraged this crowd unreservedly. "They've loose clothes, loose hair, loose morals," he said. "And loose purse-strings." Under his guidance, the bohèmes tickled my limbs with the bows of gypsy violins. Scratched me with pen nibs. Trailed paintbrushes along my soft places. With each stroke, swirls of hippocras bled to my surface. Ale, brandy, champagne, rum. One by one, the lushes lapped it all up. "They prefer drink to desserts," Javier said. Those with maudlin constitutions cannot keep anything substantial down.

"Una, *chère* Una," the bohos cried, slurring into their cups. "Promise never to leave us again."

Emotional drunks, I thought. *Glutting themselves into confusion. Muddled on passion and wine. Can't they see I'm here? I am forever here.*

"I feel—" I begin. Javier traps my jaw. Holds it still. Wary of what, I wonder? That it will fall off with talk, no doubt. That I'll run out of things to say before tonight's performance.

I feel solid, I want to assure him. I feel settled. Take it easy now. Easy. I'm going nowhere. I'm right here.

Friday's connoisseurs ate with torturous restraint.

"Pace yourselves," the women said, cracking knuckles with the sharp edges of their fans.

"Sugar is a mere distraction for the palate," said the men. "It will never satiate."

As centerpiece on their ruby tablecloth, I sat with legs pretzeled into Sadean poses. Wearing garters of hardened molasses, nothing more. By the second remove of sorbet, my contorted ankles and wrists had crumbled. I couldn't stand for all the gold in the world. My paralysis thrilled our hosts to no end—as did Javier's copper blades. Two daggers per guest. Honed to ravage goodies from my thighs, rump, belly. Tantalized, the feasters took turns at fossicking. At knifing currant ants and blackberry spiders from my innards.

"What an illusion," they moaned, crunching aniseed antennae. "So convincing, so real . . . And not even a splash of blood! When did you learn such tricks, *chère fille*? Why have you not beguiled us this way before? No matter, no matter. Bravo, *chère* Una, *et encore*!"

Tips are highest when egos are stroked, my confectioner says. When pomposity is rewarded with flirtation. So Javier slapped their bony backs. He stooped and kowtowed. I bowed as best I could. Waggling my fingers and toes. Letting them caress me long after the coins had rolled.

Rigged with peanut-brittle bones, my digits made such a gratifying snap when the party finally succumbed. When they gave into temptation. Indulged in wounding and breaking.

Javier ribbons my chin with silk to hold it in place for a few minutes. My neck needs patching; he's made quite the mess of it. He spritzes rosewater to keep me malleable, then shuffles to the stove. Bent over hotplates, he sings quietly as he stirs. His plainchant quickens the pots' ingredients. Sifted flour, hen-milk, vanilla essence. A sprinkling of salty eye-dew to bring his subtleties to life. Over and over, mournfully low, he garnishes the mixture with tears and base notes of my name.

Una, Una, he whispers, adding a pinch of cardamom to freckle my skin. *Una, this time you'll be just right.*

For tonight's outcall, Javier embeds a diadem of Jordan almonds into my curls. "The candied treasure of Priam," he says, chiseling them into my scalp. Content, he moves on to my hazel eyes. Sets them with a stony stare, like Helen's transfixed by the sight of her city ablaze. She's a favorite of Javier's. Peerless Helen. Unforgettable Helen. With that legendary face. All those ships sailing after it. Lately, while assembling and reassembling me, he's worn grooves into her story, worn it thin with retelling. The affair. The abduction. The hoopla and heartbreak. His sunken cheeks gain a healthy sheen as he talks of truces made and broken. Gifts offered, shunned, accepted. The permanence, the stubbornness of young lovers. The tale spills from him like powdered ginger, spicy and sharp, as he presses buttercream icing into my moist gaps.

While he pokes and prods, I make predictable observations. Repeating comments he himself once made. Repeating threadbare conversations. Repeating things he'll smile to hear.

From the shelf, the molds watch us, unblinking.

"Ignore them," I say, repeating, repeating. "It's just the two of us now."

Javier rubs the scowl from my forehead. Heats a spoon and melts saffron into my eyebrows. Sunshine lilts through the studio's crescent windows as he works. The deep gold of late afternoon adds fire to his story. Promises broken, omens ignored, the grief and wrath of Achilles. Every word igniting, ablaze. But when he reaches the sack of Troy, Javier pauses. Unwilling to narrate the ending, he backtracks. As always, to Helen.

Concentrating, he plunges a series of long plaits into my scalp without letting even a drop of custard ooze out. Carefully, precisely, he stretches them down my spine. I'm half-bowed under the weight of so much hair. He fusses with the braids, fusses.

"Menelaus is furious when his wife returns," he eventually says. "Can you imagine? Almost as furious as when she first left. How dare she have survived so much without him? How dare he remain such a fool in her presence."

I shrug. Javier pushes my shoulders back down, checks for wrinkles. Checks the portrait above the assembly table. Nodding, he reaches up to drape an icing chiton over my nakedness. I am taller than him by a hand, but he is clever as a monkey when it comes to climbing. Hopping from footstool to bench and back, he maneuvers around me, the long tube of material bunched in his arms. Though the gauze is thinner than faith, the strength of his recipe keeps it together.

That, and his devilish fingers.

They dart in and out, gathering, smoothing, fluffing my garment until it blouses in wondrous folds. Pins appear, disappear. Puncturing, piercing, holding the fabric in place. Javier's lips smack as he thinks, as he tucks. He steps back to take me all in. Steps up, tugs a pleat. Steps back, cocks his head.

Steps up, fidgets a cord around my waist. Steps back, smacks, annoyed. Up and back, up and back. Step-ball-change, once more from the top. Up and back in the perfectionist's dance.

At last, he is satisfied. A pendant is the final touch, a mille-feuille heart on a string of rarified gold. "You are a feast," he says, coiling the cold thing around my throat. "You are a picture." Overcome, he smacks lips and hands—and his cufflink catches on my neckline. Catches, and tears.

The robes sigh apart, exposing me from gullet to gut. Javier rushes to fix it. He flaps and gouges, making it worse. Up and back, up and back, he flaps, gouges, wrecks, and ruins. Up and back, the necklace snaps. The silver bonbons he'd spent hours spiraling around my cinnamon aureoles are scraped loose. Part of my rib cage concaves. Tiny candies plink to the floor.

But there is air in my chest. There is breath. Surely, this is good?

"And he is ever at mercy of the gods," Javier mutters, smudging my marzipan to keep the custard from seeping out. "We'll have to cancel, Una. Reschedule for another time. We can't arrive with you in this state—what will they think?"

"You underestimate—" I almost say *yourself*, but taste the error before it's spoken. A confectioner does not reach Javier's standing without resolve. Without ego. Instead, I reassure him with a familiar wink. "Tonight, I'll play the mystic. You know the routine. Smoke, mirrors, communing with spirits. It's only fitting." I look down at my Hellenistic garb. The ragged flaps of material lift easily and, thankfully, with minimal debris. I fasten them on my left shoulder, covering the worst of the mess. Leaving my heart and one flawless breast bare.

Holding his gaze, I curtsy. "A seer should ever reveal as much as she obscures. *N'est-ce pas?*"

His laugh is a sad little bark.

"And you are a vision," he says.

I am ready to go, but Javier is nervous.

I don't tell him he's being silly. Don't remind him I've survived three vigorous outings this week, mostly intact. He doesn't need to hear it.

There's no limit to his talent, no damage he can't reverse. I'm living proof, I could tell him. I'm here because of him. I'm here. But he's heard it all before.

Everything will be fine, I could say. Three faultless soirées in the space of a week. Three journeys, survived. As many trips as Helen made, or more, depending on Javier's mood when telling stories. And only a few pieces lost, despite the Sadeans. Nothing important. I'm still together—*we're* still together. Everything is fine.

Even so, Javier is nervous.

"They want to see you, Una. That's all, so they say. After so long. Only to see you." He is speaking to me, but his back is turned. Facing the faded oil painting. "They've got countless portraits, cameos, ambrotypes. Countless memories. *Insufficient*, they say. *It's just not the same.*" Javier snorts. "So now, finally, they want to see *you*."

Vacant glass eyes gaze down from the shelves. The molds sneer at me. Waiting their turn.

"I'll give it my all," I say, the phrase stale on my tongue.

"Yes, of course, *ma chère*," Javier replies to the wall. "You always have."

In the mansion's grand dining hall, dinner is imminent. The sideboard is weighed down with a hoard of gold dishes. Steaming tureens, saucières, bain-maries. The room suffocates with aromas of the meal to come. Fine claret is decanted. Muscat and champagne are chilling for later. Legions of silverware are arranged in ranks beside plates. Crystal stemware gleams. Footmen stand at the ready. Carafes of ice-water dripping condensation onto their white gloves. Poised to begin service, they look out over the room. Vigilant, unblinking.

As always, Madame dominates the table's head while Monsieur commands the foot. Eight rigid people occupy the seats between. Men sporting versions of the same black-and-white suits. Women in lusterless monochrome. All posturing, variations with the same facial features. To my left, Javier folds and refolds his napkin. A cue, perhaps? I await further signals—but like the hors d'oeuvres and drinks, none are forthcoming. For all his anxiety, my confectioner has neglected to give me instructions. Am I the centerpiece this evening? Am I the dessert? Our hosts have offered no guidance. Made no requests. The moment we entered, they simply invited me to sit. To join them at table, like a guest.

They want to see you, Javier said.

They all do, don't they? They want the same Una, over and over. I am always her. Over and over.

But tonight I am also sibyl, oracle, prophetess. Tonight I am breathless from seeing so much. Seeing and being seen.

"A striking resemblance," Maman says at last.

"We had heard," says Papa, mustache bristling. "But, you understand, we needed to see for ourselves."

"Of course," replies Javier. "Of course. Remarkable, *n'est-ce pas?*"

I shiver under their scrutiny.

"How many of these—" says the youngest Demoiselle, *la sœur*, jeweled hand fluttering. Grasping for an explanation. "How long has it been—? How did you reconstruct—? I mean, look at her. Just, *look*. Please tell me this isn't her death mask . . . "

They look and look and look away.

"Absolutely not," whispers Javier. "Does she look dead to you?"

Of course, I repeat silently. *Of course. Remarkable, n'est-ce pas?*

I reach down. Pull my legs up one at a time. Twist until I'm perched like a swami on the mahogany chair. Mousse leaks from my hips. Cream swills in my guts. I exhale and collect my thoughts. Prepare my premonitions. Summon my ghosts.

"Shall we begin?"

One of the black-ties glares at me. "Una was much more lithe," he says. "Much more vibrant. Such an exquisite dancer, such a beautiful singer. To have wasted her life on vulgar cabaret . . . "

"Slinking in alleys . . . "

"Scuffling for coin in dank, decrepit places . . . "

"Cafés and *folies*." Top-hat shakes, spits. "Damp, even in summer. Small wonder the wheeze got her—"

My joints stiffen as he speaks. Vein-syrup coagulates. Grenadine clogs my nostrils. I exaggerate a cough, swallow fizz. Use spittle and phlegm to demand their attention. "Shall we begin?"

"Heartbreaking," says another. "Clearly, a wife cannot survive on sugar, liquor, and promises alone . . . "

"A husband should provide more—"

"*Ça suffit*," says Maman. "My daughter made her own choices. What's done is done."

"But this," says Papa, crossing himself. Expression doughy. "She has had no say in *this*."

"Open your eyes," I intone with all the gravitas of Helen on the ramparts. Fire flickers in my gaze. "Open your eyes. Una is here."

Give them what they desire, my confectioner once told me, *and the audience will never forget you.*

Cardamom flakes from my cheeks as I grin, enigmatic. Remember me? Peppermint auras smoke from my mouth, sweet and pervasive. What a show we've planned! What a performance. There will be no weeping this time. No throttling chest-rattle. No thick, unbreathable air. It won't be like before.

Remember?

I am weightless, seeing them here, being seen. I am buoyant.

A fairy-floss spirit spins out of my fingertips. She clouds up to the ceiling, floats down the walls. Shrouds the gallery of portraits hung there. "Una," I say, louder now. At my command, the specter coalesces. Straight nose, high brows, Helen's fixed stare. She is the mold, the paintings, replicated in floating skeins of cotton candy. "Una is here."

My eyeballs roll back in their sockets. The undersides are concave. Hollow, but not void. Diamond-shaped dragées trickle out. Dry-tears. My pupils turn skullward, but I am not blind. I am Delphic. Past, present, future. All-knowing. All-seeing.

I look and look and don't look away.

Chairs screech back from the table. Heels chatter their exit, but not mouths. Mouths are black lines, firm-clenched or drooping. Mouths are hidden behind satin-gloved fingers, closed behind handkerchiefs. Mouths are quivering disgust. There will be no licks, no nibbles from these. No kisses.

Maman's handmaiden swats the apparition, clearing a path so her mistress can leave. Papa sniffs. Dabs his lowered eyes. Orders servants back to the kitchens. Follows them out. Javier sits rigid as meringue beside me. Will he add this story to his repertoire? Will he tell the next Una what he's told us already, over and over, so many times?

Give them what they desire, he said.

Specters, spirits, sweet subtleties.

"Wait," Javier says as his in-laws retreat from the room. Indecorous penguins, making their excuses before the entrée. "Stay! You wanted to see—"

New memories to replace the old.

Pulling, pulling, the ghost unspools from my heart. She spills. She aches.

"Is this not her face?" he says, leaning close enough to kiss. "Is Una not right here? Is she not perfect?"

"This is not her face," I repeat. Wrong, try again. My thoughts are muddled, drunk on passion and time. "You wanted to see."

Musk falls from my gums. *Bohèmes break brittle bones*. No, wait. Not quite. That's not alphabetical—macadamias, marshmallows, mignardises. Better. My fingers snap, one by one. *Bohèmes bones break brittle*. Sherbet foams from my mouth, grenadine from my nostrils. Custard seeps, melts my delicate robes. My hands find, flail, flounder in Javier's warm grip. Cream gluts from my sternum, splattering the Wedgwood. Shaking, my head teeters. Throbs. Tilts.

"She is not perfect," says the ghost.

Forced skyward, Helen's stony gaze comes to rest on the ceiling rose.

"This is not her face."

Will Javier tell the next Una this story?

Give them what they desire, he said.

New memories.

Remember?

My chest heaves, drowning in buttercream. The ghost breaks its tether, unmoors, dissolves. "This is not her face," she says. Not quite. The tone is off. The thick-glugging timbre. "Javier."

Try again and again.

"Una is not right here."

Lisa L. Hannett has had over 65 short stories appear in venues including Clarkesworld, Fantasy, Weird Tales, Apex, the Year's Best Australian Fantasy and Horror, *and* Imaginarium: Best Canadian Speculative Writing. *She has won four Aurealis Awards, including Best Collection for her first book,* Bluegrass Symphony, *which was also nominated for a World Fantasy Award. Her first novel,* Lament for the Afterlife, *was published in 2015. You can find her online at* http://lisahannett.com *and on Twitter* @LisaLHannett.

THE SENSE OF SIGHT

THOUGHTS ABOUT THE SENSE OF SIGHT

BY JESSICA BAYLISS, PHD

I F YOU WEAR CONTACT LENSES then you are one of the millions of people worldwide who touch their brain on a daily basis. How's that for a creepy fact? Yes, the eyes are part of the central nervous system.

By now, it should not surprise you that reading scary stories activates mirror neurons. The very first research into mirror neurons involved the visual sensory system, so of course, the visual mirror system is at work when we observe others' fear or even just imagine visual scenes.

But how does the brain process fear visually?

The eyes are directly wired, via the optic nerve, to the cortex where they pass through a little crossroads called the *optic chiasm*, before terminating in the lateral geniculate nuclei of the thalamus. These nuclei play a major role in visual processing, but they also help pass information on to other brain regions, including to the hypothalamus and amygdala, which turn on the fight-or-flight sympathetic response.

There are a lot of steps before visual information arrives at the hypothalamus and amygdala, so visual information takes a bit of time to trigger an emotional response. Good thing we have the auditory system; it works much faster. The visual system, however, is thought to be more important than sound when making decisions about *what* to fear. Scientists demonstrate this in the laboratory. When visual cues suggest safety, a participant's fear response to a frightening sound is not as intense.

It may even disappear altogether. But when visual cues are missing or contradictory, the research participant experiences a stronger fear response.

There are two parts to how the visual system helps us process non-visual sensory data.

First, the visual system processes the specific *characteristics* of the scene. Remember the term *cognitive schema*? Schemas are complex sets of ideas, beliefs, and expectations about what is supposed to happen across various situations, and they are essential in helping us make sense of the world. The visual system provides a way of checking in with these schemas and tells us when all is well versus when something is amiss. For example, a bunch of people shouting and clapping will be interpreted differently when the setting is a baseball game than if the crowd is made up of flesh-eating demons from the deepest pits of hell. The noise may be the same, but our eyes know the difference.

Second, the visual system interprets the *novelty* of the stimulus. If you are at a baseball game, and the person next to you suddenly jumps to her feet and starts screaming, that might startle you. If she happens to be a demon, triggering your fear response could save your life. But if we assume she is just a very loud sports fan, then there is no need to get scared over and over. For this reason, the visual system detects stimuli that are new or unusual, which is very important if you do not want to be devoured by demons, but it also habituates—stops responding—when it determines that the stimulus is not important.

The same thing happens when the visual system processes the emotional reactions of other people.

The visual cortex (including visual mirror neurons) works with the amygdala to decipher emotional facial expressions. In fact, if a person's amygdala is damaged, he or she may be unable to recognize emotions on the face of another person, particularly negative emotions. Both the amygdala and the visual cortex seem to respond to novelty, and after just one presentation, they will show less reactivity to an other's emotional state. *No, Aunt Jane isn't upset again. She's still worried about the zombie attack from this morning.* Via these subtle visual mechanisms, our brains know whether there is a new threat. An organism does not need to turn on fight-or-flight in response to old news, so this ability can preserve the body's resources for when they are needed most.

How we feel—our own affective state—is also important when it comes to deciphering the emotional cues displayed by people around us.

One study by a group of scientists in Sweden found that the visual cortex and amygdala do not habituate to emotional expressions as quickly in people with higher state anxiety. In other words, if we are already anxious, we are more likely to attend to emotional faces, and our brains will respond to them more strongly and for longer periods of time than when we are calm.

A person who just escaped flesh-eating demons will be much more responsive to their friend's scared expression than if they just escaped a horde of Golden Retriever puppies. (Unless that demon ate the person's amygdala, in which case they might not notice that their friend is scared at all!)

Our brains may need more time to process visual information, but they also store visual information more strongly than auditory. Research shows visual recognition memory is more reliable, too. It is not surprising, then, that good fiction lets us build vivid pictures in our mind—sometimes very scary pictures.

THE BEHOLDER

BY RICHARD CHRISTIAN MATHESON

EDITOR'S NOTES: Sight tends to be the foremost mode of artistic impression, for it's said that the language of visual art is *feeling*. Emotions and ideas are perceived without words through paintings, drawings, and other ocular media. Further, visual arts help give meaning to what seems meaningless and otherwise evoke a wide range of mental connections: New ideas for the viewer, new associations, even the recollection of feelings and experiences that we once had or would like to revisit again.

One of the reasons visual art is found so compelling is that eye scan patterns show artists actually see differently than other people. Most humans perceive objects—people, landmarks, etc.—for what we *expect* them to be, as icons, and then turn those sights into concepts. Artists, however, will scan the area around an object, including negative space, in order to interpret it in terms of contours, shadows, and colors. The artist's visual world—besides being filtered through their own ideals, fears, and inclinations—is conceptually different than our own.

So it is, by art, that we are invited to perceive the world in unfamiliar ways, to even become one with it . . .

Critically acclaimed and bestselling author, Richard Christian Matheson, explores one woman's vantage as she translates to canvas her mundane room and, perhaps, her own desires, while creating a still-life with uncommon paints.

Herein, see the world through the artistic eyes of *The Beholder*.

> *"As Kim painted a moon leaning casually in the black sky of the painting, the blowing leaves outside her own window began to faintly glimmer . . ."*

KIM STARED AT THE FADED ART GALLERY as if seeing something strange in a mirror for the first time.

The front window was soaped and a high banner draped where Greene's sign had hung only one week back. In perfectly painted letters, it read: *Under New Management.*

She shook her head. The gallery had been doing well enough last time she'd been in. Why hadn't Greene said something about leaving?

Switching off the car radio, she got out, walked to the gallery's door, and tried the locked knob. Glancing for the buzzer, she located a black button and pressed.

Footsteps approached within and the door was noisily unsecured. Kim tried again and, as the hinges squeaked, she entered, grasping her purse. As she walked in, the door slammed, and she spun toward it. Suddenly, she was startled by a voice from the gallery's rear.

"Sorry," said the voice. "It's only the wind."

She slowly approached the counter. To either side of the musty gallery were frames, paintings, etchings, and prints. The same stuff that hadn't sold since she'd moved in three months ago. Odd that Greene hadn't taken anything with him, she thought.

"It's why I keep the door locked. The breezes knock it open and shut all day."

He stood behind the counter in a vanilla-colored silk shirt, hair long and black. His face was classically handsome and easily more than fifty.

"Are you the new owner?" Kim asked, nerves still shaken.

He extended a friendly hand and Kim noticed the heavy rings. Too thick to be a woman's, too delicate to be a man's.

"As a matter of fact, I only took it over recently." He looked at her carefully. "My name is Christian."

Kim met his hand and was reassured by its warmth. He shared a look with her and they both smiled.

"Kim," she offered. "What happened to Mr. Greene?"

"Decided to travel through Europe. We made the exchange of the shop through the mail." He watched her. "He left rather quickly, I take it."

"Yes," Kim said. "He didn't say a word."

They regarded each other in covert fascination.

"Are you an artist?" he finally asked, searching her face.

She smiled. "No. But I've been wanting to do a painting. It struck me last night to do something about it. Isn't that odd?"

He acknowledged the thought with a small smile. "Do you need supplies?"

"Everything," Kim said, laughing. "I just moved here recently and left most of my things behind."

She looked off. Getting a place in a small town was the best thing she'd done since everything had fallen apart. Broken marriages and a new place to start; her mother had been right.

He observed her intently. "Well, I'm sure I'll have everything you'll need."

She brightened as he withdrew a large canvas from beneath the counter.

"About the right size?"

"Perfect," she answered.

Christian smiled and placed the canvas into a bag with other supplies he added to it. As he did, Kim didn't notice him looking at her. Watching.

She peeked into the bag and nodded in delight. "Well," she began, taking inventory, "all that leaves is . . ."

" . . . paint," he finished for her, causing them both to laugh. "If I might suggest something," he said, "I was never able to find colors I wanted when I painted, so I began to create my own. I have them here in the shop."

She looked into his eyes and felt something in her stomach tighten. "How wonderful," she heard herself say. "I'd love to see them."

At that, Christian disappeared into the back of the gallery and reappeared with a jeweled box. Large enough to fit into her cupped hands, it was richest gold, with gems on sides and top.

"Please," he said, indicating the box. "I want you to see."

Kim looked at him and hinged up the top without a word. Inside, a dozen, tear-shaped vials shone with lustrous color, the glowing paints inside like heavenly syrups. She held each vial to the light of the soaped window, causing each to brand regal prisms upon her face.

"They're like pieces of a rainbow," she whispered.

"These paints are *very* special," he said. "You couldn't find others like them anywhere in the world."

Kim gently returned the vials to the box, carefully arranging them as they'd been. She looked at Christian and shook her head slightly.

"They're absolutely beautiful," she said, moved by their regal mystery.

"Then you must have them. One so beautiful is the only rightful owner."

"I... couldn't," she said, suddenly struck by inexplicable doubt. Something about the paints disturbed her. Their peculiar finery was strangely frightening, and the tightening in her stomach returned.

Seeing her confusion, Christian took her hand.

"By knowing you'll create something with my paints, I gain something." He held her hand, imploringly. "It's a kind of circular intimacy; a continuation."

Kim looked at him, feeling hauntingly drawn into something she could neither understand nor resist. She could only watch without protest as Christian placed the paints in her bag, smiling.

Waiting for her to begin.

It was well past midnight when Kim set up the easel and canvas. A reticent moon lifted itself over a bank of clouds, and its light brought shapes to the countryside, outside her bedroom window.

She sat on a stool, in her nightgown, before the canvas, sipping warm tea. The house was very quiet and seemed cooperatively tranquil, wishing to aid in her creation.

She'd set the vials Christian gave her on a small tray, next to the canvas, and poised the brush, in her hand, eyes searching outside for an idea, an inspiration.

The meadows and trees outside the window and well beyond, into the open country, were in slumber, darkness blanketing their trunks and leaves. Owls hooted occasional insomnia, further defining the night's silences as they quieted.

Kim took a sip of tea.

What to paint? she wondered, staring at the taut canvas. She sipped again at the tea until the view outside drew her eye. The window was covered by French doors, the swaying fields beyond seemed, from this second story, like a restive bay of green. *The room, itself, with windows prominent and fields as evocative background, could make something lovely,* she thought.

She dipped the brush into a vial of jewel-brown paint, that Christian had given her, and began.

With its shimmering milkiness, she outlined the room, the French doors, the balcony outside, and several of the trees that napped in distant meadows.

She rinsed the brush and, with the vial of twinkling sapphire blue, finished the sky outside and colored the crystal panes of the French doors.

She shivered and took another drink of tea. It was getting cold outside and she took a sweater from her closet. Pulling it on, she began to study the painting. It needed something in the foreground.

She closed her eyes, trying to visualize what would look right. They opened quickly. Of course!

Immediately, the brush was dipped into the argent black paint, and Kim began to outline a bed. First the headboard and baseboard, finally the coverlet, yet to be colored in. As she watched her hand moving, she looked beyond it to the forming painting. It was starting to come alive and she could feel its rhythms. Its pulse.

As she painted the branches of the trees, shifting and straining in the imaginary winds of the painting, she heard the wind outside begin to stir. It rose, as she painted-in the detail of each branch. Leaves rustled against the French windows, in tangled flight. As Kim painted a moon leaning casually in the black sky of the painting, the blowing leaves outside her own window began to faintly glimmer.

But she paid little attention to these curiosities. Her hands and eyes weren't drifting much from the painting any longer. As if knowing each movement, she rinsed her brush, immersed it into the proper vial, and painted in something further, rushing the work to completion.

She repeated this, over and over, painting in the room in richer detail: an antique dresser, an arched doorway, a blazing fireplace. With the completion of the painted fireplace, her own bedroom filled with the sound of crackling logs and the swelling odor of sweet, burning pine.

She continued to paint, unaware, possessed by urges that had long since taken over. Disconnected from the room, she was linked only to the painting now. Her hands moved rapidly, over the canvas, as if conducting some mad symphony, and she began to paint someone in the bed. The form lolled under the silk comforter, that had been painted an etheric yellow, and seemed to wait for the arrival of something.

The vials were quickly emptying as Kim painted faster, giving the form in the bed more detail. There were long, tapered arms. Hair like her own. Her favorite gown . . .

Her breathing stumbled as she looked at the face. *It was her.* There was no question.

Without reacting, she began to paint with renewed fervor. More detail, ever more detail. She added a blue taper. Then, another. Both in beautiful sconces, on the painting's bedside tables, flames slithering joyously.

As she did this, the electric lights in her own room went suddenly off. Yet some strange glow remained, mysteriously filling the room. Several of the bewitching paints were now emptied from their vials and few remained. In the vial of translucent blood-red, a single drop rested at the bottom.

The painting was nearly done, and the room Kim had rendered was stunning. It was lit by tapers and firelight, and its opened French windows bid entry to a chilly midnight wind.

She felt her hair blowing and as she looked over at the window in her room, she shuddered. It was still closed.

She could feel herself reacting in fear but kept painting. As she did, noticing almost nothing of what she drew, she trembled as a warm hand touched her face.

She looked at the painting and nearly screamed. She had painted a man's hand gently resting, in the painting, on her face.

In shaken captivation, her brush began anew, slower, as if caressing the remaining portions of canvas. As the brush, moving without her conscious guidance, painted in the man's legs, she felt warm legs pressing against her own. As it painted shoulders and strong forearms, she breathed a male scent and could feel the beginnings of an embrace.

The haunting discomfiture was fading. The painting's seductions were no longer escapable, and though she fought them, afraid of what was coming, her brush continued emptying vial after vial.

She could now feel warm breath on her neck and a naked body lying next to her own, stroking it, just as in the painting. Her eyes closed completely and she could no longer see what she was painting. Nor could she separate what she painted from what she felt herself.

The two places and moments were merging.

Joining.

As she felt sensual breathing beginning to lower toward her mouth and heard her name being whispered, her brush dipped into the last available paint.

The single drop of red.

In slow motion, her arm arced from the tray of paints, to the canvas, and unveeringly sought a specific spot. Her hand found it.

As she painted in the man's lips with the single drop of red, she felt full lips lowering onto hers, warmly covering her mouth. As she responded, looking up into the man's face, the room in which she painted went suddenly still.

On the floor, the brush had fallen. There were also empty paint vials, which had scattered uselessly. Little else. Except for the empty gown which lay beneath the easel. Left behind.

As museum tours whispered by, on the floors, above and below, the small area that the exhibit occupied, a young woman looked at the paintings curiously.

"They're beautiful, aren't they?" said a friendly voice, which approached her.

"They're very strange," she said, studying them. "You can't make out the man's face in any of them."

He looked at her, watching every detail. "Perhaps he preferred it that way."

She nodded and began to walk away.

"Excuse me," he said, stopping her. "Do you paint?"

She looked at him, confused, though a bit intrigued.

And as the dozens and dozens of paintings watched, with hundreds of trapped eyes pleading to stop him, Christian withdrew the golden box from his coat pocket.

Richard Christian Matheson is an acclaimed bestselling author and screenwriter/producer for television and film. He has worked with Steven Spielberg, Stephen King, Dean Koontz, George R.R. Martin, Roger Corman, Tobe Hooper, and many others on Emmy–winning mini-series, feature films, and hit series. Matheson has had fifteen films produced and written and produced hundreds of drama and comedy television episodes, including co-creating the HBO comedy series Chemistry. *His critically-hailed, dark psychological fiction appears in his short story collections,* Scars and Other Distinguishing Marks, *#1 bestseller* Dystopia, Zoopraxis, *and over 150 major anthologies, including many Years' Best volumes. He is the author of the suspense novel,* Created By *and the Hollywood novella, "The Ritual of Illusion". He compiled and edited,* Stephen King's Battleground: A Commemoration of the Emmy-winning Television Adaptation *for which he also wrote the screenplay. A professional drummer, he studied privately with Cream's Ginger Baker. He is president of Matheson Entertainment producing film, television, and stage projects. His latest film is* Nightmare Cinema *directed by Joe Dante.*

IN THE PORCHES OF MY EARS

BY NORMAN PRENTISS

EDITOR'S NOTES: When I decided to venture on this anthology project, this next story was my first selection—really, my immediate go-to in terms of finding an assemblage of thoughtful, unconventional writings that explored the use of sense in meaningful and powerful ways.

I'd first read *In the Porches of My Ears* by Norman Prentiss several years ago in Paula Guran's *Year's Best Dark Fantasy & Horror 2010*, and the story has stayed in the back of my mind ever since. I'd thought then that I'd never read anything quite like it, and I still think the same today, with its two-story structure and ominous, subtle layering.

For what would it be like to see the world through someone else's eyes? Or, in the following case, to be without vision and have the world described to you? Sight detects obstacles and objects, the remembering and recognizing of colors and shapes, and how those have related to us individually, in our own experiences; so to explain them to others would naturally vary from one person to the next, biased by unique perspectives or, worse even, prejudices or manipulations.

Penetrating and terribly tragic, a man shares his experiences listening to an unknown woman describe the sights of a movie to her blind husband, and how the incident unexpectedly relates to the death of his own wife.

> *"His shoulders and gangly gray-fuzzed head, from my vantage, cut a dark notch into the bottom of the screen like the interlocking edge of a missing jigsaw piece . . . "*

ELEN AND I SHOULD HAVE paid more attention to the couple we followed into the movie theater: his stiff, halting walk, and the way the woman clung to him, arm around his waist and her body pressed tight to his side. I read love into their close posture, an older couple exchanging long-held decorum for the sort of public display more common among today's younger people. I felt embarrassed for them and looked away. I regret that neither my wife nor I noticed a crucial detail in time, but real life doesn't always inspire the interpretative urgency of images projected on a screen, and it's not as if a prop department provided the obvious clues: sunglasses worn indoors, or a thin white cane tapping the ground, sweeping the air.

Helen went ahead to get us seats, while I stood in line at concessions to buy bottled waters. We disliked popcorn for its metallic, fake butter smell and, more importantly, because we chose not to contribute to the surrounding crunch—a sound like feet stomping through dead leaves, intruding over a film's quieter moments. For similar reasons, we avoided candy, with its noisome wrappers, and the worst abomination of recent years, the plastic tray of corn chips and hot cheese dip. Fortunately, the Midtowne Cinema didn't serve the latter, making it one of our preferred neighborhood theaters. That, and the slightly older clientele who behaved according to that lost era, back before people trained themselves to shout over rented movies in their living rooms.

The Midtowne wasn't quite an art house, rarely showing films with subtitles or excessive nudity. Instead, it tended toward Shakespeare or Dickens or E. M. Forster adaptations, the big-screen, bigger-budget equivalents to television's *Masterpiece Theatre*, which I tended to prefer; or, closer to Helen's taste, romantic comedies more palatably delivered through British accents.

Helen had chosen the afternoon's entertainment, so we'd once again see that short, slightly goofy actor who survived an embarrassing sex scandal a few years back and still, *still* managed onscreen to charm the sandy-haired, long-legged actress (who was actually American-born, but approximated the preferred accent well enough for most, and smiled brightly enough to provoke the rest to forgive her). I brought the water bottles into the auditorium—two dollars each, unfortunately, but we broke even by saving as much on matinee admission—and searched for Helen in the flickering dark.

We were later than I expected. Previews had already started, and the semi-dark auditorium was mostly full. I knew Helen's preference for an aisle seat, on the right side of the main section, but the crowd had forced her to sit farther back than usual. I walked past her before a whispered, "Psst, Steve," called me to the correct row.

She turned sideways, legs in the aisle so I could scoot past easily. I handed her a water bottle before I sat down.

"Is this okay?" she asked.

"Fine." I responded without really thinking. It was her movie choice, so it wouldn't bother *me* to sit too far back from the picture.

Helen gestured toward the man in front of me, then forked her middle and forefinger to point at her eyes. I recognized the man from the couple I'd half-noticed on the way inside. He sat tall in his seat: his shoulders and gangly gray-fuzzed head, from my vantage, cut a dark notch into the bottom of the screen like the interlocking edge of a missing jigsaw piece. His companion was a good bit shorter, granting my wife a clear view of the film.

I knew Helen felt guilty because she liked the aisle, actually thought she *needed* it because she typically left to use the restroom at least twice during a ninety-minute film. The water bottle didn't help, obviously.

Music swelled from the preview's soundtrack, and a glossy country manor montage shimmered onscreen. Like a sequel to *Age of Innocence*, or maybe *A Room with a Different View*. "I can see fine," I assured her. Besides, the slight obstruction was better than having Helen climb over my legs several times once the film was in progress. "As long as there's no subtitles," I joked.

Helen pointed to her eyes again, and her fingertips nearly touched the lenses of her glasses. I could tell she wanted to say more, but she stopped herself.

"What *is* it?"

I spoke normally, just loud enough so she'd hear over the trailer's quoted blurb from *The New Yorker*, but from Helen's expression you would think I'd shouted, "Fire!"

"Never mind," she said, especially quiet, but her message clear.

Then the man in front of me turned his head. It was a quick motion, almost like a muscle spasm, and he held the angle for a long, awkward profile. His shoulder pressed into the chair cushion, and he twisted his head further around toward me. From a trick of the projection light, I assumed, his eyes appeared fogged, the irises lined like veined gray marble.

His companion tapped him. "The movie's about to start." As if she'd activated a button on the man's shoulder, his head snapped quickly around, face front.

"Strange," I said, barely audible, but still Helen winced. I couldn't understand her agitation. In our shared interpretation of moviegoer etiquette, it was perfectly acceptable to speak quietly during the "coming attractions" portion of the show.

The exit lights dimmed completely, and the studio logo appeared on the screen. Then before the credits, a pan over Trafalgar Square, then Big Ben, then a red double-decker bus. Quick establishing shots so any idiot would know—

"We're in England."

The woman in front of us spoke with a conspirator's whisper, a quiet, urgent tone far less musical than the lover's lilt she'd expressed earlier when she tapped his shoulder.

Jeez. Thanks for stating the obvious, lady.

The credits began, yellow lettering over a long shot of the Thames river and the London skyline. The two main actors' names appeared first, then the film title.

In that same strident whisper, the woman read aloud to her companion. The stars, the costars, the "Special Appearance by Sir James So-and-so." The screenwriter, editor, for-God's-sake the music composer, and finally the director.

He can see for himself, I thought. He's not . . .

But of course, he *was*, and I'd been a fool for not realizing sooner. For a moment I held out a glimmer of hope that the man was simply illiterate. Once the credits ended, she'd grow silent and they'd watch the movie in peace. Wishful thinking, however, because I recalled how she'd held him close coming inside the building. Guiding him.

And I knew she'd be talking over the entire movie.

If we'd figured it out sooner, we could have moved. Dark as it was, I barely distinguished a few unoccupied seats scattered around the theater—including an empty to my left—but no pairs together. Helen and I always had to sit together. If the movie ended up being ruined for us, at least it would be a shared experience.

The commentary began in earnest. "She's trying to lock the door, but she's got too much in her arms. A purse, an accordion briefcase, a grocery sack, and a Styrofoam coffee cup. The lid's loose on the coffee."

Onscreen, the Emma- or Judi- or Gwyneth-person—possibly I've conflated the actor's name with the character's—juggled the coffee cup, the lid flew up, and the liquid slipped out and over her work clothes. "Damn, damn, damn," she said in a delightful accent, and the audience roared with laughter.

"She spilled it," the man's companion told him. "A huge coffee stain on her blouse."

I hadn't laughed. The woman's commentary—I assumed she was the blind man's wife—had telegraphed the spill. Had the lid really been loose? Enough for any of us to see the clue?

"I can't believe this," I whispered to Helen, and she half-winced again. Finally, I realized the source of her tension: the commonplace wisdom that a person lacking in one physical sense gained extra ability in another—in this case, hearing.

Sure. His loud-mouth wife can ruin the whole film for us, but God forbid we whisper anything that might hurt the guy's feelings.

Helen risked a quick whisper of her own: "I'm sorry."

It wasn't her fault, of course—not really. But we'd been married almost fifteen years, and familiar intimacy brought its own yardstick for blame. The woman, her husband, the *situation itself* created the problem, and we could share disapproval of the couple's imposition, or shake fists skyward in synchronized dismay at Fates who brought us together at the same showing. And yet, Helen had eaten her lunch slowly this afternoon, had misremembered the show's start time, which in turn limited her seating options (and she *must* have the aisle seat, and *must* see these British comedies the first weekend of their release). So I blamed her a bit, then—the type of blame saved for those you love deeply, blame you savored as you indulged a spouse's habits and peculiar tastes.

Helen did the same for me. When she disliked one of my film choices—the somber violence of the latest *King Lear* adaptation, or any Thomas Hardy depression-fest other than *Under the Greenwood Tree*—I could sense her unspoken discomfort beside me, all while the film flickered toward an inevitable, tragic end. In an odd way, her discomfort often improved the experience for me, magnifying the tension of the film. Making it more authentic.

The tension was all wrong here, though, since nothing spoiled a comedy like an explanation. As the Rupert- or Ian- or Trevor-character blustered through confident proclamations, and Emma/Judi/Gwyneth mugged a sour expression, the blind man's wife stated the obvious: "His arrogance offends her. He's so self-centered, he doesn't yet realize he's in love with her."

Oh, really? Do tell.

It was easy enough to infer the same conclusions from the dialogue. I could have closed my eyes and done fine without the woman's incessant whispers. Score myself a hundred on the quiz. Besides, these romantic comedies all followed the same formula: the guy would Darcy her for a bit, she'd come around just when it seemed too late, there'd be a misunderstanding on one or both sides, until a ridiculous coincidence threw them awkwardly and then blissfully together, the end.

"Now she puts her Chinese take-out cartons in the trash, aware she's eaten too much, but also aware it doesn't matter, because she's alone."

A slight bit of interpretation there, against the whimsical Supremes song hurrying love on the soundtrack, but probably accurate. At that moment, I wondered exactly how many others in the theater could hear the woman's commentary. The people in front of them, surely, were in the same position as Helen and I: close enough to overhear, but too close to make a show of offence. Nobody else seemed to react to the voice: no grunts of disapproval, no agitated shiftings in the seats. There wasn't that ripple of cold scorn that chills the orchestra seats when a cell phone goes off during the first aria. Perhaps her whisper was one of those trained, *directed* voices, sharp in proximity but dropping off quickly with distance—as if an invisible bubble cushioned the sound into a tight circumference.

Lucky us.

I actually tried to control my indignation, for Helen's sake. We were both hyper-sensitive to extraneous chatter during a film, but this was her type of movie (though not, as was already evident, the pinnacle of the art form), and I was determined not to spoil her experience further by huffing my disapproval throughout. Instead, I touched the top of Helen's hand on our shared armrest. Our secret signal in the dark: three quick taps, for *I-love-you*.

It was a slight film, stupidly titled *Casting a Romance*: a reference to the Darcy character's job as a casting director for movies, then a pun on casting a *fishing* line, since he joins the girl and her father at a summer cottage, only to lose his stuffy demeanor amid hooks and slipping into lakes, and her getting a massive rainbow trout next to his emasculating tadpole. Somewhere along the way—about half-way between Helen's first and second trips to the Ladies' Room—I'd settled into the film, and into the commentary. I grudgingly appreciated it after a while—the woman's skill at selecting the right details, firing the narration rapidly into her husband's hungry ear. To keep myself amused, I played around a bit, closing my eyes for short stretches and letting the woman's words weave images around the dialogue. When Helen returned from the restroom, I didn't have the burden of summarizing what she missed: the woman's commentary easily filled the gaps.

After a while, I didn't mind being in the bubble with them. The shape of the blind man's head became familiar to me, atop his thin neck and leaning perpetually to one side to catch his wife's every word. That sharp underlying whisper became part of the film, like the experts' comments during a televised sporting event. I half-toyed with the idea she was an expert herself. For example, she whispered how the character left his jacket draped over the chair, and she warned, correctly, that the plane tickets would spill out. She also predicted the moment when he realized his embarrassing connection to the heroine's brother—the cad who'd tried to blackmail him into an acting job during the first reel. Her delivery was so good, that I suspected she'd seen the film before—perhaps even practiced with a notepad and a stopwatch, to pinpoint the precise moments to whisper crucial details or hiss clues that inattentive viewers might miss.

So, I'd grudgingly grown to admire her skill, almost to rely on it for my full appreciation of the movie. And then she did that malicious thing during the final scene.

She changed the ending. It was almost elegant how she did it, an interplay between the silences and the openness of the characters' final words. Onscreen, the man said, "I still love you," and there was a faint rise in his voice, maybe the actor's insecurity rather than the character's, but the woman twisted a question mark over his declaration.

"They say they are in love," she whispered, "but they don't mean it. He reaches out to hug her—" and on the screen they *are* hugging, "but she pulls away. It is too little, too late."

I realized, then, how precarious this type of movie was: a teasing, near-romance, suspended over ninety brittle minutes. The main characters' relationship is simultaneously inevitable and fragile—a happy ending endlessly deferred, the threat of ruin always beneath the comic surface.

The actress laughed onscreen, a clear display of relief and joy, and the woman said: "She's bitter. It is a dry, empty laugh. Her face is full of scorn."

I reached again for Helen's hand beside me. We didn't speak aloud; our touch expressed the outrage well enough. This horrible woman at once betrayed the movie, *and* her blind husband.

I felt certain now that she'd rehearsed the commentary. How else could she best deliver her poison into his ear—at what time, and at how strong a dose—certain no additional dialogue would provide an antidote?

Thinking back, I realized something more sinister. The woman's descriptions of the lead actor had made him taller than the visual reality, gave him a thin neck and wobbled head that tilted awkwardly to the side, very much like . . . the head in front of me, a shadow rising above the seat to darken the bottom edge of the movie frame. She'd transformed the hero into a younger version of her husband, making the character fit how the blind man—for lack of a better word—*saw* himself. For him, the disappointed ending would be particularly cruel.

The camera pulled back from the onscreen couple's happy, final embrace, and a song blared from the soundtrack. The song was allegedly a cheerful choice, with an upbeat tempo and optimistic lyrics. Most people in the audience probably tried not to dwell on how the lead singer died of a drug overdose, just as the group verged on the brink of stardom.

The blind man's shoulders shook in uneven rhythm. His head, formerly tilted toward his wife, now drooped forward. I couldn't hear over the joyful soundtrack, but clearly, the man was crying.

Still, neither Helen nor I said anything—to them, or to each other. The woman had done an awful, unforgivable thing to her husband, but we decided it wasn't our place to comment. An overheard whisper is sacred, like the bond of a confessional. We needn't involve ourselves in another couples' private drama—even if its language had been forced upon us, even if (and I knew Helen felt this more than I did) the whispered words had spoiled our afternoon's entertainment.

My wife and I didn't need to voice this decision. It was communicated though a strange telepathy, refined over many years in darkened movie houses: a released breath after an exciting chase scene; an imperceptible shift in posture to convey boredom; a barely audible sigh at a beautifully framed landscape. We felt from each other what we couldn't hear or see. Helen's soft gasp had told me, "It's not worth it." I tapped my foot on the floor, as if to say, "You're right. I'll let it go."

Like many patrons of the Midtowne Theatre, we were "credit sitters." We wouldn't stay to the very end, necessarily—even the greatest film buff has little interest in what stylist coiffed the extras' hair, or who catered lunches for the crew—but it was always worth sitting through the list of characters, to recognize an actor's name and think, "Ah, I thought I'd seen him before. Wasn't he the one in . . .?"

But the blind man and his companion began to leave right away. The woman seemed to lift him from his seat. Together, they moved slowly into the aisle. Instead of guiding him, as she had upon entering the theater, it now seemed more like she was *carrying* him out, her arm around his back and supporting slumped, defeated shoulders. The house lights were raised slightly to help people exit, and I'd caught a brief glimpse of his sad expression. I wished his wife had given him more time to collect himself, before exposing his raw emotions to the bright, sighted world of the lobby.

In a bizarre, random thought, I wondered if she'd purposely ushered him out before the rapid scroll of names and obscure job titles made a mockery of her remarkable skill. She would have short-circuited trying to keep up, like an early computer instructed to divide by zero.

Helen and I waited through the rest of the cast list, maintaining our silence even as the real-life names of "Florist" and "Waiter #4" floated toward the ceiling. About a third of the seats were still occupied when we stood to leave. After we pushed through the double doors into the lobby, my wife took a detour to the side: another trip to the ladies' room.

I dropped our empty water bottles into the recycle bin, then stood aside near the front doors. A line stretched outside, people buying tickets for the next show, and a steady trickle emerged from the auditorium doors on either side of the concessions counter. They blinked their eyes against fresh light, and all of them had pleasant expressions on their faces. Some people, at least, had been allowed to enjoy the film.

I spotted the blind man beside an arch to the side hallway. He stood by himself, slouched slightly against the wall. His head bobbled indecisively on the thin neck, as if longing to lean toward his wife's voice.

The opportunity presented itself. Despite what Helen and I tacitly agreed to, I moved toward him, my tennis shoes soundless—to me, at least—over the lobby's worn beige carpet.

"Excuse me," I said, but before I got the words out, his face turned toward me. He looked older than I'd imagined, overhead lamps etching shadows under the wrinkles in his skin. Although he was dressed in casual clothes—a light blue short-sleeve shirt and twill pants—he stiffened into a formal posture which, sadly, made him seem more foolish than dignified. His eyes were expectant and vacant and puffy red.

"Excuse me," I repeated, stalling for time even as I feared one of our wives would return from the ladies' room. My voice was loud, but I couldn't control it—as if I needed to pierce the fog of his blank stare. "I just, *um*, I just wanted to say … "

"Yes." It was the first time I'd heard him speak. His voice sounded weakened by his bout of tears, with barely strength to encourage me to continue.

People walked past us, oblivious. I squinted down the hallway toward the rest rooms. No sign yet of Helen, or the awful, whispering woman.

"The movie didn't end the way she described it to you." I blurted out the rest, before I lost my nerve. "The couple was happy at the end. Still in love. I thought you should know."

The blind man didn't react at first. Then I saw something like relief: his body relaxing, the tight line of his mouth loosening as if he sought permission to smile.

He swung his left arm to the side with a flourish, cupped his right arm over his stomach and bent his torso forward in a deep, exaggerated bow. He straightened, then spoke with a firmness I hadn't expected: "Oh, thank you. Thank you *so* much. I don't know what I would have done without your help."

It was a parody of gratefulness. The sarcasm settled into his face, an expression of scorn that immediately dismissed me from his presence.

Luckily, I spotted Helen approaching. I crossed to meet her in the archway, and I steered her across the lobby, keeping her distant from the blind man. As we reached the sidewalk outside, before the theater door swung shut with a rusty squeak, I thought I heard the blind man thank me again.

At dinner, we didn't discuss the film as we normally would. No revisiting favorite lines of dialogue, seeking subtleties in the script; no ranking of the performances or nuanced comparisons to films of similar type. Instead, we tore small pieces off store-bought rolls or rearranged silk flowers, their petals dusty in a white ceramic vase. We took turns saying we were hungry, wondering aloud when the minestrone soup would arrive.

Finally, Helen broached the subject. "I don't know what I was thinking. I wish I hadn't sat there."

"No need to blame yourself," I said. "I hadn't even noticed the guy was blind. And who'd ever expect his wife to describe the whole film for him?"

"I wish I hadn't sat there," Helen repeated.

That was pretty much all we needed to say about the matter. After the main course, though, when we decided not to stay for dessert or coffee, the waitress took too long to bring our check. In the awkward silence, I weakened and decided to confess. I told Helen about my curious encounter with the blind man in the lobby.

Helen shivered, like it was the most frightening story she'd ever heard.

Let me tell you about a different movie. It's another romantic comedy, this time about a long-married couple who stop everything so they can take a month to travel the world together. The man is reluctant at first, afraid to fall behind on his work accounts, and it's not their anniversary or either of their birthdays, and he's never been that spontaneous anyway. But she convinces him, and she's already booked the flights, the hotels, the cruise ship, and she's bought books and brochures and printed off pages and pages of advice from travel websites: little restaurants tourists didn't visit; special tours given only Sunday afternoons, *if* you know who to ask; "must see" lists for each city, itineraries to fill each day.

Before they leave, she surprises him with a wrapped package, and it's a digital camera with lots of storage space, so they can take as many pictures as they want. He'd never believed in photographs, thought taking them distracted from the experience of travel. On previous trips, other tourists were a nuisance with cameras, blocking his view or popping a flash to interrupt the soft calm of natural light. But it's a thoughtful gift, and he finds out he enjoys it: framing a waterfall or mountain or monument, with her in the foreground, and the fun of checking through the pictures that night in the hotel.

He had agreed to the trip just to please her, but soon her enthusiasm wins him over, and he ends up loving it. To be a better comedy, though, things need to go wrong: missed connections, bungled hotel reservations; a random "I'll have that" finger pointed at a menu, and lamb brains arrive at the table, or a five-pound exotic fish with bubble eyes staring up from the plate; or ill-pronounced words to a French street juggler—*fou* instead of *feu*, for instance, ("You called him crazy, *m'sieu!*")—and hilarious misunderstandings ensue.

But there's none of that. Similar things occur, but not often, nothing major. A forgotten toothbrush, rather than a lost passport. She's a fantastic tour guide, and he loves her more than ever. The trip is unforgettable, revitalizing. Okay, it's not that great a film: no conflict, no complications. But it's sweet.

After the trip, he has the memories, and the pictures. The woman smiles in all of them—leaning against the ship rail during their Hawaii cruise, the Nepali coast in the background; tiny in one corner, hair windswept, with the Grand Canyon vast behind her; at a table outside a Venice cafe, a glass of local vintage raised for the camera, and for him.

He's printed all the photos, hundreds of them. He fans a stack, like a cartoon flip-book, and the world rushes behind his wife's constant, smiling image. The heavy paper stock creates a gust of air, almost like a whisper.

Bladder cancer, it says. *Inoperable.*

Everything had seemed like one of Helen's fluffy, happy-ending movies. She kept it that way as long as she could.

The specialists call it bladder cancer, if that's where the tumor originates, even if the disease spreads to other parts of the body. Helen's frequent visits to the bathroom were a symptom, but the change happened gradually, and neither of us had noticed. By the time she got the diagnosis, things had progressed too far. Even with radical treatment, the prognosis wasn't good. When she found out, she decided not to tell me. Instead, she announced, "Let's take a trip!"

If this were really a movie, that omission makes for a more significant story. We were always a happy couple, but I was especially happy during that month-long vacation. *I* was happy. I can only imagine what really went on in Helen's mind, despite those ever-present smiles. Thoughts of aggressive therapy when she returned home; dread of long hospital days, pain still sharp through medicated fog. If she was lucky, maybe, a swift decline.

The trip wasn't for her benefit, but for mine. A beautiful, poignant farewell gift. And always, beneath the sweet surface of her romantic comedy, an awful, unnarrated tragedy.

I hate myself for not noticing it. Helen spared me the knowledge, as long as she could.

One day near the end, from the intensive care bed that she'd dreaded in silence, she revealed something very strange. I almost wish she hadn't told me—though I can understand why she needed to. Something else happened that day at the theater, after we sat behind the blind man and his talkative companion. In the ladies' room, when the film was over, Helen heard that whispered voice again, from the adjoining stall. The voice was clear and *directed*; Helen knew she was the only one who could hear it. The whisper began at the precise moment when my wife strained and began to empty her bladder. Helen remembered exactly what the voice had said: "It doesn't hurt. It's just a minor inconvenience, so you put it off. By the time you get to a doctor, it will be too late." As she repeated the words, Helen's voice, weakened by the cancer and the treatments, achieved a perfect, uncanny duplication of the woman's urgent whisper.

The hospital seemed instantly more sterile and hopeless and cold. Helen passed away that night, while I was home asleep.

And now, all my movies are sad. I go to them alone. I want to feel Helen's presence in the empty seat next to me, embrace those half-conscious signals we always shared in the dark. I want to tap the top of her hand gently, three times.

Instead, I lean my head slightly to the side. A whispered voice distorts the context of the film, makes the story all about me and my loss. It changes the ending, twists it into something horrible.

Norman Prentiss is the author of Odd Adventures with your Other Father *(a Kindle Scout selection). He won a Bram Stoker Award for his first book,* Invisible Fences. *Other publications include* The Book of Baby Names, Four Legs in the Morning, The Fleshless Man, The Halloween Children *(with Brian James Freeman), and* The Narrator *(with Michael McBride), with story appearances in* Dark Screams, Postscripts, Black Static, Four Halloweens, Blood Lite 3, Best Horror of the Year, The Year's Best Dark Fantasy and Horror, *and four editions of the* Shivers *anthology series.*

THE IMPRESSION OF CRAIG SHEE

BY DAVID McGROARTY

EDITOR'S NOTES: When I first read this next story, I was struck immediately by its depth, by the visual range expounding upon how people see or relate things differently from one another, in addition to just being a beautiful introspective piece of relationships and the search for meaning, which is both analogous to the image of self and the image of the mountain face, Craig Shee.

For visual perception is both a cognitive and a natural process: Cognitively, perceived information is transferred to the mind and related to preexisting information, finding connections, whereas the natural process is dependent on the environment, using light in the visible spectrum to find an object's edges, and constructing depth from perspective and relative size.

Interestingly, there are also a number of psychological laws relating to the process of our perception. For example, our mind will group similar items together to form a pattern; our mind will "fill in the blanks" or complete missing information (such as an incomplete triangle); and our mind will perceive an object for what we expect it to be as a whole, rather than its individual components (an image made of dots is that image, rather than a composite of such dots).

So consider such things as you proceed into the following tale: A psychologist visits the Scottish isle where her mother once lived in order to study a peculiar painting she made, famous for the disquieting effect it has on peoples' perceptions. Like its subject rock, *The Impression of Craig Shee* by David McGroarty has many takes. Be sure not to read while sitting on a bar stool.

"Much of what you think you see is not there at all . . . "

IGHT WAS INEVITABLE. In a world so drenched by the sun, for an organism to draw meaning from patterns of light, from refraction, diffusion, reflection, was always going to be a no-brainer.

Evolution has produced many, many variations on the theme of an eye. Our own camera-lens is not the most sophisticated design in the animal kingdom, and it is riddled with flaws. Of course, you would never know this; as with many of your body's shortcomings, your brain papers over the cracks. But if you knew how little information your eyes actually produce, you might be less inclined to trust them.

As a matter of fact, much of what you think you see is not there at all. (Caron Sinclair, *Perception and Deception*, Barkington, 2009)

The Isle of Porthaven is not an island. This is not the strangest thing about the place, but it can often be the thing that surprises visitors the most: to find that a narrow isthmus connects the Isle to the Mull of Kintyre, making it a part of mainland Scotland in everything but name. On the morning of Caron Sinclair's arrival at that land bridge, after a two-day cycle ride from Glasgow, a thick fog had fallen across the sea, and Porthaven was invisible. The narrow road to the Isle faded and vanished into the gray with the water, like a bridge between worlds. Caron paused at the side of the road, then walked her bicycle onto the bridge, mounted, and pedalled across.

The isthmus was a little over a mile long. Halfway over, she was able to look around and see both the Isle before her and the mainland behind, and the tenuous connection which carried her from one to the other. As she continued, the Mull of Kintyre vanished and Porthaven emerged, layer by dull layer in the fog at first, like a pop-up book, and then filling out in sharp and rich color. It surprised her that the details—a church spire, the star-shaped outline of a forest on a hillside—though they came together in unexpected ways, felt almost intimately familiar. She had never been to Porthaven, but she felt a sense of returning to a place she'd known briefly, forgotten, and then dreamed about many times.

She was inarguably in her mother's land now, more than when her plane had touched town in Scotland. Porthaven was the place that had inspired Mhairi Sinclair's greatest work, the place that had made her famous. It was also the place, many believed, that had destroyed her. On the furthest side of the Isle was Craig Shee, the Fairies' Rock, the impossible thing that had obsessed and consumed Mhairi for much of her life.

The road split into two at the end of the land bridge. A crooked signpost indicated that the town was to the left. It was the only town, and it shared its name with the Isle. She followed the road around a bend until it broadened and became a high street, lined by a squat row of whitewashed shop fronts. Caron dismounted and wheeled her bike along the pavement. It was almost noon, but the town seemed only now to be waking up. There were several shops which displayed faded prints of her mother's famous painting, *The Impression of Craig Shee*, in their windows, some of which remained shuttered. A pub seemed recently to have been named after the painting, as it still carried above the door its old name, that of the Rock itself in Gaelic form, *Creag Sìdhe*. Caron chained her bike to a fence by the seafront, sat by the harbor wall, and watched the fog lift and the sun burn through until it reflected on the sea's surface.

At the front of the pub, a few tourists clustered around a minibus, and a little red-haired woman in a parka told them stories of Fairies' Rock: how the locals had once thought the Rock to be the domain of the fairies; how Saint Columba had arrived at Porthaven from Ireland and castigated them for their fears and superstitions, had declared the Rock a miracle of God and blessed the Isle; how the Rock had later captured the imagination of Italian philosophers during the Renaissance, who tried and failed to rationalize its existence and its effects on the human mind.

Out in the open water, a ferry carried tradesmen and daytrippers around Porthaven to Mull and Bute. The air was still, the sea was flat, and it mirrored the sky.

REIFICATION: We build our own worlds, constantly, forever. In every conscious moment, we construct meaning from incomplete and ambiguous data. A smudge of tea becomes a face at the bottom of a cup. A scattering of stars becomes a winged horse in the night sky. Neither awareness of the process nor effort on our parts is needed.

EMERGENCE: When we see the whole, we see it at once. The constituent parts do not queue up for our attention. Complexity emerges spontaneously. That is a tree, not a collection of leaves. That is a house, not a collection of bricks.

INVARIANCE: The worlds that we build are robust. Their structures hold fast, even as their constituents shift around one another. If I turn the table on its side, it remains a table. If I fold my arms, they remain my arms.

MULTISTABILITY: We do not tolerate ambiguity in our worlds. A structure is what it is, until it is something else, and then the change is instantaneous and total. You see the rabbit or you see the duck. You see two faces in profile or you see a vase. You see the old woman in her scarf or the young woman with her head turned away. You do not ever see some combination of the two.

(Caron Sinclair, *Vision*, Barkington, 2010)

"You look like your mother."

The old publican stared across the bar at Caron with narrowed eyes, head cocked. She wondered if he thought that doing so might transform Caron into her mother, or if it was Mhairi's image he could see, and was trying to dispel.

She shrugged. "So I'm told."

"You don't see it?"

There was a photograph of Caron's mother on the wall behind the bar, between two shelves which were filled with various malt whiskies. In the picture, Mhairi stood beside the publican as a younger man, smiling, her head tilted to one side, her cheek resting on his shoulder. Her eyes were closed. She looked a lot like Caron.

"Did you know her?"

He nodded. "When she came to Porthaven. When she was painting that," and he pointed at the copy of *The Impression* that hung above the fireplace. "She ate and drank here nearly every night."

"I didn't know her then," Caron said.

"She was up on that cliff, making sketches, every day until it was nearly too dark to find her way back, and then she came straight to this pub. We used to be named after the Rock. This was when my old man used to run things. But these days, as much as people come to see the Rock, they're only here because of that painting."

Caron turned on her barstool to look at the picture above the fire. It was at least twice the size of the original *Impression*, which she had seen at the Gallery of Modern Art in Glasgow before coming to Porthaven. But it was not a print. It seemed to be a replica, and not a perfect one.

She supposed that it was something in the light. The main elements of her mother's masterpiece were there—the Rock jutting out of the sea, the featureless cliff face, the cave-within-a-cave, the sun-tinged clouds—but the original painting's famously disorienting effect was muted. This copy induced only a mild sensation of vertigo, which passed after a moment's closer inspection.

"It's deliberate," the publican said. "We used to hang a print up there, but punters kept falling off their stools."

"Even when you know it's a trick, you can't stop yourself."

"Are you an artist too?"

She shook her head. "I study perception."

"You mean, like, extrasensory perception?"

"No. Just the normal, everyday sensory perception. I study vision," she said. "I'm a psychologist." The publican nodded slowly, and frowned, as though this were disappointing news. She said, "How we see the world tells us a lot about our minds and how they operate. Especially when we come across images like that, which we find difficult to process."

He glanced toward the door of the pub, like he was planning his escape route. It was a look she'd seen in her students.

"Here," she said. She grabbed a beer mat, and tore back the printed surface, exposing the plain cardboard underneath, and with a pen she carried in the pocket of her rucksack, she drew onto it two overlapping squares. Then, she drew four lines, one between each of the four pairs of corners, so that the picture on the beer mat was the outline of a cube.

"Point to the front face," she said. He placed his fingertip on one face of the cube. "Point to the back," she said, and he did. Then she shaded two sides of the cube, giving it form and depth, and revealing that the front of the cube was where the publican had indicated that the back should be. He frowned, then shook his head. "It's perceptual ambiguity. There wasn't enough information to tell you what you were seeing, so your brain made it up."

"That is something," he said. He glanced toward the door again. "There's a bus about to leave for the Rock if you wanted to go."

She slid the beer mat across the bar to him, jumped down from her stool and reached for her rucksack.

"You can leave that here if you like," he said. "Come and get it when you're ready."

As she was leaving the pub she looked back. The old man leaned on the bar, turning the beer mat over in his hand and shaking his head. She left and crossed the main street, and Caron saw that there were only a few empty seats left on the minibus. The driver introduced herself as Shona, handed Caron an information pamphlet, cheaply printed and hand-stapled, and apologized for the two-pound fare. "Just keeps this old banger on the road, like."

Caron boarded and squeezed her way down the narrow aisle to the vacant seats at the back of the bus. Most of the passengers seemed to be lone travelers like herself. One or two did double-takes as she passed them, and checked against the picture of Mhairi Sinclair on the inside of their pamphlets. A pair of young men in front of her were engaged in an intense discussion in French. They continued in louder voices as the engine started and the bus began to move, only stopping when the driver, yelling to be heard over the clapped-out diesel engine, began addressing the passengers.

"Make the most of it, folks," she said. "There's no substitute for seeing it with your own eyes. Take as many photos as you like, but they won't have the same effect. You know, the Italian artist, Uccello, spent a month dangling from a rope, measuring every curve, and the most his painting ever did was give someone a tickly nose. Mhairi Sinclair is the only person to come close."

The tourists turned their pamphlets over in their hands. Caron looked out of the window. Everything in the landscape—the bent trees, the angled ridges of gray rock that pushed up through the ground—seemed to point toward her destination, to Craig Shee. The last stretch of road was a slow, steep climb, the engine of the bus whining in complaint. There was a car park at the top of the hill but, perhaps knowing the bus would not make it that far, the driver pulled it into the grass verge at the side of the road and stopped the engine.

"This is it, guys."

The journey had taken only five minutes. The passengers shuffled off the bus and onto the side of the road. While they waited in line to disembark, one of the French pair noticed Caron. He held up his pamphlet at the picture of her mother.

"You look like her."

"Yes," she said.

The sightseers started to climb the hill. They crossed the path of a party on its way down the slope to board the bus back to the town. The two groups exchanged polite smiles, and a middle-aged American man coming down the hill grinned and said, "Incredible!"

They followed a gravel footpath from the side of the car park to the summit. Caron could not see the ocean on the other side of the hill, but she could hear it, an urgent roar that seemed to occupy the air and sky. She imagined her mother making the same journey, thirty years before. There would have been no car park or gravel path, but the roar of the sea would have been the same, and perhaps the sense of anticipation, and vague dread, at the prospect of confronting such a marvel on Earth.

Boring's Figure became widely recognized in the 1930s when Edwin Boring used it as an illustration of perceptual ambiguity, but it had been in circulation as a popular cartoon since the late nineteenth century. The figure, known popularly as "My Wife and My Mother-in-law" shows a crudely drawn old woman with her head in a scarf, or a much younger woman with her head turned away. The older woman's nose is the younger woman's chin. The younger woman's ear is the older woman's eye. And so on.

What is interesting is that we never see the older woman's nose and the younger woman's ear at the same time. We see one figure or the other, entire. And if what we see shifts, it does so totally, and with a jolt that is almost palpable, so intrinsic is this process of perception to our engagement with the world around us. (Caron Sinclair, *Perception and Illusion*, Barkington, 2012)

Caron had walked out of her office at UCL after receiving an invitation to a gala screening of a documentary film of her mother's life to which she had made no contribution. She did not intend to see the film, but the invitation lay on her desk for much of the day, a distraction that became harder and harder to ignore, like the awareness of a trigger being slowly pulled. She had, for much of her adult life, politely dismissed inquiries about her mother, on the basis that she had not really known her. In her early twenties, she found that referring to Mhairi as her *biological* mother could shut down such conversations before they got going, even if she had no *adopted* mother, rather a single aunt who had taken her in during one of Mhairi's more lengthy absences.

At the end of that day, she left her desk, stopped at the faculty office to say that there'd been an illness in the family, went home to her flat, packed a rucksack, and booked a flight to Glasgow.

She knew that she had visited Glasgow with her mother as a child. Her dreams had forever been decorated with images she could not place—a cold concrete stair that smelled of urine, an old man having a fit in the gutter of a steep street. She imagined that these images had come from her time in Glasgow. All she remembered for certain was that it was a gray place, wet and noisy.

When she arrived in the city she was surprised by how much color and light there was, and how much space. She strolled on foot past grand old counting houses and assembly rooms, in elliptical orbits that always brought her back around by the gallery where her mother's famous picture hung. Eventually, on the third or fourth pass, she went inside, and climbed the stair to the room on the first floor where *The Impression* was on permanent display. The queue began at the top of the flight of stairs, and shuffled slowly into the room, which was dark and lit from the floor, like a nightclub.

The room was unusual because it had only the one painting in it, and because there was a chest-high handrail on each side of the walkway that led visitors past the display, as if it were a bridge over a deadly abyss. People grabbed the rails with both hands. One young man became transfixed on the painting, and could only be moved on when a gallery attendant flashed a pen torch in his eyes.

It angered Caron, for reasons she did not understand, that she was as susceptible as anyone to the painting's influence. The instant she saw it, the image of the impossible rocks seemed to twist and distort not only the canvas, but the fabric of space in which the painting hung, and like everyone else, she felt herself tugged into the image of the cave-within-a-cave, felt her feet lose their connection with the floor beneath her, felt the room expand around her and her own space shrink into the point of a pin. Then, she was being moved on.

There was a photograph of her mother by the exit door, dark-eyed and distant. It was the kind of image she saw often: Mhairi Sinclair, thoughtful soul, troubled genius. Caron had a particular loathing for these pictures because they showed Mhairi as she did not care to remember her. Where the casual viewer saw the haunted eyes of an artist lost in thought, she could only see the vacant stare of intoxication and depression.

Before leaving the gallery, she bought a postcard of *The Impression*, and back in her hotel room she sat on the edge of her bed and stared at it until she felt sick. In the morning, she checked out, hired a bicycle, and rode to Dumbarton, where her mother was buried, and then on to Porthaven.

What intrigues me about these so-called impossible figures is that they are patently not impossible. They clearly exist. Interpreted in two dimensions, the works of Escher, the Penrose triangle, are as mundane as any line drawing. And yet, the mind insists on interpreting these images in such a way that they

*are rendered problematic, paradoxical, brain-boggling. Why do we take this
path of greatest resistance? Why not simply see the ink and the paper?*

*We are creatures of abstraction. We sort. We order. We construct. It's as
essential to our nature as is filling our lungs with air, over and over again.*
(Caron Sinclair, *Perception and Illusion*, Barkington, 2012)

Because of who her mother was, it was not unusual for people to think
that Caron wanted to hear their theories about Fairies' Rock. She had
heard them all. Her mother, who had shaken off most of the superstitions
of her Catholic upbringing, nevertheless believed that the Rock was a
wonder of God, placed on Earth so that his children would know the
limitations of their own minds. Caron's own theory as a psychologist,
though she tried to avoid the study of the Rock, was that its paradoxical
structure would be explained by physics, and that the cognitive dissonance
it produced in its beholders was something akin to an optical illusion. It
was a fault in the way the brain parsed the eye's impression of the world,
rather than a fault in the world itself.

But standing at the top of the cliff, on the edge of the land, finally
facing the Rock, Caron was most in mind of another theory. A student,
who had later suffered a breakdown, once hijacked a one-to-one tutorial to
expound at length his notion that the entire universe was a complex
computer program. He produced screenshots from computer simulations
that had gone awry. They showed fields of grass spilling up the sides of
buildings, mountains that sank into the landscape instead of rising up,
cities that melted into the ocean, and canyons that vanished into infinity.
Fairies' Rock, he said, was like this: a glitch, a fault in the rendering of the
universe.

The roar of the sea had taken on an oppressive quality. It reverberated
across the cliff faces and between the rocks, tinny and artificial like a badly
tuned radio played too loud, and it limited her capacity to reason. She was
again imagining her mother, and the hours and days she must have sat on
the edge of that cliff, considering the Rock. Caron could hardly bear to
look at it, but she was unable to look away. The Rock, a vertical column of
granite, was of one height and aspect with the cliffside, but separated by a

stretch of turbulent water, as if the land itself had rejected it and was slowly, over eons, pushing it out to sea. The cave at its base was a terrible sight, which seemed at once to enter the Rock, to protrude from it, and to open out into infinity. The Rock gave the impression of being in constant motion, and the motion bled out of it into the sea, across the water, and even into the ground beneath her feet. Caron was overwhelmed by a sense that the Rock was not so much a wonder of God as a terrible mistake on his part, and there was no longer any reason to be certain about anything.

One of the young Frenchmen touched her gently on the back of her shoulder. "Are you all right?" He pointed down the clifftop path, where most of the party was making its way over the hill and back to the bus.

She nodded. "I think I'll walk back. It isn't far."

He smiled and turned away. Caron took the pamphlet from her pocket and turned to the image of her mother. She had thought it poorly composed, but now realized that it had been cropped out of the photograph in the pub; Mhairi was wearing the same Arran jumper and Paisley headscarf. She had the same broad smile, and her eyes were closed. As Caron looked at the image, it seemed to change instantaneously into the picture of a different woman, someone she did not know, but might have liked well.

At the foot of the Rock, the cave mouth continued to warp and stretch and swallow the fizzing sea. There was the sense of another cave within, and a cave within that, and another, forever, like a hall of mirrors, and somewhere, deep within, a source of light that was not of the Earth. Caron was consumed, fleetingly, by the urge to throw herself from the cliff and drift on the wind through the opening, imagining herself drawn into whatever state lay within.

Then she was walking away and down the hill, but something of the cave stayed with her, an impression, an awareness of a place in her understanding of the world that her consciousness could not reach, like a dream that stays just beyond recollection.

Caron found her way back to the town. The pub was hot and filled for lunch, with tourists and locals eating chips and toasted sandwiches. The old publican was busy, though apparently not so busy that he felt any need to curb his chatter. He juggled two or three conversations at once while pulling pints, saw Caron and greeted her.

"You're back," he said. "How was it?"

"It was all right," was her reply.

"All right?" he said. "Don't actually think I've heard that one before."

"It was something."

He placed two pint glasses in front of a customer, handed some change, then came over to her.

"What can I get you?"

"One of those, maybe?" She pointed at the assorted whiskies that surrounded the photograph of her mother.

He laughed. "Which one?" When she shrugged, he laughed again, and said, "Right, then."

She watched him take a bottle from the shelf, but her eyes lingered on the photograph.

"Do you have any more of those photos?"

He poured the whisky into a glass. "If it's too much I can put a little water in for you. This one can be a little intense, but it's a good one." He returned the bottle to the shelf. "No, I don't have any more photos like that one. Sorry. Actually, I don't know where that came from."

As he turned away, she said, "I've never seen another picture of her that I liked."

The whisky tasted of smoke and honey, and faintly medicinal. Caron pulled the little pamphlet from the pocket of her coat. At some point she'd folded it back on itself, so that the picture of Mhairi was at the front. It was a poor copy of a copy, dark and fuzzy, and it had crumpled in her pocket. She smoothed it on the surface of the bar, folded it carefully, and returned it to her coat. She reached across the bar and picked up a blunt and stubby pencil that lay across a notebook by the cash register and then, with the pencil in one hand and the glass of whisky in the other, started idly to sketch her mother's face onto a beer mat: smiling, bright-eyed.

She finished her whisky. The publican returned and leaned over the bar. "I thought you said you weren't an artist."

"Well, clearly, I'm not."

"How was the whisky?"

She smiled. "It was all right."

"Can I get you another?"

"I think I'm good for now."

She signed the beer mat and handed it to him. He smiled and put it on the shelf beside the photograph of Mhari. Then she grabbed another beer mat, peeled its surface away, and began again.

David McGroarty's fiction has featured in the anthologies Rustblind and Siverbright, Sensorama, Caledonia Dreamin' *(Eibonvale Press),* Astrologica *(The Alchemy Press),* Strange Tales V *(Tartarus Press),* Wordland 5 *(The Exaggerated Press), and* A World of Horror *(Dark Moon Books). He is a Scottish writer of Hebridean and Irish descent, who grew up near Glasgow and now lives in Islington, London, with his partner and two children. He is a member of Clockhouse London Writers. David can be found online at* www.davidmcgroarty.net.

THE SENSE OF SMELL

OF

SMELL

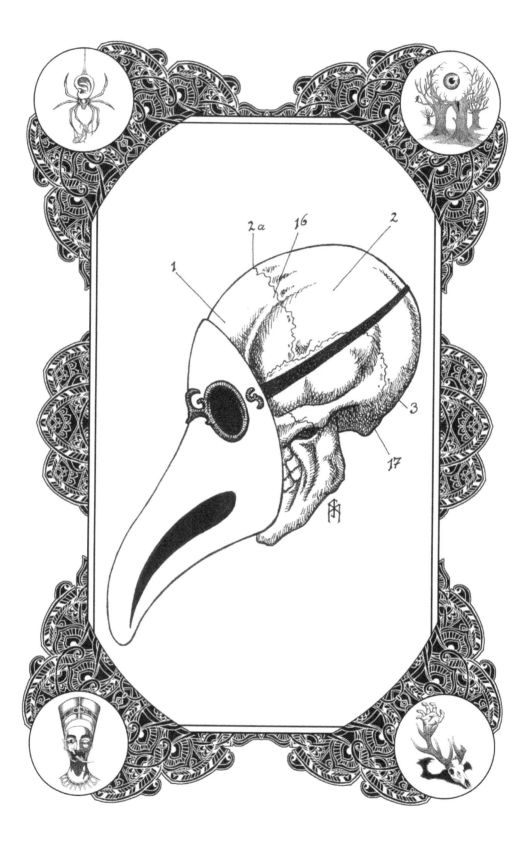

THOUGHTS ABOUT THE SENSE OF SMELL

BY JESSICA BAYLISS, PHD

L AST OF ALL THE SENSES, we come to smell. This is where things get a little weird.

We touched upon the olfactory system slightly when considering taste. These two are highly linked. In fact, much of what we experience as taste is actually attributable to smell. If you ever got sick with very blocked nasal passages, you know exactly how important smell is in the enjoyment of food.

Disgust is one of the most primal emotions, which, as we already covered, can be the result of a conditioned taste *aversion* or taste *avoidance*. Interestingly, disgust activates not only the neurons in the gustatory—taste—cortex, it also activates the neurons in the olfactory cortex, the part of the brain that processes smells. The same pattern is observed in mirror neurons: both cortical areas—taste and smell—react when we observe disgust on the face of someone else.

Disgust is not the only pertinent smell-related emotion for the fan of scary stories. There is good old-fashioned fear, itself, and researchers into this area do some pretty strange things. They actually expose participants to the sweat of other people. Yes, sweat. That's not all. They use fear-sweat—sweat collected from a person who was terrified—as well as neutral-sweat (I bet you never thought sweat could be so emotional.). But the findings are worth the weird study design, because just being exposed to sweat from a frightened person can trigger a protective response in us.

We can literally smell fear. And we react to it without even knowing.
Those deodorant commercials were not lying.

Humans can even distinguish between the sweat of people in different emotional states. They can correctly identify perspiration as being collected when the person was scared versus happy, or in a neutral mood.

So, what do we do with all this sweaty knowledge? We use it. The chemosignal of potential danger can help us when we are confronted with a task that requires focused attention—like when strategizing how to access the secret lair of the monster that is hidden beneath the city or where to run to escape said monster. We know this because, in addition to asking participants to smell other people's sweat, researchers sometimes ask participants to perform cognitively-challenging tasks while smelling other people's sweat. (I told you it was going to get weird.) The thing is, the participants who performed the tasks in the fear-sweat condition did better than those with neutral-emotion sweat. More specifically, they were slower in their responses—more cautious—but they were also more accurate or, as the study explains, more vigilant.

The people in this study did not report feeling anxious or scared themselves, though there was some stress arousal simply because they were being asked to do a challenging task; but their brains registered the chemosignal coming from the sweat pads, and gave them an edge.

Caution and vigilance are definitely assets during a life-threatening situation and can mean the difference between hiding in an ineffective spot (like the attic) or in a place where the monster is less likely to find us (say, the woods out back).

There is a difference, though, between the enhanced cognitive ability noted in this research study, from smelling someone else's fear, and experiencing that fear personally. We may be more careful and vigilant when a threat is only hinted at or is small, but once it has come at us full-force, that changes. When we are in a state of fight-or-flight arousal, our thinking often gets muddled. Some people call it tunnel vision. We lose sight of the big picture and only see what is directly in front of us. This is why it makes complete sense that a terrified horror novel character would choose to hide in the attic instead of getting out of the house and disappearing into dark shadows under the trees.

We simply do not think clearly when we are scared.

The solution to this is simple: stay home, out of dark alleys, away from zombie hordes, flesh-eating demons, ax-murderers, and that creepy voice trying to lure you into the basement.

Better to stay in the safety of your own in bed, preferably with a good book to keep you company. Like the one you're reading right now.

SHEM-EL-NESSIM: AN INSPIRATION IN PERFUME

BY CHRIS BELL

EDITOR'S NOTES: Research has shown that humans are attracted, and respond differently, to other humans based on certain telltale smells, even if we don't always know it; we send and receive olfactory messages constantly, seeking compatibility with potential long term partners. Scent is even suggested as being that hidden cosmological constant in the sexual universe, the missing factor that explains why we feel "chemistry" with one person and not another.

So it is for poor, infatuated Stan Tooprig, who's become obsessed with an enigmatic pale woman and her Oriental-scented fragrance. Tooprig's only fault it seems—besides falling in love with the odor of the woman who proves to be his downfall (and stalking her across continents)—is that he's simply more in tune with his sense of smell than the rest of us.

Adventuresome, dark, and foreboding, I've never read a tale quite like the following by Chris Bell, who takes us deep into the mysteries of 1920s Cairo. If you should ever smell *Shem-el-Nessim: An Inspiration in Perfume*, immediately, perhaps, flush the sinuses with the nearest foul-scented stink, before it is too late.

> *"Unless she could tantalize his nose, her other charms would be of no consequence, and a fragrant woman invigorated all of his senses, not merely the olfactory . . . "*

THE MU'EZZIN OF THE SULTAN al-Zahir Barquq mosque in the City of the Dead was calling for morning prayers when in one last rattling exhalation the Englishman opposite me expired. As his head fell forward, jangling our coffee cups and startling the clientele, his skin appeared translucent in the dust-dappled light. "*Shem-el-Nessim!*" were his final words. While the proprietor sent for a doctor from the Coptic Hospital on Ramses Street, I slipped the gold ring from the third finger of Stan Tooprig's left hand onto my own.

The Cairo of 1926 was the city of Moslem legend, seat of Saracen art, home of the Arabian Nights. But the coffeehouse in the Khan el-Khalili bazaar on Gawhar el-Kaid Street was so far below the domes and minarets that it didn't even merit a name. Five times a day the Mu'ezzin would summon the faithful, halting the hammerings from the silver smithy next door. But at all other times it was too noisy for us to sit outside with the pipe smokers if we wished to converse, so we were confined to the shadows within.

Most of the coffee drinkers were fantasists. In their daydreams, they would be smuggling whisky, writing novels, and returning home wealthy and triumphant. I'd met plenty who had never left Cairo and would not—at least not alive. These star-crossed fools drifted here on inauspicious currents and were marooned by ancient history. Stan Tooprig was something else altogether, and I am still not sure what. He had come here from London in search of something, or merely to escape himself. As I had done with all the rest, I struck up a conversation with him over coffee.

The unlikely surname resulted from an unusual ancestry: a Dutch trader who had made his fortune in London around the time of the Great Fire and whose descendants had been there ever since. Tooprig claimed he had always wanted to visit Egypt because his father had once produced a ring of yellow gold engraved with strange foreign symbols, and which he claimed had once belonged to a Pharaoh. He had won it in payment of a debt while on a trip to Venice, he assured the young Stan. After his father died, Stan inherited the ring, along with a considerable fortune. It was many years later before he learned that what was engraved on the ring was a cartouche of Egyptian hieroglyphs.

The Stan Tooprig I met in Cairo was no longer the well-to-do English gentleman he had once been. Behind everyday reality, there is a deeper reality so cruel that it condemns to death those whose crime is no greater than the pursuit of their own curiosity. I know this to be true because it happened to Stan Tooprig. And, as strange as it may sound, it was piqued by a woman's perfume.

Tooprig required something of women that was not physical but sensory. Although he claimed to be as partial to blondes as he was to brunettes, he had always favored the civet cat-like scent of redheads; there was a certain astringency about them he said he found entirely libidinous. Unless she could tantalize his nose, her other charms would be of no consequence, and a fragrant woman invigorated all of his senses, not merely the olfactory.

He lived just off Baker Street, on two floors, with modest living quarters for his valet. One might have described him as a gentleman of leisure; on most days, he took long walks through the city and sometimes, on a whim, would follow a particularly fragrant woman in the hope of a closer encounter. He had cultivated a succession of these, but he was fastidious and discarded his subject if she did not smell "right". He even classified them by type and aroma: Thyme and Basil (blondes); Sandalwood and Vetivert (brunettes); and Lemon and Petit Grain (redheads). But then came Shem-el-Nessim, the perfume worn by the raven-haired mystery woman. And it was in a London winter that he first crossed paths with the creature that was to be his downfall.

Klinge & Schneider, the barbershop on Jermyn Street renowned for the closest shave in London, was a haven of sandalwood and Turkish soap; a darkly timbered respite from the rumble and clatter of the city. Tooprig particularly enjoyed cold mornings when there was a touch of frost;

stepping out across the threshold, lightly powdered, with the frisson of cologne vibrant on cheeks met by the first chilled fingers of fresh air.

On this morning, his barber had left him to put the razor to the strop when a spicy, Oriental perfume wafted deliciously between the hot towel and Tooprig's nose. He didn't recognize the scent, but by the time his barber had turned back to him with a keenly glinting cut-throat, Tooprig had cast off his towel and was at the door, which was still closing against its jamb as though someone had left the shop but a moment before.

"Who was that just now?" Tooprig asked.

The barber professed to have seen no one. "Perhaps, sir, a customer too impatient to wait," he said. "It happens."

"No, this was a woman. I can still smell her." Although Tooprig had no idea what fragrance the young woman had been wearing it was on his nose nonetheless. Tipping the barber for his trouble, Tooprig resolved to follow her; the bouquet was so heady and distinctive. His eye soon settled on the only woman within a plausible distance of the barber shop door. She was waiting to cross at the next junction: a tall, even willowy creature, with her raven hair very straight and short for the fashions.

He followed her at a distance as far as the eastern reaches of the city, north of Paternoster Row, even more fascinated by her scent than by the woman wearing it. His pursuit continued toward St Paul's Cathedral, across the junction of Newgate Street, beyond the Alpine Club. She did not look back, was untroubled by the traffic and moved swiftly. Her hair had a sable quality like a broad brush. She had limbs like the legs of a racehorse, though they were barely visible beneath her long coat. Her walk was a study in poise. She paused only at side roads to ensure she would not collide with turning traffic and, in profile, her skin seemed so pale that it was almost luminous. She had slightly plump cheeks and widely-set eyes. Her face was a harmony of curves and palenesses. There was a middle-eastern turn to her features, as though her forebears might have hailed from the Orient, but then she also had something of the film star Louise Brooks as *Lulu* about her, Tooprig claimed.

It was on Newgate Street, at the corner of Ivy Lane, that the woman disappeared into a doorway. By the time Tooprig had reached it, the door had closed behind her. Tooprig had to step into the street in order to read the sign, J. GROSSMITH & SON, but there was no mention of the business being conducted within.

The door opened with a chime when he pushed against it. Inside, a display advertised what were apparently J. Grossmith & Son's products: Phul-Nana Bouquet of Indian Flowers; Old Lavender Cottage; and White Fire fragrances, along with a range of sixpenny sachets, soaps, face powders, and dentifrice.

Behind the counter, a man with a balding head and a waxed moustache eyed Tooprig who, discomfited that he had entered the store with no plan in mind, was at a loss for words. "That woman, the one who just entered . . . I, *er*, she . . . "

"You are mistaken, sir," said the man, with a hint of a foreign accent. "You are our first customer. We have just this minute opened, at nine o'clock." The man nodded politely toward a clock set above the window, which indeed showed the time to be just after the hour.

Tooprig tried to buy time as he considered what his next move might be. His gaze settled on the perfume displays. It seemed an odd but perfect coincidence. "If I were looking for a particular scent, for a lady, do you think you might carry it?" Tooprig asked.

The man smiled. "It's highly likely that we would be able to obtain it for you, sir. Or, if you can describe it to me, I would be happy to assist you in blending a scent that matches your requirements. We distil our own perfumes, and also sell a range of proprietary scents from other manufacturers."

"Well, I wouldn't really know how to describe it to you," Tooprig confessed. "It's not a scent I have ever encountered before."

The Grossmith assistant regarded Tooprig calmly and introduced himself as Monsieur Duat. "Is the scent fresh and of a citrus nature, or something deeper and more musky?"

"I can only say it had a kind of Oriental quality."

"Well sir, that certainly narrows the field. I shall be back in a moment." He disappeared into a back room, returning with a wooden box into which were set a number of vials capped by rubber bulbs. He siphoned a drop of perfume from three of the vials onto a strip of blotting paper. The scent Tooprig was looking for drew its richness—or so Duat surmised—from musk and vanilla. It was exotic and spicy rather than floral, but there was some other substance, perhaps a precious wood, that remained elusive even to the expert. Duat experimented by adding lighter, woodier notes to his existing blends.

As odd as it might seem, Tooprig had almost forgotten about the woman and was now more eager to solve the mystery of her perfume. After some deliberation, Duat produced an elaborate cylindrical carton and offered it to Tooprig. Floral designs in pink intertwined with curlicues; abstract urn shapes repeated around the base; and large, blue stylized lettering with drop shadows spelled out the transverse words SHEM-EL-NESSIM.

"I don't know why I didn't think of this before. I feel certain that this is the scent you have been looking for, Mister Tooprig." Duat dabbed a tiny quantity of the Shem-el-Nessim onto one of his blotting paper strips.

Tooprig soon ascertained that it was indeed the perfume that the woman had been wearing. It was her very essence. Duat was evidently a master *parfumier*, a veritable alchemist in fragrances, to be able to identify a perfume from the clues provided by a neophyte.

Tooprig was eager to discover Shem-el-Nessim's formula, but Duat would say only that its recipe was protected and registered "in all the leading countries of the world." He purchased as much of it as seemed judicious in a single transaction, wary that Duat might consider him unhinged, which indeed he may already have been.

In the following weeks, Tooprig haunted the British Museum's reading rooms, looking for information on Shem-el-Nessim. After a painstaking search, he found but one solitary reference, in the works of an eccentric occultist. In *The Confessions of Aleister Crowley*, Tooprig read that Oscar Eckenstein, an acquaintance of Crowley's, had suffered from an aversion to artificial scent. "One day my wife and a friend came home from shopping. They had called at the chemist's who had sprayed them with Shem-el-Nessim. We saw them coming and went to the door to receive them. Eckenstein made one rush—like a bull—for the window of the sitting-room, flung it open, and spent the next quarter of an hour leaning out and gasping for breath."

Tooprig's desire to be with the mystery woman, now that he had identified her perfume, grew like a strange addiction; he craved her closeness although he could not explain why. The days came and went, and often it was only his valet who roused him from a trance as he came into the study with his cocktail, whereupon it became apparent to him that he hadn't moved from his wing-chair since retiring there after breakfast. All the while, the scent of Shem-el-Nessim filled his senses and his mind. *What did these reveries expect of him,* he wondered; *had its mysterious wearer been but a figment of his imagination?*

It wasn't until much later that I discovered why, soon after, Tooprig booked himself a cabin on a steamer at the Port of London. And it was only my own research that led me to discover it had been on a French-registered vessel named *Cachous* that sailed to Alexandria, where he boarded a felucca up the Mahmoudieh Canal and the Nile, to Cairo.

I had been in Cairo for five years, ever since we declared Egypt a sovereign country, working mainly as a reporter for the English language *Cairo Gazette.* To my mind, we were treating the Egyptians rather more as enemies than as friends, but I was well-treated by the locals and found life in the city most pleasant. I had airy rooms off Al Geish Square and the pace of life was slower than in Europe; one achieved in a week in Cairo what one might in a day in London. The boys were alluring if not always compliant, and there was an abundance of *kif* and *majoun* with which to help stave off boredom.

But Cairo brought Stan Tooprig no luck whatsoever. When I first set eyes on him he looked emaciated. His skin had the leathery appearance of the mummified corpse of Sethos I in the Cairo Museum. He toadied up to me in the coffeehouse and, from behind the semi-transparent skin of his face, a refined English accent said, "I say, nobody else will buy me a drink. Would you?"

I acceded to his request and he rewarded me with his story. "It's quite the most remarkable thing," Tooprig claimed and, by the time I had heard the first part of it I must say I had to agree with him.

Although he had elected to live in the most luxurious hotel in all of Cairo, the hideously expensive Hotel Savoy, there was no trace whatsoever of the mysterious Shem-el-Nessim woman on either side of its daunting white façade. Although its employees were open to all manner of bribes, none even dared to feign an encounter with this woman. Tooprig hadn't yet apprised me of the reason he believed she was in Egypt—or why, apart from its magnificence, he had chosen this hotel for his accommodation.

He enjoyed no special knowledge of Cairo's geography, its businesses, or its people to help him in his quest. Since arriving, he had carried out reconnaissance missions at all of the other fine hotels to no avail. He made a mischief of himself with the officials at the British Embassy on Ahmed Raghab Street and became a regular of the expatriate cocktail circuit, but there wasn't a solitary sighting. He realized his journey had been in vain: if the woman had ever been in Cairo, she was no longer.

When he tired from the exertion of his account, we ordered more coffee and sized one another up. "There's an Egyptian chap I've heard about from my contacts on the *Gazette* who entered the grave of a Pharaoh and his Queen," I told him. "He claims to have been possessed by her perfume."

Tooprig pleaded with me to take him to this man.

I knew of Ahmed Rezk quite by chance. One evening he had told me an implausible tale about his exploits as an erstwhile grave-robber. Since Rezk's adventure also involved the supposed supernatural effects of a perfume, I agreed to arrange a meeting between them, feeling sorry for Tooprig and foolishly thinking it might comfort him. He was eating practically nothing and virtually subsisting on coffee, in the hope that if he remained awake long enough he would eventually see the Shem-el-Nessim woman again.

"Rezk broke into the undiscovered tomb in the western branch of the Valley of the Kings in Thebes," I explained as I walked Tooprig back in the direction of the Savoy. "They sold most of their spoils to foreigners around town, but Rezk retrieved a canopic jar he claims reeks of the perfume from the tomb."

Each year, in early spring, the Egyptians celebrate "smelling the breezes," an anniversary dating back to the time of the Pharaohs, over 4,000 years ago. Tooprig was so frail he could barely manage the short journey to Rezk's apartment in the old city but, with the aid of my interpreter from the *Cairo Gazette*, we eventually conquered the staircase and arrived at his door.

His wife led us to Rezk, who was on the balcony, eating *fisikh*: salted, almost rotting fish. The sulfurous stink of it was noticeable two floors below. There are many cases of food poisoning each year in Cairo, suffered by those who purchase improperly preserved *fisikh* from unlicensed salting factories. Rezk looked terrible. His skin was sallow and his breath came in wheezing gasps. His wife was clearly distraught, beseeching him to eat fruit and to drink water, but Rezk brushed her aside as she attempted to dab at his brows with a damp cloth.

Rezk and an accomplice, he purported, had tunneled through rock to the tomb's burial chamber and eventually found the king and queen in their sarcophagi. "We opened their coffins, where we found the mummy of this king," our interpreter translated as Rezk guzzled down mouthfuls of the stinking *fisikh* in the pauses in his confession. "There were amulets and golden ornaments at its throat; its head had a mask of gold upon it. The mummy was overlaid with gold, its coverings all wrought with silver and inlaid with lapis lazuli. We stripped off the gold and all the amulets and ornaments, then found the king's wife and stripped off all that we found on her, too. We stole their furniture and vases of gold, silver, and bronze. We divided the gold from the mummies, and the amulets, ornaments, and coverings between us."

Both Tooprig and I found Rezk's explanation for consuming so much of the rotting *fisikh* extraordinary, and it was linked to his confession: "It's the only way I can think of to be rid of this smell," he told my interpreter with a defeated expression on his face. Rezk went on to explain how, once the queen's mask had been removed, the chamber had filled with a beguiling perfume. The thieves narrowed down its source to an alabaster canopic urn in one corner of the tomb. They packed it into one of their swag bags and took it with them. However, upon their return to Cairo, they discovered that the urn contained but the foul, stinking viscera of the embalmed mummies, and no longer exuded the pungent perfume that had so intoxicated them. Nevertheless, it had somehow pursued the grave-robbers ever since, and they couldn't shake it; even rotting *fisikh* succeeded only in masking it slightly.

"Show me the urn!" Tooprig pleaded, but Rezk explained that his wife had forced him to abandon it in the desert, so foul had its smell become. I began to doubt Rezk's story; in particular that such a large and elaborate tomb could have existed undiscovered for so long in the Valley of the Kings, which was famously crawling with archaeologists. Rezk stubbornly refused to return to the tomb and also proved incapable of describing its location, so we had him draw a map of the site.

Tooprig was so infirm by this stage that I offered him my services and those of my interpreter to accompany him on an expedition to Thebes. It took us several days to get to the Valley of the Kings by train, by camel, and finally on foot. The place Rezk had marked for us was close to a cliff-face about nine feet high. But there was no sign of an entrance, concealed or otherwise. The wind was whipping up the dust and so, in spite of Tooprig's pleas, after several hours of searching, we were forced to admit defeat as the sun began to rise.

When, at Tooprig's insistence, we returned to Cairo and to Rezk's dwellings, we found his wife in mourning. Her beloved Ahmed, she said, had stopped eating altogether—even the stinking *fisikh*—and had wasted away. The identity of his accomplice thus went with him to his grave.

Tooprig and I would meet once a week for coffee at the Khan el-Khalili coffeehouse and each week he would appear thinner and to have lost a little more of his feeble grip on life. Occasionally, he would be roused from a reverie to ask me the time or the date; annoyingly, often several times in the same morning. Then once, quite out of nowhere, as though there had merely been a brief pause in a long stream of conversation, Tooprig lit his final cigarette and wheezed, "I say, do you know what happened to me at The Savoy in London? It was quite the damndest thing. Buy me a coffee, and I shall tell you all about it."

About a week after his first encounter with the woman, it seemed, on a quite separate errand off Bond Street, Tooprig fancied he saw her again. She had emerged like an apparition between behatted heads and traffic, bobbing on her long limbs as if to gyroscopically navigate herself through the crosshatching of obstacles.

As he drew closer to her, the woman's scent became unmistakable. He followed her to Trafalgar Square, around which she walked before stopping in her tracks and turning to face him. She didn't speak, just looked at him and smiled. "There was something terrifyingly lascivious about her lips," Tooprig claimed, trembling as he recalled her. She held up a key to Room 941 at The Savoy Hotel, proffered it, then turned and continued on her way along the Strand and into the hotel lobby. When the elevator door opened, the woman entered it, and turned to look at Tooprig with a sphinx-like smile. He followed her only after an interval and discovered her waiting outside the door to Room 941.

When he unlocked the door with the key she had given him, the room was dark and all the air had gone from it. In the twilight, she took off her coat and threw it onto the bed. Her clinging black dress was the next to go, and soon she was naked, skin shimmering and pearlescent with the sheen of shot silk.

They lay together into the failing light of a late afternoon, all the while the indescribable Oriental fragrance of her skin buffering the room's airlessness. Hardly a word was spoken by either of them, but there was a prevailing tenderness, a lightness of touch, and from what Tooprig told me, it was not spoiled by the directness of their passions; at least not at first.

"Her body was warm, and yet she seemed to be draining me of heat," he said. "I felt the life being sapped out of me. Her ministrations were tender, and yet it was as though she were embalming and not making love to me. Her kisses tasted salty and bitter."

Tooprig said he felt an obstruction in his airways, as if something viscous and too large for the passages was being pulled out of him. "I had my eyes closed and yet, when I attempted to open them to see what was happening, it was as though I was asleep—I simply didn't have the energy to lift my eyelids. A vinegary odor filled the room, as though of some unctuous preservative."

All at once, there were not merely two but a manyness of hands upon him; not soft and womanly, but large, coarse, and oiled. "They sought and prodded, poked and peeled to such an extent that I could no longer keep track of their location on my body. I felt a sharp stroke below my left ribs and a sensation of something being quickly removed. I grew even weaker.

My heart was suddenly heavy, as though it were about to fall through both me and the bed and onto the floor. And yet, *her* hands were soft, like clean linen. I felt as though I was being wrapped in her arms. But I could not defend myself against the other violations—whatever they were—and I began to feel afraid. All the while, my eyelids were as though sewn shut. I tried to call out, but I couldn't; my senses were paralyzed. And although my heart was beating hard, my blood felt sluggish in my veins."

The darkness throbbed and, out of it, he seemed to hear male voices chanting. Tooprig claimed he felt something peppery with the texture of grit being inserted into his nostrils, but he found it impossible to provide resistance to the sensations assailing him, and soon fell into unconsciousness.

"Afterward, I was numb. In a dream of red velvet drapes, I smelt her perfume again: sweeter than any bloom; warmer and more satisfying than any musk; fresher than any exotic fruit. And, like a dream, it dissipated as I woke, until I was left with nothing, for when I awoke she had gone."

It was only when Tooprig left The Savoy that he fully became aware of Shem-el-Nessim again, because traces of it had been left on his clothing and skin. It was the perfume from his dream, and it had been with him permanently ever since—night and day, no matter where he went.

Sometime later, he returned to The Savoy and approached the concierge's desk, where he engaged him in conversation about his liaison with the woman. "She was staying in Room 941," he said. "We met for tea. It was a Tuesday—I distinctly remember that, and the date must have been late in January, perhaps the last day of the month."

"Sir, no such rendezvous can have taken place in this hotel," said the concierge.

Tooprig was infuriated by such impertinence. "Dash it all, man, are you calling me a liar?"

"Not at all, sir, but no such liaison can have taken place in that room, as there is no Room 941 in The Savoy Hotel."

Tooprig turned from the counter, quite sure that he had not misremembered the room number. He decided to try a different approach and bribed a bellboy who claimed to remember such a woman from Tooprig's description. Although the boy didn't recall the woman's name, Tooprig asked where she had gone after she had checked out. He slowly spelled out a word he had memorized from the label on her cabin trunks: K-A-I-R-O.

Stan Tooprig had spoken to me often of returning to London, but he never did. He spent his final days in the coffeehouse in Khan el-Khalili, and a man more out-of-sorts with himself you couldn't hope to meet. It was soon after recounting his tale that he died. He was buried here in Cairo: at the Beb el-Wezir cemetery with a view of the Citadel and the Mohammed Ali Mosque, beyond.

In everything there is an element of the mysterious, and yet we know the world can only be this way. For, as the biologist J.B.S. Haldane observed, "The Universe is not only queerer than we suppose; it is queerer than we *can* suppose." It is with a heavy heart that I acknowledge the mystery of Shem-el-Nessim might never be solved. Whether that woman existed only in the mind of Stan Tooprig has never been entirely relevant to me since, once imagined, she existed for him as did everything else in his world.

I am old now. I have memories, and that is all I have. They are like the loose leaves of a book that has lost its binding; the pages are in the wrong order, are torn and discolored. Each year, on the anniversary of Tooprig's death, his haunted, bony face comes back to me, and each year I doubt the veracity of his story more—he had woven a tale as one might a ghost story, seemingly omitting anything that did not assist his narrative.

But recently I have reproached myself for questioning Tooprig's honesty. In recording the foregoing events, I was forced to refer to some back issues of the *Cairo Gazette*. And so, one evening, I found myself in the reading rooms of the Al-Azhar University library in the shadow of the Fatima az-Zahraa mosque. In an issue from the spring of 1926, I turned the page from an account of the Palestinian labor camps to a full-page advertisement for the company J. Grossmith & Son. It featured a drawing of a turbaned woman on a nighttime camel ride in front of the Great

Pyramids. She had some of the allure of Louise Brooks. Two oversized bottles of Shem-el-Nessim hung like water vessels from either side of her camel as she smiled gaily at me from the newsprint. The advertising copy read:

SHEM-EL-NESSIM, SCENT OF ARABY:
AN INSPIRATION IN PERFUME

While gazing at the woman's face I was struck by an intense fragrance; something Oriental laced with spice and perhaps a suggestion of sandalwood. It filled my nostrils, lungs, and my imagination, and I almost swooned. I tried to ascertain its source but, apart from me, the room was unoccupied and quite still, save for an odd shadow that paused fleetingly against the open door and a curtain that billowed over a window left ajar.

The Shem-el-Nessim woman may have been an inspiration to Monsieur Duat and the *parfumiers* of J. Grossmith & Son, but her "scent of Araby" was tainted by the miasma of early death. I myself fell ill soon after that visit to the library. My vitality has been sapped, and I doubt I shall live to see my seventieth birthday. She, though, will never grow old, and I fear the lifelong curse of her fragrance, which seduced me like a memory of London long ago, will be on the air long after we are all gone.

Chris Bell was born in North Wales. After working in London as a musician, record company messenger, freelance music journalist, and as editor of Soundcheck!, *he moved to Germany where he was employed by a guitar company and a music publisher before emigrating in 1997 to New Zealand, where he works as a writer. His short stories have appeared in* The Third Alternative, Postscripts, Grotesque, The Heidelberg Review,

TransVersions, Not One of Us, The Mammoth Book of Best New Horror, That Haunted Feeling, *and* Takahe. *His story collection,* The Bumper Book of Lies, *received an honorable mention in* The Year's Best Fantasy & Horror (10th Annual Edition). *His poetry has been published in* Workshop New Poetry, Snorkel, foam:e, *and the* New Zealand Listener. *His first novel,* Liquidambar, *won UKAuthors' "Search for a Great Read" competition. He recently published a speculative trilogy about the power of music, consisting of* Songshifting, Requiem For Stage Diver & Bass Guitar, *and* An Audience with the Impresario; *a second short story collection,* Faces In Things; *as well as* Deadpan, *a short comic novel; all in his own wordsSHIFTminds imprint.*

THE SCENT

BY JOHN F.D. TAFF

EDITOR'S NOTES: Although I've been reading John F.D. Taff for several years, I wasn't previously familiar with this next story, coming from his collection, *Little Deaths*, that was referred to me through a mutual contact.

This selection was <*wince*> "on the nose" for what I was seeking, an example of prose rich in olfactory detail. Even more, the scents around the character, William, are used as a vehicle of change, setting the scene of his journey, growing danker, more corruptible as he progresses through the city. And the power of the scent is the actual catalyst for his journey—it compels William. He identifies differences between the unexpected and the familiar in his surroundings, so that the aromatic deviation from his routine acts as lure, as impetus.

Interestingly, medical studies have shown that high scent sensitivity can lead to increased anxiety, particularly if smells make a person self-conscious or hyper-aware of their surroundings, of menace or foreboding... rather fitting for the situation William finds himself in, as he follows *The Scent*.

"William sniffs the air again deeply, half expecting the smell to have vanished. But, instead, it has grown stronger..."

HE STEPS OUTSIDE, PAUSES on his front stoop.

William is not an old man, not by today's standards, but he is a hat man. He is not bald or even balding, but he is a man who believes in hats. He believes in the fashion of hats, the safety of hats. What a hat says about its wearer.

In an age when men no longer wear hats, William wears hats.

And not just any hats. Not baseball hats or any of their varieties, to be sure—'gimme hats' with the names of insurance companies or local feed stores, caps emblazoned with the logos of college or professional teams or even caps with rap words on them, meant to be worn bill-backward.

A hat, to William, means a fedora with a crisp crease, perhaps a staid, squat bowler, or a conservative Homburg. Even a cool Panama or a rakish pork pie like those worn by Sinatra or Martin. On occasion, he's even been known to step out in a Stetson.

Today, he wears a tawny suit of tweed topped by an expensive beaver felt fedora; a rare and expensive hat, it makes him feel stylish and gives him a jaunty, nostalgic air.

He fingers its brim as he stands there, azaleas in bloom on either side of his porch. The cherry and dogwood trees are in blossom, too, and their over-sculpted, fuzzy pink and white blossoms give them the look of poodles standing on their hind legs.

As he adjusts the angle of the fedora, he inhales deeply their mingled odors: the fruity, flowery scents, mingled with the musky, almost sexual smell of the Bradford pear trees lining the street, brazenly announcing their availability to every passing bird and bee.

William walks to work, as he does each day, rain or shine. It is why he bought the condo in this marginal neighborhood on the verge of downtown St. Louis. Gutted and rehabbed throughout, William's townhouse is beautiful: all hardwood floors and pristine, white gallery walls, and stainless steel appliances.

Outside, though, the neighborhood is gutted. To either side of his condo are decaying tenements, collapsed warehouses, and piles of bricks and debris that once, when whole, might have housed livery companies or taverns or rendering plants.

His neighborhood is marginal, yes, but he has had few troubles. With no car, he's not experienced any of the multiple thefts and break-ins many of his other gentrified neighbors have been subject to. His townhouse is fully outfitted with a state-of-the-art security system, which in the two years he's lived there has only gone off twice, and one of those occurrences had been caused by him. His backyard patio-cum-garden, small though it might be, is enclosed by a solid brick wall ten feet in height, topped by a "decorative" row of iron spikes.

On his walks to and from work, he has never been mugged or assaulted. He is, though, constantly approached for money by men and women who plead various needs, all jointly understood to be false. The mother who needs an operation. The bus ticket for some vital trip. Money for a meal or to bail a loved one out of jail. William gives money or not depending on his mood and the creativity of the story, bestowing it when he does as much as an award as charity.

Having set the tilt of his fedora to keep the sun from his eyes, he steps down onto the pristine sidewalk that bisects his small, merely ornamental front lawn and sets off. The crisp, level lines of this sidewalk give way quickly to cracked and shattered pavement. In some places, great swaths of it are picked away like scabs, revealing the shocking red of cobblestones beneath; the desiccated, jumbled flesh of an older time; the time, perhaps, of the livery and the rendering plant.

William steps gingerly over these scars, barely noticing them anymore. He crosses Tamm and then Pestalozzi Streets, skeletal buildings lining each side like pallbearers. The trees give way to stunted, sprawling bushes whose flowers are small and stingy. Their odors are sharp, spicy, unpleasant, though they cover, somewhat, the musty, mothball aromas that waft from the abandoned buildings along this stretch of his path.

Here, a structure that once housed a carriage company. Here, a tannery. Here—disturbingly, right next door—a butcher shop. All closed, all gone years ago. Their faded signs, ghostlike on the brick sides of their buildings, give tantalizing clues to what they offered. Igloo Ice and Cold Storage. Renner's Valves and Boilers. The Eston Millinery Co. (William once peeked inside this building, through a hole in a boarded window. He saw nothing but dark emptiness. The intense, acrid smell of urine kept him from exploring further.)

All that is left of these places now are their sagging brick husks and the smell of their decay—dusty and moldy with the generic, loamy odor that all things offer up when they finally return to the earth.

But these were all old and accepted parts of William's world by this time. In the two years of walking back and forth to work, he'd seen all of these, noticed them in their turn as some piece or part of their structures caught his eye. He'd had time to study those things that held his attention, until they drifted again to the background, allowing some other detail or structure to come forward.

But now all is background to him, and he rarely devotes any time these days to thinking about his surroundings.

So, he walks, humming to himself, enjoying the coolness of the air, the shade cast onto his face by his hat.

When he smells it: *a scent.*

A new scent.

Not the death dust of the buildings, collapsing like shriveled lungs.

Not the chemicals of the ancient factories, still wheezing out their toxins.

Not the jungle aroma of the weeds tangled in the overgrown lots.

No, this is new. At once flowery and bitter, sweet and burning. He inhales, and it leaves his nostrils and throat feeling raw, abraded.

And it is disturbingly, elusively familiar.

He turns completely around, slowly. But there's nothing new here, nothing that could be giving off this increasingly intoxicating scent.

Here is the baby carriage factory, empty and heartbreakingly austere. Across the street, the low, ramshackle remains of the stables for the St. Louis Municipal Police Mounted Patrol, abandoned for nearly a century, still exuding the aroma of dry hay and moist droppings. Further up, a bicycle repair shop and the collapsed remains of a fur exchange, whatever that was.

William sniffs the air again deeply, half expecting the smell to have vanished. But, instead, it has grown stronger.

Hints of juniper make him think of gin and tonics taken on his patio, complete with their final acid twist of lemon. But the scent also evokes hyacinth and honeysuckle, and even—briefly, lightly—tea roses.

William has never, in his two years of walking this route, never smelled anything even remotely like this.

But that's not true, he dimly knows, not entirely . . .

Something vague and shadowed lurches in the lizard part of his brain that processes smell. It fires synapses meant to bring forth memories. But there is a gulf here, a span, an abyss that cannot be bridged. So William's brain twitches with the smell, but cannot identify it, cannot place it in its rightful context.

He breathes it in again, a heady, pleasurable lungful. His eyes roll up into his head like the wheels of a slot machine, slowing to reveal their cherries, lemons, or bars.

What is it? he wonders. Then, tripping on its heels, *I have to know.*

He readjusts his brim with a quick, defiant snap, then lifts his nose into the air, turning and drawing deep breaths in through his nostrils as if he were a champion bloodhound.

It seems stronger behind him, to his right.

He turns, walks back past the boarded and graffitied windows of the Applewaite & Sons Trucking Co. He smells rot and old wood, oil and the phantom vapors of ancient gasoline, and, as everywhere, the flat, soupy tang of urine.

But above it all, rising like an aching high note over a bass choir is the scent: sweet and hinting of foliage and flowers. Cartoonlike, it reaches tenuous, smoky fingers out to him, fairly pulling him along.

A dark, narrow alley runs between the Applewaite & Sons building and its neighbor, Mugler Publishing & Printing. The alley's uneven surface is strewn with broken bottles, an old tire, a rickety stack of warped wood pallets, and the ubiquitous single shoe.

William pauses, momentarily brought to his senses by the instinctive alarm the alley sets off in his urban brain. At its end there is a wedge, a sliver of brilliant light, where the sun shines through to the ground again. To get to that light, though, he must pass through a space that is dark and dank, restrictive, with many potential hiding spots.

But the scent is insistent, overpowering his sharper senses.

He breathes deeply, coating his lungs in it, and steps into the alley.

It is like stepping into another world, another time.

The smells here are stronger, deeper. There is a womblike thickness to the air: liquid and organic with undertones that speak of grit and decay.

William steps forward cautiously, the scent lulling him, urging him on by degrees.

He nears the alley's exit. The wedge of sunlight has become a panel, narrow and tall, that rises above him. It reveals the space between the rears of the buildings, with the gaping, toothless mouths of their dark loading bays. Doors dot the brick structures here and there, some wooden and warped like badly set bones, others metal and rusting like oozing sores.

He puts a foot forward, out of the dark and into the light of this industrial courtyard, when he hears it . . . *them*.

Sounds.

Voices, muffled and constrained.

He freezes, dark, rainbow-sheened water soaking into his loafers.

The voices are not speaking.

What he hears are not words, not conversation.

But there is a definite sense of command and protest, of compulsion and repulsion.

Of desire and fear.

He hugs the edge of the rusted and sagging remains of a fire escape, peers slowly around the corner of the building.

The elusive, ephemeral scent that has led him here takes on a forceful physical presence; it goes from ghost to revenant with shocking rapidity, striding from the shadows, the dappled sunlight and striking not just his nose, but his entire body.

William recoils from this blow. But his eyes do not close, nor do his nostrils stop bringing the scent inside of him; he takes it in gulps as if it, and not the air it is carried on, is what his lungs, his body, his mind craves.

It is flowers now, the scent: strongly, assertively floral. But there are so many colors to it, so many tones. Sharp lime and pine. A crisp, astringent soapiness. And underneath, barely perceptible but pervasive, a sweet reek of rot.

Still, he takes it in as his eyes take in movement in the mottled shadows. A figure, tall, heavy, masculine, looms over another, smaller, thin, feminine.

Their heads incline toward one another, their lips almost touching.

The man is all shade and outline. The woman, wearing a tight, bone-colored dress, reveals him beside her more as an absence, something missing. One of her hands, long, tapered nails painted eggplant, is flat against his chest. The other is not visible. One of his hands is cupping her chin, lifting her face to his.

Shaking his own head dully, William realizes what he's stumbled onto. Lovers or whatever passes for lovers in this rundown, scabrous neighborhood. A village Romeo and Juliet meeting in the ruins for sex. If he stays, William knows that afterward, in addition to the crude sex, he's likely to see an exchange of money or drugs . . . or both.

Slinking back around the corner of the building, he frowns, the power of the scent broken. It was only cheap perfume, after all, something to cover the other less pleasant odors of her addictions—the unwashed body of her customer, the meth-rotted teeth, dirty hair that reeks of sour sweat and cigarette smoke.

He takes a deep breath and exhales sharply. How could he have found the odor pleasurable, much less intoxicating? The scent is oily, cloying. It seems to ooze on the air, cover his skin in a sticky layer of scum. He feels it at the back of his throat now, coagulated there like blood.

He turns to head back down the alley, disgusted and disappointed.

A gurgle, liquid and strained.

He stops moving.

The blood within him stops, too—hesitates.

Suddenly, he is horribly sure that what he has just seen is not a prelude to sex . . .

Slowly, he advances to the corner again, edges around it.

The hand that William had thought rested lightly on the man's chest now looks stiff and clenched, its muscles taut with the effort to repel.

The hand that William had thought lifted her chin delicately now grasps her neck, squeezes tightly.

Another bubble of air escapes her lips.

The man's other hand appears now, arcing over his head like a dark wing unfurling.

A shiny talon at the tip of that wing descends powerfully.

Raises. Lowers.

Again.

Again.

Something that sounds like drops of rain patters to the ground, pools in the shadows at their feet.

Then, the man, the shadow, the shape turns toward William, fixes him with his eyes.

Instead of recoiling, reeling from the man's glare, William freezes.

The man's eyes glow from beneath the brim of his hat. They are hot, laval, and they roil in their orbits like balls of incandescent gas.

Hat . . . ?

William notices, for the first time, the hat worn by the shadow.

Unconscious of what he's doing, his hand moves to the brim of his own hat, strokes it as if to reassure himself that it still sits atop his head.

The shadow smiles at him, his fiery orange eyes flashing, his teeth a white and even arc within the dark of his face.

He turns, fades away, and is gone, lost within the denseness of the worn buildings.

William remains still for a time. The shape of the woman is abstract against the relentless pattern of the cobblestones. She is all curves and spirals and glistening pools of red and cream. She is a painting now; he has reduced her to a kind of art.

He takes a single, tentative step forward, stops.

Two things come to him immediately, like sudden electric bolts.

There is the smell of blood: metallic, and as intimate as the change in his pocket. It floats on the air, recrimination and guilt, and it envelops him in a cloud.

Then there is the scent again, above, below, inside him.

It is bitter now, like old limes: sharp and too sweet, with a powdery tang like the taste of aspirin crushed between dry teeth.

And it is him, he realizes.

Me. My scent.

But William wears no cologne.

What he smelled today, noticed for the first time, is not the city around him, not the scent of its life and decay. Rather it is the scent of *him*: his shampoo, his soap, his shaving cream.

More, it the essential smell of him, his skin, his sweat, the whiskers that push up from beneath, and the blood that pulses through him. It is the smell of his failures and successes, his faith and fear, his affectations and the true self that lies quivering at his center.

It floats from him, wicked from his pores, surrounds him in an aura of his own making.

Another realization sweeps through him, impatient, yet seemingly content to wait for these first two to have their effect.

It is *his* scent, too.

His knees give, and he falls forward like a penitent, vomits onto the cold, slick ground.

His head bows forward until he feels the cool grit of the cobblestones pressing his forehead.

That's why it was so strong here . . . so overpowering.

I never smelled it before, but he wore it like a cape, like the shadows he shrouded himself in.

He wore it as if he knew it.

And he smiled at me because he recognized it.

Recognized me.

Weakly, he pulls himself to his feet, absently wipes his mouth.

He backs away from the woman's body, down the alley, back onto the street.

It is raining now, lightly, and it is as if a gauzy curtain has been draped over the city, softening its rougher features.

The sights, smells are familiar once again, but he draws none of them in any longer.

His own smell fills his nostrils now, plugging them against all else.

With a hesitant look in the direction he'd set out in this morning, toward his office, he turns back to his home, sets out through the rain that way instead.

When he arrives, he enters, locks the door behind him, goes to his closet.

On the patio in his backyard, within the ten-foot walls with their iron spikes, he burns all of his hats one by one, watching their dark smoke drift up into the misty, impersonal gray of the sky and fade, fade, fade . . .

John F.D. Taff has been writing for about 25 years now, with more than 85 short stories and four novels in print. His collection, Little Deaths, *was named the best horror fiction collection of 2012 by HorrorTalk.* The End in All Beginnings, *his collection of novellas, was published by Grey Matter Press in 2014. Jack Ketchum called it, "the best novella collection I've read in years," and it was a finalist for a Bram Stoker Award for Superior Achievement in a Fiction Collection. His work has appeared recently in* Dread: The Best of Grey Matter Press, Gutted: Beautiful Horror Stories, The Beauty of Death, Cutting Block Book's Single Slices, *and* I Can Taste the Blood. *Additionally,* Little Deaths: The Definitive Collection *was released by Grey Matter Press in 2017. Keep up with Taff at his blog,* johnfdtaff.com; *follow him on Twitter* @johnfdtaff, *on Instagram at* johnfdtaff, *or visit his Amazon Author Page.*

THE ODOR OF VIOLETS

BY JOHN FARRIS

EDITOR'S NOTES: This final selection was one of my more pleasing finds in the reading search for scent-related tales. I was, of course, already familiar with John Farris's works, and had the opportunity to correspond with—and later meet—him and his son on behalf of a horror convention souvenir book I edited a couple years ago. John was as gracious and contemplative in person as his writing is complex and engaging. So to find a tale from a luminary such as him that was both fitting and entertaining for this anthology was a fortuitous high point.

What is it about a smell that causes us to associate it with a person's *character*, whether the smell is of them or is simply a factor of the surrounding environment? Jubilant qualities may be assigned to any cruel brute in smelling range of something pleasant as vanilla or honeysuckle, and loathsome attributes given to anyone unfortunate enough to have caught the linger of a malfeasant stink, even if that person is otherwise kind, generous, and loving.

Western culture tends to do this subconsciously, while there are many peoples around the world whose social order and community interaction are purposefully built around their smells, often fittingly referred to as the "aroma-force." The Ongee of the Andaman Islands define themselves by touching the tip of their nose in greeting, meaning both *me* and *my odor*. The Serer Ndut of Senegal believe our scent has two purposes, not only as physical identification, but also a spiritual definer, revealing the true virtue of a person.

Then there is the following, in which scents seem to follow or "attach" to people, which is also a fitting allegory for the characters themselves, especially when contrasting the finale's more disturbing effluvium against the motif fragrance of *The Odor of Violets*.

> *"Each day the odor of violets, mysteriously present, masked the odor of dissolution . . . "*

I WAS COMPLETING MY LAST LAP of the day on the rutted cinder track when a man in a trench coat and a muffler appeared out of the fog and called my name.

"Mr. Mayo, sir?"

Not as if he knew me by sight. I was tempted to pass him by with a curt shake of the head, since at the time I was nearly three months behind on my car payments, and ripe for repossession. But immediately after calling, tentatively, to me, the man in the trench coat was taken with a fit of coughing, like a volcano trying to erupt. He leaned against the chain link fence surrounding the track and the Sprayberry College football field ("Home of the Purple Maulers"). Instinctively, as I jogged nearer, I felt that he was not going to threaten me with harsh reminders of past-due bills. He seemed to have no business being there at all, in the dank night air. Nonetheless I stopped well short of where he stood, trying to arrest his cough, holding with one hand to the fence for support and clutching, under his other arm, a bulky manila envelope.

Jogging in place, I spoke to him. "Yes?"

He got control of himself and straightened, breathing hard. Light from the sodium vapor lamp above the end-zone gate, now almost invisible in the fast-moving fog, touched his face; it was a glowing, unhealthy shade of red, as if from St. Anthony's fire. Although we were early into February, the air growing chillier by the minute, he was perspiring. He had a brown ruff of beard along the jawline, like a worn-out strip of welcome mat, and not much hair on his head.

"You *are* Jack Mayo—the author?"

His accent was softly southern; I was reminded of pleasant bourbon-saturated evenings in Key West in the company of Tennessee and dear, doomed Carson McCullers.

"Yes," I admitted impatiently, now paying more attention to the telltale envelope he'd brought with him. He was of late middle age; I assumed he was not a student here. At least I had never noticed him on campus, or heard that distressing cough before. Sprayberry was a rather small and thoroughly déclassé institution, near the sea's edge and forever on the brink of insolvency. "Who are you?" I inquired.

He spoke slowly, and in a low tone, as if constantly needing to strangle the urge to cough. "David Hallowell, sir. You have never heard of me. But I am a writer, too."

"I see," I said unencouragingly, and decided to forgo the last hundred yards of my final lap. I began doing exercises so as not to cool off too suddenly and risk taking a chill. "If you're interested in signing up for one of my seminars in creative writing, then I suggest that you contact the admissions office."

"No. I—I don't have time for that," Hallowell replied, and he smiled deprecatingly before he began to cough again, into a soiled wad of handkerchief. When he regained his voice, he said, "But it doesn't matter. I have nearly finished it. My book, I mean. Another two weeks—three at the vereh most. I wanted you to see it now. Then my fondest hope is that you will be willing to advise me. I know nothing about the publishing business. I do not know what I should do next. Of course, it *will* be published. It's good—vereh good. Superb, in fact. Yes, it should be a vereh great success."

"Really?" I grunted, touching my toes, feeling fire in the tendons of my thighs, the old bursitis that plagued my right shoulder. I was amused and, I suppose, a trifle irritated by his presumption. "What is it you've written? A novel?"

"Yes, sir. That I have."

"You want me to read it, and find you a publisher."

I couldn't keep the sarcasm from my voice: too many years of practice at the expense of mediocre scribblers unable to retaliate in kind had perfected my killshots. He drew back a little, shifting the position of the large envelope until it covered him like a buckler. But I had no desire to shatter his pathetic dignity.

"I'm much too busy," I said, "with teaching. And then my own work—"

"Oh, I know that!" he said, trembling now. "It's only that I have admired your writing so much. I must have read each of the stories in *Tug of War* a dozen times. The craftsmanship, the complexity, the humor—your talent inspired me from the beginning of my own poor ambition, and I—well—" He thrust the envelope at me, holding it at arm's length. His eyes pleaded for me to take it. "I owe so much to you."

"Mr. Hallowell—"

"Please! You'll like it, I know you will. Here is my *life*, sir—all that has kept me alive these past two years."

The coughing again. I felt a twinge of alarm and then, vaguely, guilt for not accepting his manuscript, making him suffer all the more in the fog and the cold.

"Yes, I suppose I could find the time. All right."

He stumbled forward eagerly, pressing the envelope into my hands. Quite heavy, there would be well over three hundred pages, I thought. At least I could glance at it before dismissing his labor with a few noncommittal words. Up close I saw how bad his eyes looked, like runny egg congealing on a cheap plate, how thin and ragged he was. I could not imagine him straying very far from the Salvation Army shelter, much less finding the high purpose and energy it took to write a novel.

"You're very ill," I said. "Are you seeing a doctor?"

He shook his head. "It's my lungs. I was a sickly child, and at fourteen I was made to go to work in my uncle's mill, on the Alabama side of the Chattahoochee River. It was an old, primitive, turn-of-the-century place, and the air was always thick with cotton dust. I contracted brown-lung disease while still a young man. And, well, nothing can help me now." His face screwed up in an agony of pride and he whispered fiercely, "I will finish my appointed task, however. I already have the last few chapters in mind. Just a few more nights—"

"You really ought to be in a hospital," I said.

He smiled, astounded, perhaps deeply touched that I might care whether he lived or died. Tears flowed from his red-flecked eyes. He seized my free hand and shook it. I felt as if I were grasping the bony hand of Death itself.

"You can't know how happy you've made me, sir! A year ago I couldn't imagine even meeting you, and now—you're going to read my novel!"

"Yes, certainly I'll read it, Mr. Hallowell. But I can't promise anything—"

"You'll do what you can!" he cried, ecstatic, his weeping eyes wandering from my face; almost instantly he appeared to be in a feverish fugue state. He babbled. "You're a man of high talent, a good and generous man!"—as if these qualities must be synonymous. "I only regret I shall not be here to read *your* novel. I know it's going to be a masterpiece, after all the years you've spent writing it—"

"Well, I'm afraid I still have far to go," I said, an automatic response. "Now, you really must put yourself to bed, take care of that cough."

Even as I spoke, his efflorescence was fading in the voracious Pacific fog, and I was left standing there holding a torn and seedy envelope I had no real desire to open.

"Good-bye—good-bye, Mr. Mayo! My address is on the title page. If you could see your way clear—I'm so very anxious to know what you think—"

"I'll read it immediately!" I promised rashly, now talking only to a ghost as he vanished beyond the gate. I shuddered, then began to jog again in the opposite direction and away from the sea, across the rolling campus to my studio in the faculty apartments.

After a shower and a light supper I applied myself to the chore of reading my students' work, fortifying myself at intervals with double scotches. I had put the envelope containing David Hallowell's manuscript far back on my already cluttered worktable. For the next two hours my mood worsened steadily as I looked for some gleam of talent in the pile of chaff before me. Influences in style ranged from Saul Bellow to Erma Bombeck and, yes, even hoary old Hemingway. I gave up when a headache like a spike between my eyes diminished my ability to concentrate. I drank the last of the scotch in the bottle (remembering, too late, there would be no more credit at the liquor store), and went to bed.

Scarcely three hours later I was suddenly wide awake on the Hide A Bed, roused from an unmemorable dream; I had heard, or thought I heard, a tortured cough. And there was an unfamiliar odor in my cramped studio, the sweetness of wild violets.

I got up and turned on a lamp, but I had no company except for the memory of David Hallowell's face in the fog. I felt amazingly refreshed on a short ration of sleep. It was half past three in the morning; I didn't want to go back to bed. I made coffee. The odor of violets faded gradually as I stood at my windows looking at the campus lights through slow spirals of fog. Then I turned to a bookshelf and took down a copy of *Tug of War*. I looked at the dust-jacket photo of myself—leaner and with a thicker head of hair in those days when I had been, in pugilistic terms, a "comer." I knew the brief biography by heart, my present state of futility summed up in the last line: *Mr. Mayo is currently at work on a novel.*

The collection of eight stories in my hand, my only published work, was thirteen years old. Each year's crop of "comers" had pushed me farther and farther into the dim background of the literary scene. The novel blithely referred to on the endpaper was not forthcoming. In thirteen years I had managed less than a hundred pages. Not one word for the past two years. I was still not well recovered from the depression caused by my fiftieth birthday.

I set aside *Tug of War* and glanced at my worktable, now seeing only the soiled envelope with David Hallowell's manuscript inside. I felt annoyed with him; he was terminally ill, yet he had nearly finished a novel while I could not write at all. Assuredly it would turn out to be a dreadful piece of muck . . . but his dedication, his belief that he had a story worth telling, merited respect.

I opened the envelope, and a thick bundle of yellow pages torn from legal pads fell to the floor. It was a holographic manuscript, and he wrote, like Eugene O'Neill, in a cramped, miserly hand; there must have been half a thousand words on every page. But he composed so painstakingly that every word was legible without a magnifying glass. I scanned the first page casually after finding the title provocative, turned to the second, sat down slowly on the Hide A Bed with that untidy bundle in my lap.

By daybreak I had read all of *Angels and Aborigines*. I'd been powerless to stop reading. It was marvelous: a comic, picaresque *Lear*. Hallowell's protagonist, an old poet, and three randy daughters careered like tornadoes through his pages. He satirized (and often tore to shreds) academia, government, religion, the full spectrum of intellectual pretentiousness and cultural folderol of our times. I turned over the last, incomplete page knowing that David Hallowell was a literary titan. My first thought, with nothing more to read, was an earnest entreaty to the gods that Hallowell be allowed to live long enough to finish this masterwork.

My second, distantly corrupting thought was, *This is the novel I was meant to write.*

I had been almost childishly pleased to note that there were echoes of the old, the good Jack Mayo, in those pages. It was true, as Hallowell insisted, that I had served him in some small way.

After my morning classes I drove down from the hills to the old section of San Augustín. David Hallowell was living in a *barrio* by the sea where the dreary fog lingered at noonday. The streets were narrow, the houses ramshackle, with a few hang-dog date palms and rusting pepper trees in the sandy yards. There was truculent graffiti in Spanish on every side wall of *laundería* and *bodega*. It took me quite some time to locate him.

The squat Mexican woman who responded to my inquiry on Portales Street had a baby on one hip and toddlers clinging to her skirt.

"Dah-veed, *sí,* is living here." She looked hopefully at me. "You are friend?"

"We met only yesterday," I said.

"Oh. Dah-veed very sick, is always—*tosiendo.*" She translated the word for me by coughing into her fist.

"Yes, I know. Could you take me to him?"

She led me through her squalid house and out the back door to a *casita* set against the alley fence. There were chickens in the bare yard, discarded beer cans, and rusted parts of automobiles. A stench of garbage saturated the fog. I could hear the surf just two blocks away. I also heard him coughing as we reached the *casita* door. The Mexican woman shifted her fretting half-clad infant from one chubby arm to the other.

"All night he is like that," she said of the coughing. "I go make tea for him now." She smacked one of her toddlers, who was bending over poking a finger into a fresh pile of chicken shit, and returned to the house.

I knocked at the *casita* door. Muffled coughing, but no other response. I shivered in the damp grayness. The door was unlocked, so I let myself in.

There was, unexpectedly, a sweetness in the air: violets, a welcome contrast to the sour spoor of the chicken-blighted yard. The one-room *casita* was quite dark, shades pulled down over the remaining panes of glass in the door and the single small window. I could make him out lying in a narrow mission-style bed, huddled under a blanket, coughing pathetically, rocking the springs with the violence of his affliction.

"Mr. Hallowell?" I said. "David?"

He gave a start, one bare foot kicking out from beneath the blanket, and sat up, peering at the doorway.

"Yes—yes. Who is it?"

"Jack Mayo."

"Oh, Mr. Mayo! I apologize, sir, I—please, if you would give me a few moments—"

"Certainly. I'll wait outside."

"No! No! Stay! I'm just waking up. I work nights, you see." He was having difficulty getting his breath. "If you wouldn't mind—on the table there—a bottle of tequila."

I raised the window shade, letting in some pallid light. I poured a shot of tequila for him and, at his urging, a shot for myself, as he had a supply of paper cups to drink from. I didn't entirely trust his explanation of the illness from which he suffered, and I have always been more than mildly phobic about germs. Fortunately there was no atmosphere of the sickroom, because of the remarkably pleasant odor of spring violets. I saw none growing in the room, however; and no potentially flowering seed would have survived for long out-of-doors. Perhaps it was perfume, a recent female visitor—

When I mentioned the odor to him he looked puzzled. His face was flushed and glistened from perspiration, his eyes were unfocused as he sipped his tequila.

"Oh, yes, I did smell violets in the beginning, I suppose. But that was so long ago I've become used to it. I hardly notice anymore."

His explanation was far from clear, but I had no good reason to question him further. And my attention had been drawn to the pile of yellow paper on his writing table, beside a cracked pair of wire-rimmed reading glasses and a jar crammed with ballpoint pens, the cheap variety given away by every sort of business establishment. It was difficult for me not to pick up the new pages and begin reading on the spot. Instead I smiled at David Hallowell.

The tequila seemed to have temporarily suppressed his cough, although it lived on in his skinny chest, as a low dangerous rumbling. His complexion had cleared somewhat. My smile was unexpected; it caused him to flinch, and then he returned an abashed smile of his own.

"Was I right? It is good, isn't it?"

"I think you're a genius," I said.

He scratched his head and trembled; he began to weep and shake the bed in a paroxysm of joy and thanksgiving. A little overcome myself, I fed him more tequila, and wondered how his heart could stand up under the strain. Some of the tequila dribbled into the ruff of his coarse beard.

"But surely," I said, "others have told you that."

"No. Not another living soul but you has read a word of my book. I moved to San Augustín because—I knew that you were here."

Rather than watch him suffer through more agonies of gratitude. I turned again to his worktable, noticing a copy of *Tug of War* atop a pile of badly worn paperback dictionaries. I picked up the book, which obviously he'd rescued from a stall in a secondhand store. Just inside the cover was a recent clipping from the local newspaper, my photo accompanying an announcement of the summer writers' workshop I had established on campus.

By now the odor of violets was all but gone from the room; I could smell his trickling toilet in one corner, and the sordidness of the *casita* became oppressive to me. Obviously before David Hallowell settled in, the *casita* had served as lodging for numerous wetbacks. Chickens quarreled in the yard; a child wailed.

"How long have you been living here?" I asked him.

He shrugged. "I don't know. Three months? Closer to four."

"And where is your home? I believe you mentioned Alabama."

"Eufaula, Alabama. That was a vereh long time ago. I haven't been back since—" It was an effort, or an ordeal, for him to recall. "Anyway," he said quietly, "there's no reason for me to go back. Everyone dear to me has long since passed to his or her reward."

"You have no family?" He shook his head. "Oh, I'm very sorry. David."

"An insufficiency of the genes, I'm afraid. No Hallowell or Radburne was ever celebrated for longevity." He clutched his blanket more tightly around him, smiling wanly at his expected fate. Then he looked at me with the sweet, devoted expression of a setter dog. When it was I who should have been wagging my tail at him.

"You will be celebrated," I assured David Hallowell, "beyond your wildest dreams. Leave that to me."

"Thank you," he said. "My friend."

I was braced for tears again; but the Mexican woman came to the door of the *casita* with a little tray: she had brought tea, some sugared oatmeal in a bowl. I took the tray from her. She look worried.

"Eat nothing," she said. "Many days, no *comidas*."

"I'll see that he has some of the oatmeal. *Muchas gracias*."

David was willing to be fed. But after a few gummy spoonfuls and half a cup of dark, aromatic tea he could manage no more. He lay down wearily, eyes closing.

"I'll sleep for a few hours," he said. "Until my muse shows up."

"Do you have much more to go?"

"It's almost done," he murmured.

"With your permission, David, I'll take these pages you've completed." I hesitated. "You have a copy of the manuscript, of course."

"No. Couldn't afford to make copies."

"Well, then. I'll see to it. And I'll be back tomorrow."

He thanked me, coughed, pressed a fist to his mouth, and drifted off to sleep that way. I let myself out and all but ran to my car.

I read the twenty new pages then and there, in an excruciating state of excitement. They were excellent. The wasting of his body and quantities of tequila had not in the least diminished his art. He was Faulknerian in his prodigality. Oh, a word might be changed here and there, a redundancy deleted. Nothing more.

For the next four days I arrived promptly at noon. I had forsaken pride and borrowed a hundred dollars from a faculty colleague with whom I had had an affair and who still entertained some hope the affair might be renewed, although she was one of those women for whom the sexual act seems to have the caloric input of a two-pound German chocolate cake: she had put on forty pounds through trysting. I purchased cough remedies which had only a temporary flagging effect on David's consuming cough, more tequila, painkillers. And many legal pads: David was using up more than one a night in a rage of completion. Each day the odor of violets, mysteriously present, masked the odor of dissolution in the *casita*. I was frightened for David, nearly sleepless at night for fear he wouldn't, after all, reach the dizzying conclusion of his novel.

A week after our first meeting on the running track at Sprayberry, I let myself in, and took a few moments to adjust to the portent that the odor of violets was absent from the *casita*. David Hallowell lay very still on his back, his eyes open and staring, a slight smile of peace on his lips. His ordeal had ended. In his right hand there was a note to me.

We have done it!

It was signed, *David*.

I gathered up the last pages of *Angels and Aborigines* strewn across his worktable and stumbled sobbing into the chicken-infested yard. The Mexican woman, children dangling haplessly from her swirling skirt, hurried outside and, hearing me, began her own lamentation. The children, one by one, contributed their voices. Dogs barked mournfully up and down the *barrio*.

"He has no family," I told the coroner. "He was the last of his line. And, except for Mrs. Cerador and myself, he had no friends."

I sold my car, one jump ahead of the repo man, raising enough cash to retire the note and afford David Hallowell a modest but decent funeral.

The night following his burial I assembled all of the yellow pages in my studio, changed the ribbon on my Smith-Corona electric, drank two double scotches to fortify myself, then began typing the book I had been born to write.

ANGELS AND ABORIGINES
a novel by
Jack Mayo

I made a few editorial changes as I went along. Nothing major. Ten days later I mailed the typescript to an editor who had almost forgotten I existed, at an august publishing house in New York. The manuscript went through the house like wildfire. It knocked them all on their asses.

Angels and Aborigines was published the following spring, in a first
edition of half a million copies. The Book-of-the-Month Club ordered an
additional quarter of a million. Word of mouth secured the number one
position on the *New York Times* best-seller list two weeks after publication.
The novel stayed at number one through six additional printings, for
eighteen glorious weeks. The reviews—ah, God, the reviews! Each one a
nutritious sweetmeat, a seductive paean, an exaltation of a unique talent! I
swept all of my peers under the rug that season—Norman, Philip, John.
Even they came forth with tributes for the literary event of the decade. The
King Rat currently in residence at the Dream Factory snatched the cheese
from all the other rats, paying an unheard-of sum for movie rights.
Thirty-three foreign editions were planned. The appeal of my novel was
universal.

My novel, yes. Mine by escheat, if you will.

I had known what I must do, even before David Hallowell was laid to
rest. Because—to be brutally honest about the matter—if I'd simply
arranged for posthumous publication of the novel, it would have done far
less well with his name on it. Perhaps *Angels and Aborigines* would have
been grievously neglected. Those things happen. The bald truth is,
publishers and the literati take little interest in dead authors, particularly
those who have had the bad fortune to die without first establishing a
reputation that will, you might say, tide them over. In taking credit for
what David had written I was, in fact, ensuring the widest possible
circulation for a great book. I assumed the role of literary celebrity and, I
must say, played it with panache. This was a requirement for bestsellerdom
that had to be fulfilled. It kept me busy for months. And as I read and
reread the novel (some of the more wittily salacious passages made for
uproarious cocktail party entertainment), it became rooted in my soul that
I was the true proprietor of the words I recited.

For my services as executive consultant to the film version of *Angels
and Aborigines*, my Hollywood agent obtained a fee equal to half the
national debt of Ecuador. Production plans and major casting coups were
to be announced and celebrated at a wingding hosted by the producer and
the director, a thirty-year-old *Wunderkind* who—bless his heart—had yet
to taste failure.

Much of the fun of having a party in Hollywood is to have it at a *boîte* which is so desirable that code names are assigned to the famous few allowed by the management to make reservations. There is more fun in deciding whom not to invite, and delivering invitations only on the day before the event. The howls of pain and outrage from the uninvited thus are concentrated into a short period of time, and the maneuverings of the newly disenfranchised to be included becomes a frantic shadow dance up and down the corridors of Tinsel Town.

I adored it all: exiting from a massive silver limousine, the press of *paparazzi* and plain folk swamping the sidewalk outside Gepetto's, the monstrous energy of allure released inside the packed café, the director's acknowledged indebtedness to me for providing the "raw material" for his next megahit; the camaraderie of the charmingly maniacal actor, a two-time Oscar winner, who was to essay the character of Lordy Lambkin in the screen version . . .

"I wonder what David would have thought?"

I was near the bar, looking for a refill, when she spoke. Perhaps not to me. But I turned anyway because, in spite of the atmosphere in the chic café, the mild scentings of fresh flowers and drop-dead perfume all around, the odor of violets was suddenly pervasive.

The room was filled with glamorous, world-famous women, but even in their company the youthful creature watching me with a questioning smile was unique. Perhaps because she seemed perfectly at ease when everyone else was trying a little too hard. She wore her red hair pulled severely back from her forehead; it was gathered in a cunning Psyche knot. There was a sweetness in her oval face, but not naïveté. Her gaze was direct, coolly sensual, slightly mischievous. She wore an almost piously simple, rather old-fashioned off-the-shoulder gown of some neutral, crushed fabric that shimmered with exotic color, like sunlight in the sea, each time she moved.

"I beg your pardon?" I said, sniffing audibly. I couldn't help myself. Her scent was familiar, and although it should have been pleasing, I had an adverse, almost allergic reaction to it: my skin suddenly felt clammy, my heart raced.

She edged past an old man in pigtails and a pink leather suit and stood in front of me, never taking her vivid blue eyes from my face. She was drinking one of those abominable Fuzzy Navels. Her nearness, the pungency of violets, made my eyes water.

"David *wouldn't* have liked it," she said thoughtfully, lowering her long-stemmed glass after a sip. "All the hoopla. I think we would have been someplace else right now, working on a new book, isn't that what *you* think, Mr. Mayo?"

"I'm afraid I don't know what you're talking about," I said, too fascinated to avoid her strict gaze.

"I'm talking about David Hallowell," she replied. "The author of *Angels and Aborigines.* The book you stole from him."

"What a preposterous accusation! I don't know any David Hallowell!" A skeptical dimple appeared on one perfect cheek. I glanced around to see if anyone had overheard us, but the party babble was at such a level that our conversation, thus far, had been private. "Who put you up to this ludicrous jape? Who are you?"

"I'm Dierdre. I was David's muse."

I began to laugh, although I felt panicky. Somehow, somewhere, this beautiful, merciless girl had known David Hallowell, and he had told her about the book he was writing. What was she doing here now, and what did she have in mind? I could only try to bluff my way out of this predicament without exhibiting any sort of anxiety and thereby allowing that her accusation might be true. But my nostrils had dilated; I was again nearly anesthetized by the odor of violets.

"I think," she said, "you've recognized me already. Although, of course, since David worked nights we were never introduced."

"Are you an actress?" I asked her, manufacturing an air of good-humored resignation. "You're quite good. I hope you're going to be in the film. Would you like to meet the director? By all means, let me introduce you. Because you're wasting your considerable talents on this crude and rather insulting—"

"I have several hundred pages of an earlier draft of David's novel. Handwritten, on legal pad paper. A draft you never saw. Post Office copyright. It proves beyond any doubt who wrote *Angels and Aborigines.*" She said all of this without rancor, as if she had no interest in intimidating me; a rueful little smile appeared as she finished. One eyebrow was slightly raised, inviting the denial she knew it was not in me to attempt.

"You were—a friend of his?" I said, when I could speak again.

"More than that. Much more. I told you. I was David's muse."

There was a twitching muscle near one corner of my mouth that I couldn't control. "Oh, yes," I said desperately playing along. "Your perfume—the odor of violets. Is that what the gods are wearing on Olympus nowadays?"

"It isn't perfume. It's my natural essence."

"And your name is Dierdre. Forgive me, I thought I knew the names of all the muses. Calliope, Thalia, Terpsichore—and so forth. Not a Dierdre in the lot, however."

"I'm an apprentice."

"Oh, well, that does explain it."

"With everybody and his brother writing or composing something these days, they need so many of us. The Association took on ten thousand new apprentices the day before yesterday."

"I hope they all look like you."

"We come in all shapes and sizes," she said, not smiling now. "Why don't you have that drink you came over here for? You look as if you're going to pass out, Mr. Mayo."

I could see no reason for her to continue this labored and unfunny pretense, the exercise in humiliation she seemed determined to put me through. Obviously it was money she was after.

"How much?" I asked Dierdre. "How much do you want to keep your mouth shut?"

Dierdre lowered her eyes, and sighed. "I don't think this is the time, or the place, to discuss restitution."

"All right, when?"

"I'll be in touch. After the next Association meeting."

"The Association? What is that?"

"I'll let you know. Later." She raised her glass in a mock salute, smiled guilelessly, slipped suddenly through a gap in a shifting group of bodies. I started to follow her, felt a tug at my sleeve, looked down. It was our producer, a hunchbacked albino renowned for his conquests of ravishing women.

"Come with me," he said. "Want you to meet someone." He named a prominent studio honcho.

"Do you know who that girl is?" I demanded of him.

He looked around with alert bunny eyes. "If she works in the Industry, I know her. Which lovely do you have in mind?"

"There—the redhead." But when I searched for Dierdre in the mob I couldn't find her. I turned back to the producer. "The one I was just talking to."

"You've been standing here by yourself for the last ten minutes mumbling in your beard. Frankly I thought you'd had a couple too many snorts."

"You didn't see—"

"You look devastated, Jacky. Want a woman? Pick one. I'll personally see to it she's delivered to your doorstep at the hotel by one a.m."

I said something to the effect that I could handle my own love life and went with him. I did not ask him if he also smelled violets. But the hypnotic odor persisted, like an olfactory illusion, although it weakened by the hour as I lay sleepless in my bungalow at the Beverly Hills Hotel. Wondering what the outcome would be and if, after all, it was only money that Dierdre desired.

I cursed myself for having believed David Hallowell's assertion that only the two of us had ever laid eyes on *Angels and Aborigines*. The solitude of the writer's trade can be agonizing: we must all, from time to time, seek the release of the confessional. The amateur wordsmith is particularly unable to keep silent about what he is up to. He must talk about his aspirations incessantly, even to a stranger on a bus. "I'm writing a novel." And so forth. Dierdre claimed to have an earlier manuscript... what, exactly, was her game? And who *was* she? How could I find out? After an hour of pacing and cigarettes I concluded that there was nothing I could do until she put an end to my speculation by contacting me again. I would simply have to wait.

For the next three days I stayed close to the hotel, anticipating, dreading her phone call. It was impossible not to think about Dierdre for more than a few seconds at a time. Despite the very great threat to my well-being she represented, I was perversely attracted to her, so much so that I scarcely paid notice to the numerous starlets and harlots available in the sexual marketplace where I was staying. Had she and David Hallowell been lovers? If so, then I was envious—of a man in his grave, from whom I had already appropriated everything.

Everything but Dierdre.

I swam in the pool, and at poolside I had meetings with the screenwriter, a well-respected hack who expressed reverence for my novel and seemed to have a few worthwhile ideas for translating it to the screen. The gardens of the hotel were lushly in bloom, there was a heated scent of roses outside my bungalow, but no violets to soothe my riddled nerves.

Her call came as I was having my sideburns darkened by Alberto in the hotel barbershop.

"Do you know what day this is?"

"The twenty-fourth of February," I replied, my heart pounding. "Why?"

"I thought you might remember," she said softly. "Well, never mind."

"Where are you? I want to—I think it's imperative that we get together."

"Do you know where the Bistro is?"

"On Canon Drive."

"I'll be in front at five o'clock." She hung up without another word.

I was driving a vintage Mercedes sports convertible, which the producer had made available to me during my stay. Like many of the paranoids in his profession, he was terrified of muggers and kidnapers. He belonged to the Beverly Hills Gun Club. He had weapons in all of his automobiles. He proudly had shown me the hiding place built into the driver's seat of the Mercedes, the push-button release that ejected into his waiting hand a pearl-handled pistol with considerable stopping power.

At the end of the hotel driveway, waiting for the light on Sunset to change, I checked to make sure the gun was still there. The butt slapped into my palm with a little metallic click. I didn't know then why I found that so satisfying, why it made my scrotum crawl with pleasure. I've fired pistols, but I'm not an aficionado. I had never conceived of the possibility that I could do bodily harm to someone.

Even though it was growing dark I identified Dierdre's flame from two blocks away as I drove south on Canon in the rush-hour traffic. I was on the wrong side of the street to pick her up. I made a left turn into the driveway beside the Bistro, waving the parking valet away. Dierdre got in. As slender as I remembered her; "so coldly sweet, so deadly fair." Byron, I believe.

She wore tinted glasses and a fawn-colored pantsuit. Her red hair was loose and flowing. She carried a big purse like a saddlebag. She didn't say hello. The odor of violets was chilly in the weather she brought with her, exhilarating as the bouquet of a great wine.

"Where are we going?" I asked her.

"Up the coast. To San Augustín."

San Augustín. I hadn't been back since resigning my teaching position at the college, shortly after the acceptance of my novel. My throat tightened.

"Why?"

"It's been two years," she replied, looking straight ahead. "We owe David a visit, don't you think?"

I realized then why she'd asked me on the telephone if I knew what day it was. February 24. The day David Hallowell died.

"Is that necessary?"

She looked at me, two seconds, her expression neutral. "Yes."

I could have refused. In traffic it would take more than three hours to drive to San Augustín. But the long drive would give me my chance to find out everything I wanted to know about Dierdre: the full story of her relationship with David Hallowell. It was even possible that—for her sake—I could persuade her not to take any action against me.

And if I couldn't—

Unfortunately she was not talkative on the trip up the Pacific Coast Highway. She answered questions sparingly or not at all. She seemed to be under a strain, not the assured, tantalizing amateur blackmailer I'd met three nights ago. Finally I gave up trying to talk to Dierdre, willing to wait her out. Without harming my perceptions, the odor of violets had a beneficial, lulling effect on me. I drove north with the confidence that the situation ultimately would be resolved in my favor.

The fog was rolling in as we reached San Augustín. The cemetery in which David Hallowell was buried lay on the slope of a hill only two hundred yards from the sea. With the fog lights on I crept up the winding access road past drab and dimly seen monuments to small deeds and inconsequential passions. The fuming fog cut visibility to less than ten feet. I had forgotten where he was interred. Dierdre seemed to know exactly, as if she had made many visits, after dark.

"To the left up ahead. There's a stand of oak trees and a crypt with a plinth. He's just down the path from there, near a wall that's parallel to the cliff."

"Now I remember," I said, my sense of well-being wearing a little thin. I wondered, for the first time, if Dierdre was in on this alone; if she was, then what was her real purpose in bringing me to a wayside cemetery under cover of the winter fog? The situation I had felt to be within my control was now unappealing.

Nevertheless, I stopped the small car by the trees, leaving the fog lights on. Dierdre got out immediately. The leafless branches dripped moisture onto the canvas cover. I heard the swish and boom of surf across the highway below. There was a flashlight in the glove compartment. Before getting out from behind the wheel I reached down and released the pistol from its hiding place, slipping it into my jacket pocket as I closed the door behind me.

I didn't know what lay ahead, in the fog; but Dierdre looked back at me impatiently, waiting. Not as if she had devastating mischief in mind. Her blue eyes were wide and unwinking, like eyes in a portrait.

"This way." She led me to David's plot along a narrow path of stepping-stones, her essence—as she called it—sweetening the dismal, dripping air. I cast the flashlight beam on the little bronze marker, flush with the ground, that I had purchased. The sight of it brought back memories but prompted no remorse, if that's what she expected. If not for me, *Angels and Aborigines* probably wouldn't have been finished. And in what anonymous grave, crowded close to unwanted and unremarked men, would he now be lying? I was tired of indulging her fantasies of revenge, whatever they might be.

"What do you want, Dierdre?"

She looked up slowly from contemplation of the grave.

"I was hoping," she said quietly, "by now you would know what you must do."

"For a start, I want those pages you told me about. The earlier draft. Name your price."

She frowned, then opened her purse. I tightened my grip on the pistol in my pocket. But all she brought out was another bundle of the familiar yellow pages.

"I have them here."

"Just drop them on the ground." She did so. "There are no more pages anywhere?"

"No."

"I wonder why I don't believe you."

She turned her face toward the sea, livelier than this boneyard, but invisible. "I'm going away tonight. I won't be back. It doesn't matter if you don't believe me. What matters is that you make restitution, in David's memory."

"I'm afraid that would mean the end of my career."

"You might try writing something of your own," she said sharply.

The night breathed mistily on my brow, its chill sinking to the roots of my heart. I suffered a momentary pang of self-loathing, and I hated her for judging me. She was very young; how could she know what it felt like to be out of the running all of your life?

I took a step toward her. Our eyes met in a dead heat. I was shaking from anger, and desire. Goaded by her essence, repelled by the setting of death in which my lust was manifest.

"If I had the right muse—" I said, now throwing her own joke back in her face. "Why don't you consider taking the job? I'll treat you better than David Hallowell ever could."

She shook her head slightly. "I'm not the muse you deserve. But one will be provided—once you've admitted that you stole David's novel, then done everything in your power to ensure him full credit. That is the will of the Association."

"Goddamn you! What difference does it make to David now?"

"It's the right thing to do."

I knew then that she would never let me touch her. That she meant what she had said. She was going away. But I couldn't bear the thought that Dierdre would be forever beyond my reach—the one who *knew*, unforgiving.

I took the pistol from my pocket and shone the beam of the flashlight full in her face. She looked steadily at me, not blinking, bold eyes with no appreciation of danger in them, no fear.

"That doesn't mean a thing," Dierdre said. "You can't hurt me. I'm immortal."

"You're crazy," I said. "Or we both are." I raised the pistol a little higher and shot her between the eyes.

Something seemed to uncurl from the fog like the lash of a whip and snatch the flashlight from my hand. Dierdre disappeared without a sound; I was blind in the fog. Moments after I fired the shot I was seized by a clonus—a series of violent muscular spasms. Involuntarily I dropped the gun, then went to my knees beside David Hallowell's grave crying incoherently, anticipating some lethal, otherworldly blow that would end my own life.

But nothing happened. No one was there. I had no company but the disinterested dead, who now included Dierdre among their number. The flashlight, still in working order, lay a few feet from where I was kneeling. Perhaps, unable to bear the sight of murder, I had flung it there myself just after pulling the trigger.

I picked up the gun again and crawled to the flashlight. I looked through the fog for Dierdre's body. The purse she had brought to the cemetery lay near the low brick wall at the edge of the cliff. Gasping for air, I went to the wall and looked over it. The beam of light, diffused by fog, afforded me a glimpse of her tumbled body fifty feet below.

I wanted to search her purse, find out who she really was; but I couldn't chance leaving a fingerprint behind. I gathered up all of the loose yellow sheets of the draft manuscript, frantic that I might miss one, thus leaving behind a clue that eventually would point the bird dogs of the law in my direction. When I was sure I had them all I returned in a deathly cold sweat to the Mercedes and climbed inside. The pistol was in my pocket. I planned to pull off the highway on my return to the City of Angels and fling it well out to sea.

Before starting the car I looked through the legal pad pages I had carefully gathered up. David had written nothing on them; they were blank. Dierdre had been bluffing. She had no evidence of theft on my part. A pathetic attempt at blackmail had cost her her life.

But was it blackmail that she had in mind? I could no longer be certain. Perhaps she had prudently left the incriminating first draft with someone else for safekeeping. In that case, I was as good as cooked.

I was too traumatized to do anything but put some distance between myself and the lonely cemetery. Back at the Beverly Hills Hotel I opened a bottle of scotch, drank from the bottle until I was dizzy, then swooned across the bed. I dreamed, ghoulishly, of executions. Dierdre's. Mine.

I awoke, in a fever of apprehension, to the odor of violets in the bungalow. I sat up, a sob in my throat. I heard the clink of a bottle neck against the rim of a glass, the soft gurgle of liquor poured over ice.

She came toward me illuminated in her own pure radiance, holding the glass out to me.

"Drink this," she said. "You probably could use it."

"Killed you," I said in a pitiful croaking voice; my heart was slowly squeezed to the size of a peanut by a fist of iron.

She was wearing a simple white shift with a gold ceinture. One shoulder was bare. She had bound up her abundant, cedar-colored hair. Her forehead, where the bullet had smashed it, was now unblemished. Her expression was businesslike, as if she were there only to serve me.

"I told you," she said. "I'm immortal."

I took the whiskey from her hand—real flesh and blood to my own, stony fingers—and gulped it. The fist that gripped my heart relaxed and blood surged to my nearly comatose brain. I found that I could breathe.

"I really hoped you wouldn't fail me," Dierdre said. "That you would want to do the right thing. But I guess it isn't in you, Jack."

She spoke mildly, as if rebuking a puppy that had displeased her. I said nothing, only stared into her bright, strict eyes. Was I dreaming? Insane? If this was insanity, I was willing to make the most of it.

"What do you want me to do now?" I asked, desiring nothing more than a smile of favor in return for my capitulation.

She didn't smile. "You're strong. Healthy. Good for another twenty years, at least."

I nodded hopefully.

"Now you will get the chance to earn the fame you've had so cheaply."

"How?"

"You're going to *write*, Jack. Write, and write, and write. As many as eighteen or twenty hours a day your muse will be with you, scarcely letting you rest."

"Doesn't sound so bad," I said, and reached out to pull her into bed with me.

She drew back politely before I could touch her.

"Oh, no, Jack, it won't be me. I have another assignment. You'll be getting a different muse."

"Who?"

Dierdre looked away from me. "The muse you deserve," she said. "The Association is adamant about that."

"That isn't fair! I deserve you! I'm famous! I want—"

Her celestial light dwindled to the size of a rubied ladybug in a corner of the dark room, turned scintillatingly and took wing, flew through the wall. I tumbled frenziedly out of bed and went to the spot where she had disappeared, standing on a chair to reach it. The spot was warm and glowing to my touch; an essence of fresh violets stung my eyes. And then the ravishing odor faded. I felt deserted, bereft. And a little frightened.

I poured myself another three fingers of scotch. The clock on the mantel in the living room whirred and chimed, four times.

A noisome odor was seeping into the bedroom, perhaps from outside the bungalow. An effluvium of Southern California's patented smog, mixed with—oh, God—dead cat and overripe refuse and spoiled eggs, almost everything unpleasant and sickening that memory could recall. I had to soak a handkerchief in scotch and hold it to my nose as I went out to the living room, intending to ring the front desk and complain.

It was sitting in a wing chair by the fireplace, facing me. If it could be said to have a face. Watching me. If it could be said to have eyes. It waved a hand—no, no, no, how could one call such a barbed and bloated thing a human hand!—leaving a phosphorescent wake of putrefaction in the air. There was a seething corona, as of tainted, primordial gas, all around it. The thing belched more gases and rumbled and laughed at me. Yes, that sound could be interpreted as a laugh, though it was so dreadful I knew I was condemned to hear it repeated even in those few hours of exhausted sleep I would be entitled to for the rest of my natural life.

"Long as you're up, pal," my muse said to me, "why don't we get to work?"

John Farris is an American writer, known largely for his work in the southern Gothic genre. He sold his first novel, Corpse Next Door, *the summer after he graduated high school in 1955. In 1959,* Harrison High *became his first million-seller.*

Apart from his vast body of fiction (over forty suspense and horror novels to his credit and a short story collection, Scare Tactics), *his work on motion picture screenplays includes adaptations of his own books (i.e.,* The Fury), *original scripts (such as writing and directing* Dear Dead Delilah), *and adaptations of the works of others (such as Alfred Bester's* The Demolished Man). *He's had several plays produced off-Broadway, and also paints and writes poetry. In addition he's found the time to raise a family and inspire dozens of up-and-coming writers, including his own sons. At various times John has made his home in New York, southern California, and Puerto Rico; he now lives near Atlanta, Georgia.*

ADDITIONAL MATERIAL

UNDERSTANDING AND INCORPORATING THE FIVE HUMAN SENSES INTO MODERN HORROR SHORT FICTION WRITING

BY ERIC J. GUIGNARD

"There are some things that are real, that you can see, that you can observe, like the moon, and grass and things. But for ideas to become real, they have to be played on your senses."

—Jane Campion

OUR IMPRESSIONS OF THE WORLD are formed by our five senses, and so too is writing made resonant and meaningful that manages to capture these senses. By exciting the perceptions of sight, sound, taste, hearing, and touch, writers transport us into the lives and memories of fanciful characters and evoke rich emotion, especially in the atmospheric-laden genre of horror.

Writers have long sought to entice readers through empathy and shared experiences, writing from what they know, or *think* they know, to engage us in colorful and alluring tales. In the field of horror authors, none are discussed more than Poe and Lovecraft, who are widely recognized as the champions of poetic and descriptive prose. Yet Lovecraft perished over eighty years ago, and Poe near a century before that. What they wrote that incorporates the senses is still compelling today, but so too do we have a better understanding of the brain, and how we are shaped by our perceptions, and how, too, our perceptions are shaped by our environment.

Consider that the cubist artist and theorist, Fernand Léger, wrote, "A modern man registers a hundred times more sensory impressions than an eighteenth-century artist." (Lanchner, Hauptman, and Affron, 1998, p. 75.)

Though surely one would expect such insight to have been authored in the age of the internet, Léger proclaimed it over a century ago, in 1914. Imagine the exponential increase for sensory overload in *today's* modern man!

So given that modern (postmodern) authors may not be studied in the same academe as our scribbler forefathers, there is also an increased validity that make today's writers more relatable to our lives, and there's also the opportunity to tap into the scientific advances of our surroundings. Why is it that sound affects our taste, or that smell triggers our memory? Why does touch set our expectations and foreshadow future events, or how can we depict visual elements using succinct and culturally-meaningful descriptors?

The following overview touches barely upon the wealth of reading and information available, but will, hopefully, inspire and enlighten writers and readers alike as to the interaction of the five senses with fiction literature, combining both a focus on scientific research and the short form of horror and dark fantasy within the last seventy-five years.

THE SENSE OF TOUCH

"You raise yourself, muscles shuddering with the effort, your cheek chafing against the wood of the stair..."

—"Heading Home" by Ramsey Campbell
(first published in *Whispers #11-12*, 1978)

From temperature to texture, pressure, pleasure or pain, the sense of touch is the most important sense associated with life and survival. This sense is responsible for things we feel, such as the tickling of a mosquito on our neck or the vibration of the ground as a train nears. Further, the sense of touch is the sense that leads to greatest reaction. If you touch something hot, the reaction is to jerk back and let go.

In writing, descriptive details of sensations leads to receptivity in readers, and the capacity to relate to characters: An erotic kiss from the dark mistress sends shivers of desire through our longing hero until the cold steel of her razor neatly slices open his neck; he feels the splatter of hot blood down his chest, the unexpected rush of chilling air into his opened throat, the adrenaline spike at her betrayal . . .

This sense of touch—both the largest of the senses, and the first of the senses to develop in an embryo—is a product of the somatosensory system, which is an immense network of nerve endings, neural fibers, and tactile receptors. These are responsible not only for physical receptivity, but also for forming our expectations of what *should* occur with the touch.

According to David J. Linden, PhD, "The genes, cells, and neural circuits involved in the sense of touch have been crucial to creating our unique human experience . . . where sensation and expectation collide, allowing for powerful effects of life history, culture, and context." (Lindon, 2015, p. 5.)

Part of this "unique human experience" is the *emotional* context associated with touch, known as the Haptic Sense. This means of communication is vital in touch to interpret the *intent* of physical contact, particularly in relationships. Consider when someone places a hand on your—or your character's—forearm, what does it mean? The experience of the same physical touch changes, depending on who it's coming from: a sensual lover, a disapproving manager, a playful friend, or a threatening stranger. The ensuing reaction changes as well: an emotional response of arousal, loathing, friskiness, or fear, and so too comes the physical response . . . we know in each of those scenarios what *should* occur next from a character, but will they respond naturally or will they surprise even themselves by an unexpected behavior that advances the scene or adds depth to their role?

Connect your reader *emotionally* through the sense of touch, in addition to setting those expectations for their physical environment.

Fun fact: Humans can survive without the other four senses, but the sense of touch is deemed *necessary* for life.

THE SENSE OF HEARING

"With each swing of the brass pendulum there was a resonant echo, like the striking of a padded hammer on wood."

—"Sounds" by Kathryn Ptacek
(first published in *Masques IV*, 1991)

Sound is a limitless source of information about our surroundings and plays a central role in communication. Conscious thought and visual recognition take about the same rate of time to occur—micro-fractions of a second—while the sense of hearing is up to one hundred times faster. We are surrounded by acoustic signals, and they reach us so frequently and so much quicker than other senses, that it alters all other input, modifying and preparing our other perceptions of what next we should see, taste, feel, and smell.

Writing to the sense of hearing can immediately grab a reader's attention or evoke emotional response, particularly of sounds that are a recurring motif. Consider the soft thump of nearing footsteps in an otherwise empty underground garage, or the thunderous buzzing of a circling mosquito. The terrifying roar of a vicious animal, the slowing gasps of a dying loved one, the resonant shriek of gunfire or jets screaming overhead. Even the use of onomatopoeia—words that read as they sound (most notably used in comic books and Adam West's *Batman*)—can be powerful opportunities to create a sonorous and interesting scene.

Every time we hear a sound—whether through solid, liquid, or gaseous matter—we're receiving information about something. According to psychologist and sound engineer, Seth Horowitz, hearing cannot be turned off, and there is no place in the universe that is completely silent. Sounds operate at all decibel ranges around us, even in the acoustic properties of the environment, though most are outside our range of hearing (about 20 Hz to 20 kHz). "Your auditory system has evolved a complex and automatic "volume control," fine-tuned by development and experience, to keep most noises off your cognitive radar unless they might be of use as a signal that something dangerous or wonderful is somewhere within the kilometer or so that your ears can detect." (Horowitz, 2013, para. 1.)

Sound waves are heard by entering the ear canal (outer ear) and making the ear drum vibrate, which moves the ossicles bones (the tiniest bones in our body) to "knock" on the membrane of the inner ear, the cochlea, that in turn causes fluid in the cochlea to move. The cochlea also contains tiny hair cells (cilia) which react to these sound waves, triggering chemicals that are sent to the brain as nerve impulses. Diminishment of these sensory hairs by loud noise is the primary cause of hearing loss.

Our brain craves to make sense of patterns in sounds that have mathematical regularity, while sounds without patterns are those that cause us alarm. Through rhythmic sounds, we can find hypnosis or other mind-altering states; without rhythms, our brains can be led to fury, panic, or insanity, particularly through the condition of Misophonia, which is the dire hatred of certain sounds.

Fun fact: The word "noise" comes from the Latin word "nausea," meaning sickness.

THE SENSE OF TASTE

"The absinthe cauterized my throat with its flavor, part pepper, part licorice, part rot."
—"His Mouth Will Taste of Wormwood" by Poppy Z. Brite
(first published in *Borderlands 1*, 1990)

Taste is perhaps the most underused sense in fiction writing, generally engaged only when a character is actively eating or drinking, or in scenes of physical affection and sexual encounter.

The human tongue identifies five basic tastes: sweet, bitter, sour, salty, and—most recently discovered—savory (called umami), a brothy taste associated with mushrooms and meat. Similar to smell, taste can be used as a medium to exhibit emotion: Remember the expression, "You are what you eat." Your character may eat food that is bitter, which is symbolic for his/her mood or circumstance, or it could be used to play against flavor, a foreshadowing of something dreadful set to occur.

Interestingly, tastes are affected by external factors: Air temperature, expectations, even color and environment. According to the *Journal of Sensory Studies*, "Auditory stimuli... significantly impacts the overall amount that people consume... it heightens our enjoyment and experience of food and drink." (Spence & Shankar, 2010, p. 416.)

If background music is soothing, we tend to eat more and at a slower pace. At very high decibel levels, our taste perception goes down, meaning loud music causes food to have less flavor. Conversely, potato chip bag manufacturers design their bags to be noisy for the sensory experience to compliment eating noisy chips.

Taste also leads to ingestion, which makes this the most intimate and invasive of our senses. So taking it a step further, consider that as taste can be manipulated by external factors, this affects anything entering and *becoming* a part of who we are.

Carolyn Korsmeyer observes, "The objects of taste are taken into one's own body: they become one. Because tasting and eating alter one's very constitution, their exercise requires trust." (Korsmeyer, 1999, p. 189.)

And, as we all know, taste (and accompanying flavor) is corruptible. It can be used against us, affects every person's health and self-image, is used as a behavioral reward, and as an emotional crutch. In depression, we eat.

So for writers, don't just explain the taste, but explain *why* it tastes as it does: When I eat a warm slice of pumpkin pie, I'm struck first by the aroma of spicy ginger and rich cinnamon. It takes me back to family holidays, and memories of laughter linger in the air as much as the hint of cloves. Its color is of Thanksgiving and autumn, of falling leaves and cooling sun. Then the first taste of the pie is immediately associated with comfort: it's sweet, soft, enticing. It also causes me to crave more. How long will I give into the craving? Or, has something else occurred? Have my expectations of this pumpkin pie not been met? Is there some slow-acting bitterness reminiscent of old, earthy vegetable roots that is unexpected, disrupting my fond memories, or does it sadden me that in some current circumstance, my past pleasures cannot ever seem to be recaptured again?

Fun fact: Each person's sense of flavor is as unique as their fingerprint, shaped by both genes, life choices, and external factors, and it's continually changing with each new meal.

THE SENSE OF SIGHT

"... His shoulders and gangly gray-fuzzed head, from my vantage, cut a dark notch into the bottom of the screen like the interlocking edge of a missing jigsaw piece."

—"In the Porches of My Ears" by Norman Prentiss
(first published in *Postscripts #18* (*This is the Summer of Love*), 2009)

Our eyes are the strongest muscles in our body relative to their duties, and contribute roughly 85% of our knowledge, with about half of the human brain dedicated to seeing. It's no surprise, therefore, that sight is credited as the strongest of our five senses, and is also the sense overwhelmingly utilized most by writers in descriptive prose. Every page of a story is filled with visual elements: details describing garment appearance, household setting, oncoming danger, appealing destinations, or even the dreaded character's own reflection when he describes himself while looking into a mirror.

Consequently, what then becomes important in writing is the *choice* of character's observations; we must see the world through their eye. The human eye is capable of processing 36,000 pieces of information per hour or, in terms of focus, about 50 things per second, so succinct and *meaningful* descriptors must be used. Interestingly, the most common types of descriptive terms—*good, bad, beautiful, ugly*—are also the most universally misinterpreted, known as *Empty Descriptors*. Different readers' interpretations of vague terms such as, "The room was ugly," could mean ugly-70s' plaid to one reader, or ugly Gothic-black to another, or ugly Victorian-floral to someone else.

Sufficient illustrative information must be used: The reaching shadow of the beast began to grow distinct, larger than a tusked boar, yet upright. At that moment, a fleeting beam of pale moonlight fell upon it, briefly revealing scaled arms that protruded from a cobbling of feather tufts, gray sinew, and ebon-black knobs of horned muscle. The creature's eyes were gold as sun-bronzed coins, though mere small dots in a domed head, which was most all a single snarl-toothed mouth. Unshrouded from the darkness, it moved neither faster nor slower, but ambled only steadily nearer, its singular purpose without doubt . . .

Utilize all the tools of observation when writing. Highlight shapes and forms, color, light and shadow, relatable size, texture, etc. to help readers see what your character sees.

In addition to visual cues, sight also helps us interpret distance, an important part of describing landscapes and cityscapes in setting. Jennifer Kahn explains: "Vision demands that the brain differentiate foreground from background, and edges from lines . . . otherwise a chair and desk would be perceived as a single flat image, like an abstract painting made of rectangles. Optical illusions work by exploiting the mind's tendency to try to find order in patterns—a face in the pockmarks on a cement wall—or to make sense of an impossible image, like the endless climbing staircase in an Escher drawing." (Kahn, 2012, para. 1.)

Herein lies the opportunity for misdirection in what characters see, or *think* they see, in the distance of mirage, tricks of the light, or other deceptive appearances and illusions which add interest to a story. Characters who are near-sighted or far-sighted, color-blind, or can't judge the afore-mentioned depth, will all "observe" the world in a different perspective than other people.

Know also, that vision is different amongst organisms. If you are writing of what is seen by an animal or a fiendish monster, their ocular capacities are not constrained to human limitations. For instance, birds can see the earth's magnetic fields; snakes can detect heat with their eyes; and certain fish can see above and below water at the same time!

Fun fact: A genetic mutation found in approximately 2–3% of women allows them to see up to 100 million different colors (including the ethereal "Impossible Colors"), which is one hundred times more than the rest of us.

THE SENSE OF SMELL

"At once flowery and bitter, sweet and burning. He inhales, and it leaves his nostrils and throat feeling raw, abraded."
—"The Scent" by John F.D. Taff
(first published in Little Deaths, 2012)

The cinnamon scent of freshly-baked apple pie may often remind one of being a child in their mother or grandmother's kitchen. The smell of white craft glue recalls school projects from long ago. A certain cloying perfume or a heady cologne reminds us of old flames, whether in longing or in fury.

Of our five senses, that of smell is the most acute, and also most closely linked to triggering vivid memories and awakened emotions.

Writing to the sense of smell is a great opportunity to transition into a flashback scene: *The burned-out detective is walking through the cluttered aisles of a used book store; here the air is musty, stifling warm, it smells of moldering pages, a sweet fragrance that is both vanilla and woody musk. It reminds him of happier times, of sitting as a boy in his grandfather's study late at night, safe and warm, as wind and rain beat the rattling windows. He'd stay up through the night reading those mysteries of Wilkie Collins and Arthur Conan Doyle, dreaming he was Chandler's Marlowe in youth... back then, there was no mystery he could not solve. All he had to do now was recapture that spirit of confidence, of fortitude!*

Scientifically, smell is the oldest sense and the first to evolve; its origins are traced even to the rudimentary senses for chemicals in air and water, and smell was also the first sense to evolve in animal species; as the sense of smell increased in mammals, so too did the size of the brain. In addition, the sense of smell is located in the same seat of the brain that processes memory, emotion, and associative learning, and has shown to be controllable through aromatherapy and pheromones.

The psychologist and smell expert, Trygg Engen, explains: "[Smell] is very sensitive, learns quickly, and forgets nothing, but it has no judgment about what ought to be remembered and what might as well be forgotten ... it ensures the identification of odors vital to the individual's physical and psychological well-being." (Blodgett, 2010, p. 69.)

Smell has the strongest psychological effect of all our senses, and so too are odor-evoked memories more emotionally valid than other forms of evoked memories. In writing, describe pleasant scents to make a scene or location seem comforting, offensive smells to induce an impression of unease or fear. Particularly when a character enters a new environment (walks through a door, exits a train), the use of smell is most relevant.

Fun fact: A loss or diminished sense of smell is considered an early sign of Alzheimer's or other memory-degenerative ailment.

In Closing

So it is that the five senses define our experiences of the world around us in unique ways, translating physical phenomenon to our brains to help us enjoy, interact with, and even just survive our environment. Sight, sound, taste, hearing, and touch: Readers most deeply relate to writers who utilize these impressions, providing meaningful details and shared experiences of characters who exist in their own worlds of fictive sensory input. Particularly in horror, fill the pages with rich emotions and resonant characters, for life is complex, vivid, and evolving, and we yearn for writing to be the same.

WORKS CITED

Blodgett, Bonnie. (2010). *Remembering Smell: A Memoir of Losing—and Discovering—the Primal Sense*. Boston: Houghton Mifflin Harcourt.

Horowitz, Seth S., PhD. (2013). The Science and Art of Listening. *New York Times*. Retrieved from http://www.nytimes.com.

Kahn, Jennifer. (2012). What Your Nose Knows. *Parade Magazine*. Retrieved from http://communitytable.parade.com.

Korsmeyer, Carolyn. (1999). *Making Sense of Taste: Food and Philosophy*. Ithaca: Cornell University Press.

Lanchner, Carolyn, Hauptman, Jodi, and Affron, Matthew. (1998). *Fernand Léger*. New York City: The Museum of Modern Art, New York.

Linden, David J., PhD. (2015). *Touch: the Science of Hand, Heart, and Mind*. New York City: Viking Press (Penguin Books).

Spence, C. and Shankar, M. U. (2010). The Influence of Auditory Cues on the Perception of, and Responses to, Food and Drink. *Journal of Sensory Studies*, 25, 406-430.

AFTERWORD: SENSATION AND PERCEPTION

BY K. H. VAUGHAN, PHD

T RADITIONALLY, THERE ARE FIVE human senses: sight, hearing, smell, taste, and touch. This is not literally true, because some of our senses (e.g., touch) are made up of multiple systems that we group together, and which include additional, less familiar senses such as our vestibular, kinesthetic, and interoceptive senses. That is, our concept of sensation is artificial: a convenient fiction that is good enough for everyday use. This is appropriate because our perceptions also are a "good enough" fiction, at least to some degree. There are things we perceive that are not there, things there that escape our perception, and what we do perceive is not the raw data of experience, but a processed construct. Our senses lie to us, or, at least, our brains do.

At this point, in the interest of full disclosure, so do I. This commentary, and those that accompanied each section of the anthology, are written for writers and fans of horror. In trying to balance truth and the needs of the audience, there is much here that is simplified or distorted, and even more left out. I hope that you will at least get the flavor.

Before talking about specific senses, we need to draw a distinction between sensation and perception. Sensation is the mechanical process by which physical stimuli in the world (e.g., electromagnetic radiation, sound waves) act on receptors in our nervous system. These receptor cells encode that data and transmit it to the central nervous system where it is processed and interpreted. Perception is the process of interpreting these signals so that we have a coherent experience that is imbued with meaning, and we'll return to that topic after we work through the basics. Sensation comes first.

SENSATION

It's important to understand that this is all a physical process. It would be possible for humans to hear sounds pitched higher or lower than we do, or to have the same resolution in our peripheral vision that we do in the center of our focus. There is no reason, in principle, why we couldn't have the ability to sense electrical voltage the way sharks can, or the orientation of the Earth's magnetic field as do migratory birds. Evolution is a series of compromises. We happen to occupy an environmental niche, and our senses are adapted to be generally good enough for it. We could have more, or different, or better senses, but there is a cost: it would take up more space and use more energy. All sensory systems require these minimum physical elements: receptors, nerves, and brain tissue to process the data. Taking this to horror fiction, does a monster or alien species occupy an ecosystem? They might not, but if they do, then their sensory systems must fit their niche.

Receptors: Sensation begins with special nerve cells (neurons) that detect specific features of the physical environment. The material world acts on these sensors, triggering them to signal the presence of whatever it is that they have evolved to detect. Anything you can sense exists in the physical world in some way, and we can only sense those things that we have receptors for. Your tongue has receptors that signal when they come in contact with certain chemicals such as salt. There are other chemicals, such as water molecules or nitrogen, that we don't have receptors for, and so they have no taste. Even when we have receptors to detect a phenomenon, we may only be able to pick up a specific range of that stimulus. Human ears can detect sound waves between 20–20,000 Hz. Sound waves at higher and lower frequencies are around us all the time, but we do not hear them. If it doesn't interact with the body, we can't sense it.

Sensors can be damaged, miscalibrated, or wear out over time. Different creatures have different types of sensors and in different numbers. A grizzly bear's superior sense of smell begins with the fact that the bear has around a billion smell-detecting cells compared to the five to ten million in your own nose. A shark can sense the slight electrical charge created by the muscle movements of fish, something we do not have sensors for at all. All creatures live in a specific sensory world, and many of them are profoundly unlike the one we take for granted.

Nerves: Once a stimulus is detected, the sensors must send that signal across physical space to the brain in order for that data to be processed and (perhaps) contribute to our experience. Those signals have to travel across a distance. Distance matters because distance equals time.

The scale may seem small (individual nerve cells are microscopic in most species), but imagine stepping on a Lego with your bare foot in the middle of the night: that signal has to physically move from the bottom of your foot up the leg to the spinal cord, and then up to the brain before you can feel anything. And although you may know that neurons communicate via an electrochemical process, it is far slower than the speed of electricity. The sense of pressure, as your foot conforms to that hard, sharp piece of plastic is conveyed to the brain at about 76 meters/second. The sense of pain arrives later on at a rate of around .6 meters/second, so perhaps 2–3 seconds afterward for an average adult. Now imagine the nerve fibers of a blue whale, which may be 30 meters long, or the nerve fibers of some dinosaurs, which are estimated to have been as long as 50 or 60 meters. That's a long distance to carry a signal.

Now, back to that Lego. You say that's happened to you, and you felt the pain immediately? Most likely you just didn't notice the pressure until the pain hit, and folded these separate experiences into one. You say you're positive you felt the pain immediately? Well, maybe you did "feel" it before the signal from your foot got to your brain. Pain is strange. Perhaps your brain anticipated the pain based on experience and got a head-start once it learned of the pressure. Your eyes live right by your brain. Your brain may have seen you step on the Lego well before it actually felt any of it. Remember, your brain lies to you all the time. One of the lies is that our conscious experience is a seamless, unitary phenomenon.

The other thing about nerves is that their size is directly related to how much information they can carry. The central trunk line of the body (the spinal cord) carries the most data and is up to half an inch thick. This mass of nerves is maintained by an infrastructure of blood vessels, protective membranes, insulation, cerebrospinal fluid, and the vertebrae of the spinal column. That's a lot of tissue to power and maintain. It takes up room and adds weight. Suppose humans had more sensitive vision. We would need more receptors, and, ultimately, fatter optic nerves. These thicker nerves would need bigger passages through the skull and take up more space. If you have a media cabinet, you have to have holes for the cables to pass through. The same is true of the body. Better vision would change the internal architecture of the skull.

Last, like any cable, nerve fibers can be pinched, cut, or damaged. When this happens, the signal is degraded or even lost. Your sensors pick up the information and call the brain, but they cannot get through; they range from barely noticeable to catastrophic in terms of impact.

Brain Tissue: The brain is a tremendously complex system containing around 100 billion neurons, each connected with up to 10,000 of their neighbors. Different sensory inputs enter the brain in different areas (often more than one), and each sense has brain tissue devoted to processing that incoming data, initially in very raw form (putting basic features together), and then in more complex ways involving meaning and associations. Damage to brain tissue dedicated to processing sensory information can disrupt or eliminate the perception of that experience. In this case, the signal has reached the brain intact, but it is decoded incorrectly, or not at all. Because the brain is a very complex system, the types of processing deficits can be very specific, with some functions perfectly intact and others destroyed. And, it is an oversimplification, but neurons are not replaced when destroyed, in the way we make new skin cells to replace the old. If a neuron is damaged, it may attempt to regenerate itself, but if it dies, it's gone forever. As a rule of thumb, damage to the peripheral nervous system tends to heal, and damage to the central nervous system (the brain and spinal cord) does not (although the brain may compensate for the death of cells by reorganizing those functions when possible).

The human brain is about as big as evolution will allow without technological intervention. We already cheat in order to get the most brain we can. The ligaments connecting the bones of the mother's pelvis soften during labor and stretch in order to make more room for the head to exit safely. The infant is born with the plates of the skull not fused, so that it can compress on its passage through the birth canal. The infant brain is not fully developed, and will take years for all of the connections to be made, pruned, and insulated; brain development is not complete until we're aged in our twenties. Despite these cheats, childbirth carries danger for the mother and infant, and is still a significant cause of death and disability. We will not have bigger brains without scientific intervention, and it is a myth that we have untapped reserves of brain capacity to unlock. It's all in use.

Neurons also burn a lot of energy. The human brain accounts for about 20% of your entire metabolism even though it is only 2% of the total weight of an average adult. Space and energy are costly. In order to have the skin on your back be as sensitive to touch as your fingertips, you would have to devote more of the brain to processing that information. Is that necessary, from an evolutionary perspective? What would be the advantage? What other processes do you eliminate or short?

For there is no room inside the skull to spare.

The specifics of how the different sense inputs enter the brain will wait, but it's a good idea to briefly look at the geography of the brain. The human brain developed over millions of years. Primates have been around for some sixty-five million years, and the branch of what became humans split away from the other great apes around six to eight million years ago. As we evolved, we added new capacities and more processing power on top of the existing structure, much like adding rooms to a treehouse. We built up, out, and around. If you cut away the wrinkled exterior of the cerebral cortex (like cutting the florets from a head of cauliflower) you are left with a stem with an enlarged stump at the top. These subcortical structures are ancient and deal with simple reflexive behaviors, metabolism, appetites, reproduction, and keep the heart and lungs working. We sometimes call this the *reptile brain*. Reptiles do not have a rich emotional life. They do not engage in complex problem solving, or learn many tricks. They hunt, defend themselves, eat, and make more reptiles. The reptile brain primarily controls the "Four F's": fighting, fleeing, feeding, and mating.

Fast forward millions of years and add some tissue around the reptile brain. You begin to get a brain that looks like the brain of a cat or a small monkey. Mammals demonstrate more learning capacity, and more complex emotions. Your lizard doesn't really miss you when you are away, but your dog sure does. This *paleomammalian* brain includes the limbic system: structures related to emotion, attachment, and memory. Wrap even more tissue around that and you get the *neomammalian brain* or *neocortex*. The neocortex is associated with complex problem solving and social networks, abstraction, language, self-awareness, higher forms of reasoning, and executive functioning. Among the mammals with above-average neocortical development are the great apes, dolphins, elephants, some species of whale, and, of course, humans. Humans most clearly demonstrate these capacities.

This model is a gross oversimplification, of course, and there is more than one way to wire a brain. Octopuses are excellent problem solvers and may engage in observational learning. Some members of the crow family use tools and demonstrate self-awareness. Intelligence takes many forms. The thing to remember about the evolutionary history of the brain is that as we added new tissue, we didn't replace and rewire the old tissue. If you've lived in an old home that has had additions over the decades, the flow from room to room doesn't always work and the wiring doesn't make sense. You have switches that don't seem to do anything, and the circuit that controls the third floor outlets also controls the porch light. You cannot run the kitchen microwave and the living room air conditioner at the same time without tripping a breaker. In the evolution of the brain, we never stripped the place down to the studs and did a complete renovation. It's a series of adaptations to solve specific problems with the new rooms and wiring kluged together as we went along. This has implications for how the brain works (or doesn't) in a wide range of situations.

The mind is not a single process, but a number of semi-independent processes that more or less work together. Perception, and consciousness, emerges from a complex interaction of these systems.

PERCEPTION

Perception is far more complicated and far less understood than sensation. Sensation is mechanical and automatic, while perception is a process of interpretation. What we perceive is a function of the sensory input, our learning of history, mood, expectations, level of alertness, and many other factors.

I have to confess, this next section was tough to write, because the bottom line is that we really don't understand much about how perception really works. As a science, we're just scratching the surface and trying to describe the more basic elements. Not to put too fine a point on it, but the reality is that for most of human history we have merely learned about how the brain functions by identifying people who had disorders, waiting for them to die, and then trying to figure out what was broken. We can do research on animals to explore sensation effectively, but animal models start to become less and less relevant as we get to higher-order perceptual processes. Human perception requires examining human brains, and we've only been able to look at what live human brains are doing for a very brief period in time. Safe, non-invasive neuroimaging techniques were only invented around the 1970s, and it was years before they became widely available. Even now, this research is expensive and fairly crude. You will often see news reports of "what your brain looks like" on different drugs or when doing different activities, but these are always gross oversimplifications. Most of what we know is descriptive, and this is fine; science starts with description. But, the specifics of how the raw input of your sense organs is transformed into a conscious perceptual experience? We have a lot to learn. There are many wonderful and potentially terrifying issues that emerge from all of this.

Does a reality exist independently of our perceptions?

How accurate a representation of that reality do we have (assuming there is one)?

How different are my perceptions from yours?

Can perception be trusted at all?

What happens when I discover that I can't?

There is terror in not seeing things for what they are, or in not being able to trust your own mind, whether that illusion is due to brain disorder or the efforts of supernatural forces.

When people first started to apply science to the process of perception, a common belief was that the physical world acted directly on the mind. Non-human animals were thought to function much like automatons made of meat. When Ivan Pavlov discovered learning by association, or "classical conditioning," he was trying to study the reflexive mechanism that caused dogs to salivate when food touched their tongues. Everyone has a calling, and Pavlov's was dog spit. He thought there would be a hard-wired neural circuit, and sensors on the tongue would function like a switch that would open a spigot. Human cognition, until recently, was considered fundamentally different than animal cognition, just as "mind" or "spirit" or "soul" was thought to be somehow separate from the substance of the material world. Although humans were (generally) thought to have free will and the capacity for reason, it was still thought that the mind passively received sense impressions and conformed to them automatically, much like a pin art frame creates a three-dimensional relief when something is pressed against it. Sir Francis Galton, polymath and eugenicist, believed that differences in human intelligence were due to differences in sensory acuity; the "dull" sensed less than the "eminent," and so had less information to work with. Our mental representation of the world was at least assumed to be a simple and direct reflection of the world at large.

It did not take long before scientists realized this was far from the truth. We do not experience the raw sensory data of the world. The data "out there" starts being processed and manipulated at the level of the receptors cells even before it gets sent to the brain, and is then processed, processed, and processed some more in order to create the experience we have. So, assuming our sensory receptors are detecting *something*, what do we perceive?

For starters, many sensations are detected by our sense receptors, but at such a low level that we don't become consciously aware of them, such as a sound that is too quiet, or a smell that is too faint. If an eyelash falls on your forearm, your skin may register the contact, but the touch is so light that it falls below the absolute threshold of perception. We simply cannot become consciously aware of it. There is a fuzzy boundary between the things we cannot perceive consciously and the things our brain will register at some level. *Subliminal* perception falls in this range. Subliminal stimuli can have subtle but measurable effects on behavior in laboratory experiments. For example, a picture flashed on a screen so quickly that the subject only "sees" a flash of light, although a researcher can detect changes in emotional or sexual arousal in the subject. These techniques have been employed in advertising and in self-help audio tapes. There's little evidence that they have an impact outside the carefully controlled setting of the lab, but the possibilities in fiction for gaslighting, brainwashing, and manipulation are extensive.

So, sensors receive information, send it to the brain, and this is what we experience, right? *No.* Of all the information that we take in, we only notice a fraction of it. We have limited ability to process and pay attention to it all, so we pick and choose what to focus on.

Detectable sensory impressions enter the brain and are temporarily stored in a sensory buffer. Sensory memory lasts after the stimulus is gone. Light travels at 186,000 miles per second, so consider that stars we see in the sky may have been dead for millions of years before their light reaches us; we're seeing a reflection of the distant past when we look up at the night sky. This is also true of the things around us, although the scale is greatly compressed.

Light travelling toward you flashes past long before you process any of the information it carried. *Iconic memory* is a brief store of visual data that lasts no more than one second. We believe that this aspect of visual memory is critical for experiencing the visual world as continuous despite the constant changes we see. The appearance of motion when we watch a series of still images flashed at twenty-four frames per second during a film is a function of this. *Echoic memory*, the storage of auditory information, lasts as long as three to four seconds. You have probably had the experience of someone asking, "are you listening to me?" when you weren't paying attention. In that moment, you can sometimes search your echoic memory and "hear" what they said just before that question. The sound is gone, but we can still perceive what we didn't consciously hear at first. For the most part, we're processing the memory of events that have already occurred. It is possible to search iconic memory as well, although it is so short that we need a laboratory experiment to demonstrate this.

The next level of perception is attention. We do not perceive everything we sense because we aren't focused on it. Attention is a limited capacity, and we can easily become overwhelmed with information. Imagine a juggler being thrown another ball every second. He or she will reach their limit and start dropping things fairly quickly. Of all the information we sense, we have to focus on what matters to us the most at any given time. Think of attention like a spotlight; we direct it toward some things and pass by others. That spotlight may also be adjusted to be broader or more narrow depending on our alertness, interest, and intentions. When things escape our attention, they are gone from our awareness.

There is a phenomenon called *weapon focus* that occurs when people witness a crime. When people are confronted with a gun during a robbery, the weapon commands their attention so much that they may have trouble remembering anything else about the robbery with any accuracy. Stage magicians, shoplifters, and pickpockets also use the attentional spotlight in their work. They (perhaps with the help of an accomplice) draw attention away from an act they want to commit covertly with a distraction. A skilled magician (or thief) can do this while you watch them, as we can't perceive everything we see. This is true in daily life as well: Texting while driving is very dangerous. Research suggests that texting raises your risk of an accident by about as much as drinking four beers and getting on the road. People seem to think that if they glance at their phone quickly, they should still be able to see what's happening around them in their peripheral vision. What they don't understand is that, even if you held your phone up front so that your field of vision encompassed the road like it would normally, it doesn't make a difference. The extra load on attention narrows the area of the road we physically scan and then we do not attend to what the eye sees. The light reflected off of the truck, or pedestrian, or traffic signal might hit your eyes and be registered by your nervous system, but your attention is focused elsewhere and so you will not "see" that bit of information even though it is in your sensory field. We just aren't wired to multitask. We focus on one thing, and the rest is background. The thing you hit didn't "come out of nowhere" as the sensory information was there, but, since you didn't attend, it may as well have.

All right. Assuming that information enters your brain and gets through the bottleneck or filter of sensory memory and the attentional spotlight, how does it all get put together? Remember, we do not see what Kant called "the thing in itself." We get information that is essentially meaningless without context and experience. Much more brain tissue is devoted to interpretation and meaning than to raw sensory input. What we perceive is the result of probabilistic inferences, pattern recognition, and expectations. As a general rule of thumb, the brain will commit to an interpretation and it will force ambiguity and anomaly to fit within the boundaries of what it knows. Once we've decided what something is, it can be very hard to perceive it differently. The overwhelming majority of this process occurs outside of our awareness. *How* we perceive is not available for our conscious inspection most of the time.

In February, 2015, a photo of a dress exploded on the internet. "The Dress" was of a solid color with horizontal lace striping, but people could not agree as to whether it was white with gold stripes or black with blue stripes. Millions of people were divided, and the original Tumblr post was being viewed up to 14,000 times per second as people tried to figure it out. Two people, side by side, could see the dress and disagree, each disbelieving what the other saw plain as day with their own eyes. In reality, the dress was black with blue lace stripes. Neuroscientists have theorized that the difference is due to the brain's effort to correct the color of the dress in response to the lighting conditions in the picture. The quality of light changes during the day, but we don't experience objects as changing color as that happens—we perceive the color as constant, and the light as shifting. People saw the picture and made an automatic color correction based on how their brains interpreted the illumination. The discovery that others were seeing something so obvious and objective as very different was profoundly disorienting. To this day, I see white with gold, and have been unable to adjust my perceptions to see black and blue in the original photo.

I don't want to suggest that how we perceive the world is completely arbitrary or that the perceptual experiences that you have are incommensurable with the perceptual experiences of other people. Our brains are the product of millions of years of shared evolution, and the physics of the world act on all of us in the same way. We exist within a specific cultural and linguistic space that is common to others and shapes our perceptions. But, at the same time, there are individual differences in sensory packages; no one else shares your exact learning history, and the specific network of neuronal connections in your head is unique. We also do not have any direct experience of the perceptions of others. We live within our own.

I used to have a copy of a cartoon, back when I was taking a lot of undergraduate philosophy and cognitive science courses. I haven't been able to find it since, and can't source it, but as I recall, a dog is talking to a fish in a bowl. The fish asks the dog where he's been and the dog says he's been taking a nap in the corner. The fish replies, "what's a corner?" "Corners" are something so alien to the experience of the fish that it can't imagine what such a thing it. How well our own experiences match up to those of others is tricky business.

Another question might be whether or not it really matters how close to objective reality our perceptions are. The evolution of the brain is the product of objective reality, but that doesn't mean that it is adaptive to perceive the world as it really is. Perception is about compromise, priorities, and a constant trade-off between being accurate enough versus being quick and efficient. The purpose is to reduce ambiguity and allow decisions. Evolution rewards "more likely to not get you killed and promote the survival of your genes," not accuracy of representation. If short-cuts, illusions, and inaccuracy promotes survival, then that is what nature will select for. A systematic lie might serve us very well. There isn't necessarily a benefit to having "God-mode" objectivity.

Our perceptions are the only reality we know directly. How well one reality matches up with another is an open question. Pragmatically, I'm inclined to think that the overlap is fairly significant. Day to day life functions far too well for our fishbowls to be radically different in critical ways. But at the same time, when you buy a new model of car, you suddenly notice all of the other cars of the same model on the road around you. Those cars were there before, but you process them differently now. I see a painting of a woman posed with a sword and a severed head. Another might see a depiction of *Judith with the Head of Holofernes*, and yet another, the specific study of the subject by Cranach the Elder from the

Burrell Collection in Glasgow, one of eight known versions Cranach and his students produced. Judith beheading Holofernes was a popular subject in the Renaissance and Baroque periods of European art. But while Cranach's *Judith* wears Renaissance finery and a somewhat wicked smile, the *Judith* of Caravaggio is depicted in the act in simpler garb and with a trace of discomfort with the bloodiness of the event. The *Judith* of Riedel is a proud and confident warrior, and the *Judith* of Klimt erotic and dangerous. The artists interpret the event according to their perceptions, and then we interpret their paintings in an ever-expanding web of associations. How well does the Venn diagram of my perceptions overlap with yours? How well do my perceptions map with objective reality? There is no way for any of us to know.

The Five Senses of Horror, in commentary and fiction, explores some of the weirdness of the perceptual world. There are things you perceive at this very moment that are not there, and many others that you do not perceive at all. There are aspects to this that are hardwired and others trained through experience. Above all, remember that it is not to be trusted. There is a lot of terror to be found in the strange world contained within our skull as it tries to connect with the world outside itself.

K. H. Vaughan holds a doctorate in clinical psychology and has taught a wide variety of graduate and undergraduate courses over the past twenty years. He has worked and trained in a variety of clinical settings including inpatient, outpatient, residential, correctional, and forensic consultation. His academic interests are in decision theory, research methods and philosophy of science, psychopathology, and forensic topics, including the psychology of mass violence and genocide. He also writes dark fiction and regularly appears as a panelist or moderator at conventions.

SUGGESTED ACADEMIC READING FOR FURTHER STUDY OF THE FIVE SENSES INCLUDING ITS INTERACTION WITH FICTION WRITING

F or those interested in further academic reading, I've compiled a list of books and articles below that either I read or was recommended to me during my study of the five human senses. The following material relates to either scientific understanding and/or how the senses are—or *can* be—integrated best into fiction writing.

Ackerman, Diane. (1990). *A Natural History of the Senses*. New York City: Vintage Books.

Aspell, J. E., Lavanchy, T., Lenggenhager, B., and Blanke, O. (2010). Seeing the Body Modulates Audiotactile Integration. *European Journal of Neuroscience*, 31: 1868–1873.

Baddeley, A. (1992). Working Memory. *Science*, 255: 556–559.

Berger, John. (1985). *The Sense of Sight*. London: Chatto & Windus.

Blodgett, Bonnie. (2010). *Remembering Smell: A Memoir of Losing—and Discovering—the Primal Sense*. Boston: Houghton Mifflin Harcourt.

Calvert, G. A., Hansen, P. C., Iversen, S. D., and Brammer, M. J. (2001). Detection of Audio-Visual Integration Sites in Humans by Application of Electrophysiological Criteria to the BOLD Effect. *Neuroimage*, 14(2): 427–438.

Carlisle, Janice. (2004). *Common Scents: Comparative Encounters in High-Victorian Fiction*. Oxford: Oxford University Press.

Carlson-Smith C., Wiener, W.R. (1996). The Auditory Skills Necessary for Echolocation: A New Explanation. *Journal of Visual Impairment & Blindness*, 90(1): 21–35.

Deutsch, Laura. (2014). *Writing from the Senses: 59 Exercises to Ignite Creativity and Revitalize Your Writing*. Boulder: Shambhala.

Feng, Albert and Ratnam, Rama. (2000). Neural Basis of Hearing in Real-World Situations. *Annual Review of Psychology*, 51: 699–725.

Garrington, Abbie. (2015). *Haptic Modernism: Touch and the Tactile in Modernist Writing*. Edinburgh: Edinburgh University Press.

Goodale, M. A., and Milner, A. D. (1992). Separate Visual Pathways for Perception and Action. *Trends in Neurosciences*, 15(1): 20–25.

Grossenbacher, Peter G. and Lovelace, Christopher T. (2001). Mechanisms of Synesthesia: Cognitive and Physiological Constraints. *Cognitive Sciences*, 5.1: 36–41.

Hadhazy, Adam. (2011). Tip of the Tongue: Humans May Taste at Least 6 Flavors. *Live Science*. Retrieved from http://www.livescience.com.

Hertel, Ralf. (2005). *Making Sense: Sense Perception in the British Novel of the 1980s and 1990s*. Amsterdam: Rodopi.

Herz, Rachel S. and Engen, Trygg. (1996). Odor Memory: Review and Analysis. *Psychonomic Bulletin & Review*, 3(3), 300–313.

Horowitz, Seth S., PhD. (2012). *The Universal Sense: How Hearing Shapes the Mind*. New York City: Bloomsbury USA.

Horowitz, Seth S., PhD. (2013). The Science and Art of Listening. *New York Times*. Retrieved from http://www.nytimes.com.

Jacobsen, Michael Hviid, Drake, Michael S., Keohane, Kieran, and Petersen, Anders (eds). (2005). *Imaginative Methodologies in the Social Sciences: Creativity, Poetics and Rhetoric in Social Research*. New York City: Ashgate Publishing (Taylor & Francis Group).

Jastorff, J., Huang, Y. A., Giese, M. A., and Vandenbulcke, M. (2015). Common Neural Correlates of Emotion Perception in Humans. *Human Brain Mapping*, 36: 4184–4201.

Kahn, Jennifer. (2012). What Your Nose Knows. *Parade Magazine*. Retrieved from http://communitytable.parade.com.

Korsmeyer, Carolyn. (1999). *Making Sense of Taste: Food and Philosophy*. Ithaca: Cornell University Press.

Lanchner, Carolyn, Hauptman, Jodi, and Affron, Matthew. (1998). *Fernand Léger*. New York City: The Museum of Modern Art, New York.

Lessard N., Pare M., Lepore F., and Lassonde M. (1998). Early-Blind Human Subjects Localize Sound Sources Better Than Sighted Subjects. *Nature*, 395: 278–280.

Linden, David J., PhD. (2015). *Touch: the Science of Hand, Heart, and Mind.* New York City: Viking Press (Penguin Books).

Man, K., Damasio, A., Meyer, K., and Kaplan, J. T. (2015). Convergent and Invariant Object Representations for Sight, Sound, and Touch. *Human Brain Mapping*, 36: 3629–3640.

Mayer, R.E. and Sims, V.K. (1994). For whom is a Picture Worth a Thousand Words? Extensions of a Dual-Coding Theory of Multimedia Learning. *Journal of Educational Psychology*, 86: 389–401.

Rasley, Alici. (2010). How to Enhance Your Character's POV. *Writer's Digest.* Retrieved from http://www.writersdigest.com.

Renier, L. A., Anurova, I., De Volder, A. G., Carlson, S., VanMeter, J., and Rauschecker, J. P. (2009). Multisensory Integration of Sounds and Vibrotactile Stimuli in Processing Streams for "What" and "Where". *The Journal of Neuroscience*, 29(35): 10950–10960.

Robertson, Lynn C. and Sagiv, Noam (eds). (2004). *Synesthesia: Perspectives from Cognitive Neuroscience.* Oxford: Oxford University Press.

Rozelle, Ron. (2005). *Description & Setting: Techniques and Exercises for Crafting a Believable World of People, Places, and Events.* Cincinnati: Writer's Digest Books.

SEG Research. (2008). *Understanding Multimedia Learning.* (White Paper). New Hope: BrainPOP, LLC.

Shockman, Elizabeth. (2016). How Music Can Affect Your Sense of Taste. *Public Radio International.* Retrieved from https://www.pri.org.

Solander, Tove. (2013). *Creating the Senses: Sensation in the Work of Shelley Jackson (Umeå Studies in Language & Literature)* (Doctoral Dissertation). Umeå Universitet, Umeå, Sweden.

Spence, C. (2013). Just How Important is Spatial Coincidence to Multisensory Integration? Evaluating the Spatial Rule. *Annals of the New York Academy of Sciences*, 1296: 31–49.

Spence, C. and Shankar, M. U. (2010). The Influence of Auditory Cues on the Perception of, and Responses to, Food and Drink. *Journal of Sensory Studies*, 25, 406–430.

Sweller, J. (2003). Evolution of Human Cognitive Architecture. *The Psychology of Learning and Motivation*, 43: 215–266.

Thaler, L., Milne, J. L., Arnott, S. R., Kish, D., and Goodale, M. (2014). Neural Correlates of Motion Processing Through Echolocation, Source Hearing, and Vision in Blind Echolocation Experts and Sighted Echolocation Novices. *Journal of Neurophysiology*, 111(1): 112–27.

Venter, Enette. (2015). The Power of Smells in Writing. *Enette's World*. Retrieved from https://enetteventer.com/2015/08/11/the-power-of-smells-in-writing.

Ward, Megan. (2008). *Feeling Middle Class: Sensory Perception in Victorian Literature and Culture* (Doctoral Dissertation). Rutgers University—New Brunswick, New Brunswick, NJ.

Zimmer, U. and Macaluso, E. (2007). Processing of Multisensory Spatial Congruency Can Be Dissociated from Working Memory and Visuo-Spatial Attention. *European Journal of Neuroscience*, 26: 1681–1691.

Zucco, Gesualdo M., Herz, Rachel S., and Schaal, Benoist (eds). (2005). *Olfactory Cognition: From Perception and Memory to Environmental Odours and Neuroscience*. Philadelphia: John Benjamins Publishing Company.

A BRIEF READING LIST OF MODERN FICTION SHORT STORIES WITH RELATION TO THE SENSES (1940–2015)

HEREIN I'VE LISTED A BRIEF selection of recent works within the last seventy-five years (1940–2015) that have a distinct association with one or more of the human senses.

By no means were these stories selected on a basis of them being "better" than any other story, but rather that by their whole, the below reading list helps to push the boundaries of scope and diversity in exploring this subject.

The primary criteria I used in making selections included:

- Work must be a story of short fiction, approximately 8,000 words or less (i.e. no novelettes, novellas, or longer).
- Work must include some speculative, supernatural, or horror element.
- Work must first have been published within the last 75 years, between 1940 through 2015 (*all stories sought during 2016).
- Work must be available in the English language (whether by original language printing or through translation).
- Authors cannot be listed more than once.

Whether sights of sparkling refraction, sounds of chirruping frogs, or smells of flowering pear trees, the human senses have consequential impact on storytelling, and the following are some examples of merit:

THE SENSE OF TOUCH

1948: "The October Game" by Ray Bradbury (*Weird Tales*, May: Weird Tales); A frenzied husband enacts a plot of revenge against his wife—whom he levels all woes and wishes to hurt in ways worse than murder—by playing a simple children's game.

1978: "Heading Home" by Ramsey Campbell (*Whispers #11-12*, October: Stuart David Schiff); A dastardly scientist is determined to wreck vengeance against his adulterous wife and the butcher who's brutally dismembered him … if only he can put himself back together. *

1981: "On the Uses of Torture" by Piers Anthony (*The Berkley Showcase: Vol. 3*, an anthology: Berkley Books); A sadistic prison warden is appointed ambassador to an alien civilization that measures worth by pain endurance; the warden is prepared to prove his resolution.

1986: "The Skins You Love to Touch" by Janet Fox (*Shadows 9*, an anthology: Doubleday); Two wealthy antique shoppers discover an off-road country store where the proprietor crafts his own unique furniture.

1990: "Soft" by Darrell Schweitzer (*Weird Tales*, Spring: David Terminus); After a monumental argument, Richard lies in bed next to his wife while contemplating divorce. He tries to remember just one "perfect" moment with her, and if only he could mold her … *

1997: "Autopsy Room Four" by Stephen King (*Robert Bloch's Psychos*, an anthology: Cemetery Dance Publications); An otherwise healthy man awakens temporarily paralyzed on an autopsy table. He must somehow signal the mortician he's still alive before the dissection begins.

2000: "Dead Like Me" by Adam-Troy Castro (*A Desperate, Decaying Darkness*, a collection: Wildside Press); Instructions for the hapless survivor of a zombie plague on how to mimic the undead and otherwise "fit in" with them so as not to be discovered as living foodstuff.

2013: "Feel the Noise" by Lisa Morton (*Shivers VII*, an anthology: Cemetery Dance Publications); A disabled veteran suffering from "systemic synesthesia" must translate rewired senses—tastes that have become smells, sounds turned to touches—while trying to find a murdering ex-superior. *

THE SENSE OF HEARING

1945: "The Music-Box from Hell" by Emil Petaja (*Weird Tales*, May: Weird Tales); A scheming nephew arranges for the death of his wealthy aunt by way of a cursed music-box.

1959: "Eminent Domain" by Cecil Dawkins (*Charm*, October: Street & Smith Publications); An elderly woman who cannot hear is swindled by a man she takes for the devil.

1984: "Sound Is Second Sight" by Lynne Sharon Schwartz (*Triumph of the Night: Tales of Terror and the Supernatural*, a collection: Silver Salamander Press); A lonely farmer first finds companionship in a barking dog, then in a wife with a beautiful voice. The wife and dog die, but their voices can return.

1991: "Sounds" by Kathryn Ptacek (*Masques IV*, an anthology: Maclay & Associates); A woman with hyper-sensitivity to sound bemoans every noise in life. *

1999: "Burden" by Michael Marano (*www.gothic.net*, March: Gothic.net);
A gay man is haunted by the ghosts of friends and lovers who died
from AIDS, as he tries fleeing his past and the terrible burden of
remembering them.

2003: "Sounds Like" by Mike O' Driscoll (*Gathering the Bones:
Thirty-Four Original Stories from the World's Masters of Horror*, an
anthology: Voyager/ HarperCollins (Australia); Larry Pearce has
exceptional hearing, which helps him excel at a job listening in on
customer service phone calls. His hearing, however, seems to keep
sharpening, or is it the stress which makes every noise unbearable?

2010: "Malleus, Incus, Stapes" by Sarah Totton (*Fantasy Magazine*,
December: Prime Books); A boy discovers a trunk containing relics
from his dead father, including an object that allows him to listen to
the past as heard through his father's ear. *

2015: "In the Cave of the Delicate Singers" by Lucy Taylor (*www.tor.com*,
July: Tor); A woman gifted with synesthesia—the ability to feel sound
waves—uses her endowment to embark on a rescue mission of cavers
who have gone missing in an underground system that is rumored to
drive people mad. *

THE SENSE OF TASTE

1945: "Taste" by Roald Dahl (*Ladies Home Journal*, March: Meredith
Corp.); A willful stockbroker bets his connoisseur-dinner companion
that he cannot name the locale of a certain wine's vintage by taste alone.
The companion accepts that bet, and by blustering, each begins to
increase the stakes.

1981: "Dante's Bistro" by Carolyn L. Bird (*The 22nd Pan Book of Horror
Stories*, an anthology: Pan Books); The celebrated chef and
restaurateur, Gothric O'Hooligan-Dante, must continually push the

boundaries of exotic dishes he serves or suffer among elitists the ignominy of irrelevance.

1984: "A Matter of Taste" by Parke Godwin (*Shadows 7*, an anthology: Doubleday); A rarefied gourmand laments the failings of his dating life, for he can find no match to his self-professed highest standards of taste, until he meets Pristine Solent . . .

1990: "His Mouth Will Taste of Wormwood" by Poppy Z. Brite (*Borderlands 1*, an anthology: Maclay & Associates); Two young men who know no taboos grow bored with all life has to offer, even when grave robbing from forbidden tombs. *

1998: "Cassilago's Wife" by Sarah Singleton (*Interzone*, #137, November: David Pringle); A lonely traveler finds hospitality at the home of an herbalist and his much younger wife. *

2009: "A Delicate Architecture" by Catherynne M. Valente (*Troll's Eye View: A Book of Villainous Tales*, an anthology: Viking); The daughter of the best confectioner in the land grows up well-loved in a world of sweets, only to discover the reason she is so loved, in this reimagining of a famous folktale.

2012: "Sweet Subtleties" by Lisa L. Hannett (*Clarkesworld*, #75, December: Wyrm Publishing); Una Belle is French confectioner Javier's greatest creation, a culinary fantasy to be dined upon by whatever the audience wishes her to be, although she finds the hardest tastes to satisfy are those of disappointed family. *

2015: "Hungry Daughters of Starving Mothers" by Alyssa Wong (*Nightmare Magazine*, October: Nightmare Magazine); A vampire who feeds on the manifestations of bad thoughts struggles with dating, an overbearing mother, and a cruel love-interest who is too much like herself.

THE SENSE OF SIGHT

1949: "The Girl with the Hungry Eyes" by Fritz Leiber (*The Girl with the Hungry Eyes, and Other Stories*, an anthology: Avon Publishing Co.); A mysterious girl finds sensational fame as a billboard model; she is secretive, never smiles, and her images show a strange hunger in her eyes . . .

1953: "The Living Eyes" by Justin Dowling (*Weird Tales*, May: Weird Tales); A teenage boy is horrified to learn his widowed father plans to marry a wealthy older woman who is partly-paralyzed, cruel, and has bulging, veined eyes that seemingly are alive in their own way.

1969: "The Movie People" by Robert Bloch (*The Magazine of Fantasy and Science Fiction*, October: Mercury Press, Inc.); A filmgoer befriends a romantic bit-extra actor who's found a sort of immortality by hiding in the background crowds of movie scenes.

1983: "The Beholder" by Richard Christian Matheson (*Whispers IV*, an anthology: Doubleday); A woman inspired to create a painting has found her favorite gallery mysteriously taken over by a new owner who provides her with uncommon paints for her art. *

2009: "In the Porches of My Ears" by Norman Prentiss (*Postscripts #18 (This is the Summer of Love)*, May: PS Publishing); In a story within a story, a man relates his experiences listening to a woman describe the sights of a movie to her blind husband. *

2012: "Some Pictures in an Album" by Gary McMahon (*Chiral Mad*, an anthology: Written Backwards); A visual exploration of seventeen Polaroid photos taken by a man's father and arranged in a photograph album leads the man to understand a horrific secret about himself.

2013: "The Marginals" by Steve Duffy (*The Moment of Panic*, a collection: PS Publishing); Howard begins a new job, sitting in a hidden trailer and carefully logging each person he should see passing by. Except whenever he glances away, more people have appeared... or disappeared.

2015: "The Impression of Craig Shee" by David McGroarty (*Sensorama*, an anthology: Eibonvale Press); A psychologist visits the Scottish isle where her mother once lived in order to study a peculiar painting she made, famous for the disquieting effect it has on peoples' perceptions. *

THE SENSE OF SMELL

1946: "Whiffs of the Sea" by Sir Andrew Caldecott (*Not Exactly Ghosts*, a collection: Edward Arnold); A wealthy gentleman tells of an ominous painting he once purchased that smelled of the sea and the accompanying nightmares it brought.

1966: "I Mnemagoghi" (English: "The Mnemogogues") by Primo Levi (*Storie Naturali*, a collection: Einaudi); A scholarly doctor collects in small vials the scents of his memories.

1971: "The Smell of Death" by Dennis Etchison (*The Magazine of Fantasy & Science Fiction*, October: Mercury Press, Inc.); The owner of a roadside diner with a dark past shares a car ride with a reporter searching for an ex-soldier who escaped a NASA experiment after murdering the rest of his team.

1988: "The Odor of Violets" by John Farris (*Scare Tactics*, a collection: Tor Horror); A struggling author comes across the unpublished novel he was meant to write, accompanied by a strange fragrance of violets. *

1996: "I Am Not My Smell" by Elizabeth Massie (*Shadow Dreams*, a collection: Silver Salamander Press); A disabled homeless woman who has given up hope against her own repugnance finds a final purpose in life by sacrificing for another.

2007: "Shem-el-Nessim: An Inspiration in Perfume" by Chris Bell (*Zahir*, #13, Summer: Zahir Publishing); A wealthy 1920s Londoner becomes obsessed with an Oriental-scented fragrance, and pursues to Cairo the mysterious pale woman who wears it. *

2012: "The Scent" by John F.D. Taff (*Little Deaths*, a collection: Books of the Dead Press); A man walks to work through his aged, declining neighborhood and confronts a luring, unknown scent. *

2013: "Jasmine and Opium" by Rebecca L. Brown (*Eulogies II: Tales From the Cellar*, an anthology: Horror World Press); A sociopath driven by exceptional aromatic perception follows a woman he desires.

---

* Story reprinted within this anthology

PERSONAL ACKNOWLEDGEMENTS

T HOUGH I IMMERSED MYSELF for half a year in Everestian mountains of short story volumes (anthologies, magazines, collections, etc.), searching for the right mix of fiction voices and techniques, I also opened up through social media, requesting recommendations, for in the sagacity of others do we grow wiser.

Over my reading window I actually received so many suggestions that if I tried to enumerate them all here, this book would double in size. But know that I did look into every one, and while most weren't quite what I was searching for, several individuals did provide advantageous advice.

So thanks to the following for either suggesting (or in some cases "reminding me of"!) stories I found most useful, and that I either accepted as a selection into this anthology or at least included as a recommendation in the Suggested Reading List compilation (see: *A Brief Reading List of Modern Fiction Short Stories with Relation to the Senses {1940–2015}*):

Angela Slatter for suggesting Lisa L. Hannett's "Sweet Subtleties"
David E. Cowen for suggesting John F.D. Taff's "The Scent"
Kealan Patrick Burke for suggesting Mike O' Driscoll's "Sounds Like"
Max Booth III for suggesting Alyssa Wong's "Hungry Daughters of Starving Mothers"
Sanford Allen for suggesting Ray Bradbury's "The October Game"
Sean Eads for suggesting Fritz Leiber's "The Girl with the Hungry Eyes"
Todd Austin Hunt for suggesting Roald Dahl's "Taste"

And thanks to John Joseph Adams for connecting me with Sarah Totton, whom I could not otherwise reach.

Thanks also to Tim Curran. Although I didn't use material from his collection of short stories, *Bone Marrow Stew*, I highly recommend it for horror reading.

Great thanks to contributor, Jessica Bayliss, PhD, for her compelling commentaries, and to illustrator, Nils Bross, for his gorgeous artwork.

And, lastly, thanks most of all to the authors included within for allowing me to reprint your wonderful works!

ACKNOWLEDGEMENT IS MADE FOR REPRINTING THE FOLLOWING MATERIAL

"Heading Home" © 1978 by Ramsey Campbell. First published in *Whispers #11-12*, October, Stuart David Schiff. Reprinted by permission of the author.

"Soft" © 1990 by Darrell Schweitzer. First published in *Weird Tales*, Spring, David Terminus. Reprinted by permission of the author.

"Feel the Noise" © 2013 by Lisa Morton. First published in *Shivers VII*, edited by Richard Chizmar, Cemetery Dance Publications. Reprinted by permission of the author.

"In the Cave of the Delicate Singers" © 2015 by Lucy Taylor. First published in *Tor.com*, July, Tor. Reprinted by permission of the author.

"Sounds" © 1991 by Kathryn Ptacek. First published in *Masques IV*, edited by J.N. Williamson, Maclay & Associates. Reprinted by permission of the author.

"Malleus, Incus, Stapes" © 2010 by Sarah Totton. First published in *Fantasy Magazine*, December, Prime Books. Reprinted by permission of the author.

"His Mouth Will Taste of Wormwood" © 1990 by Poppy Z. Brite. First published in *Borderlands 1*, edited by Thomas F. Monteleone, Maclay & Associates. Reprinted by permission of the author.

"Cassilago's Wife" © 1998 by Sarah Singleton. First published in *Interzone #137*, November, David Pringle. Reprinted by permission of the author.

"Sweet Subtleties" © 2012 by Lisa L. Hannett. First published in *Clarkesworld #75*, December, Wyrm Publishing. Reprinted by permission of the author.

"The Beholder" © 1983 by Richard Christian Matheson. First published in *Whispers IV*, edited by Stuart David Schiff, Doubleday. Reprinted by permission of the author.

"In the Porches of My Ears" © 2009 by Norman Prentiss. First published in *Postscripts #18 (This is the Summer of Love)*, May, PS Publishing. Reprinted by permission of the author.

"The Impression of Craig Shee" © 2015 by David McGroarty. First published in *Sensorama*, edited by Allen Ashley, Eibonvale Press. Reprinted by permission of the author.

"Shem-el-Nessim: An Inspiration in Perfume" © 2007 by Chris Bell. First published in *Zahir #13*, Summer, Zahir Publishing. Reprinted by permission of the author.

"The Scent" © 2012 by John F.D. Taff. First published in *Little Deaths*, Books of the Dead Press. Reprinted by permission of the author.

"The Odor of Violets" © 1988 by John Farris. First published in *Scare Tactics*, Tor Horror. Reprinted by permission of the author.

ALSO FROM ERIC J. GUIGNARD AND DARK MOON BOOKS:

A WORLD OF HORROR

Every nation of the globe has unique tales to tell, whispers that settle in through the land, creatures or superstitions that enliven the night, but rarely do readers get to experience such a diversity of these voices in one place as in *A WORLD OF HORROR*, the latest anthology book created by award-winning editor Eric J. Guignard, and beautifully illustrated by artist Steve Lines.

Enclosed within its pages are twenty-two all-new dark and speculative fiction stories written by authors from around the world that explore the myths and monsters, fables and fears of their homelands.

Encounter the haunting things that stalk those radioactive forests outside Chernobyl in Ukraine; sample the curious dishes one may eat in Canada; beware the veldt monster that mirrors yourself in Uganda; or simply battle mountain trolls alongside Alfred Nobel in Sweden. These stories and more are found within *A World of Horror*: Enter and discover, truly, there's no place on the planet devoid of frights, thrills, and wondrous imagination.

> "This is the book we need right now! Fresh voices from all over the world, bringing American audiences new ways to feel the fear. Horror is a universal genre and for too long we have only experienced one western version of it. No more. Get ready to experience a whole new world of terror."
>
> —*Becky Spratford; librarian, reviewer,* RA for All: Horror

Order your copy at www.darkmoonbooks.com or www.amazon.com
ISBN-13: 978-0-9989383-1-8

ALSO FROM ERIC J. GUIGNARD AND DARK MOON BOOKS:

Death. Who has not considered their own mortality and wondered at what awaits, once our frail human shell expires? What occurs after the heart stops beating, after the last breath is drawn, after life as we know it terminates?

Does our spirit remain on Earth while the body rots? Do the remnants of our soul transcend to a celestial Heaven or sink to Hell's torment? Can we choose our own afterlife? Can we die again in the hereafter? Are we given the opportunity to reincarnate and do it all over? Is life merely a cosmic joke or is it an experiment for something greater? Enclosed in this Bram Stoker-award winning anthology are thirty-four all-new dark and speculative fiction stories exploring the possibilities *AFTER DEATH . . .*

"Though the majority of the pieces come from the darker side of the genre, a solid minority are playful, clever, or full of wonder. This strong anthology is sure to make readers contemplative even while it creates nightmares."

—*Publishers Weekly*

"In Eric J. Guignard's latest anthology he gathers some of the biggest and most talented authors on the planet to give us their take on this entertaining and perplexing subject matter . . . highly recommended."

—*Famous Monsters of Filmland*

"An excellent collection of imaginative tales of what waits beyond the veil."

—*Amazing Stories Magazine*

Order your copy at www.darkmoonbooks.com or www.amazon.com
ISBN-13: 978-0-9885569-2-8

ALSO FROM ERIC J. GUIGNARD AND DARK MOON BOOKS:

Exploring Dark Short Fiction #1:
A Primer to Steve Rasnic Tem

For over four decades, Steve Rasnic Tem has been an acclaimed author of horror, weird, and sentimental fiction. Hailed by *Publishers Weekly* as "A perfect balance between the bizarre and the straight-forward" and *Library Journal* as "One of the most distinctive voices in imaginative literature," Steve Rasnic Tem has been read and cherished the world over for his affecting, genre-crossing tales.

Dark Moon Books and editor Eric J. Guignard bring you this introduction to his work, the first in a series of primers exploring modern masters of literary dark short fiction. Herein is a chance to discover—or learn more of—the rich voice of Steve Rasnic Tem, as beautifully illustrated by artist Michelle Prebich.

Included within these pages are:

- Six short stories, one written exclusively for this book
- Author interview
- Complete bibliography
- Academic commentary by Michael Arnzen, PhD (former humanities chair and professor of the year, Seton Hill University)
- . . . and more!

Enter this doorway to the vast and fantastic: Get to know Steve Rasnic Tem.

Order your copy at www.darkmoonbooks.com or www.amazon.com
ISBN-13: 978-0-9988275-2-0

ALSO FROM ERIC J. GUIGNARD AND DARK MOON BOOKS:

Exploring Dark Short Fiction #2:
A Primer to Kaaron Warren

Australian author Kaaron Warren is widely recognized as one of the leading writers today of speculative and dark short fiction. She's published four novels, multiple novellas, and well over one hundred heart-rending tales of horror, science fiction, and beautiful fantasy, and is the first author ever to simultaneously win all three of Australia's top speculative fiction writing awards (Ditmar, Shadows, and Aurealis awards for *The Grief Hole*).

Dark Moon Books and editor Eric J. Guignard bring you this introduction to her work, the second in a series of primers exploring modern masters of literary dark short fiction. Herein is a chance to discover—or learn more of—the distinct voice of Kaaron Warren, as beautifully illustrated by artist Michelle Prebich.

Included within these pages are:

- Six short stories, one written exclusively for this book
- Author interview
- Complete bibliography
- Academic commentary by Michael Arnzen, PhD (former humanities chair and professor of the year, Seton Hill University)
- . . . and more!

Enter this doorway to the vast and fantastic: Get to know Kaaron Warren.

Order your copy at www.darkmoonbooks.com or www.amazon.com
ISBN-13: 978-0-9989383-0-1

ALSO FROM ERIC J. GUIGNARD AND DARK MOON BOOKS:

Exploring Dark Short Fiction #3:
A Primer to Nisi Shawl

Praised by both literary journals and leading fiction magazines, Nisi Shawl is celebrated as an author whose works are lyrical and philosophical, speculative and far-ranging; "…broad in ambition and deep in accomplishment" (*The Seattle Times*). Besides nearly three decades of creating fantasy and science fiction, fairy tales, and indigenous stories, Nisi has also been lauded as editor, journalist, and proponent of feminism, African-American fiction, and other pedagogical issues of diversity.

Dark Moon Books and editor Eric J. Guignard bring you this introduction to her work, the third in a series of primers exploring modern masters of literary dark short fiction. Herein is a chance to discover—or learn more of—the vibrant voice of Nisi Shawl, as beautifully illustrated by artist Michelle Prebich.

Included within these pages are:
- Six short stories, one written exclusively for this book
- Author interview
- Complete bibliography
- Academic commentary by Michael Arnzen, PhD (former humanities chair and professor of the year, Seton Hill University)
- …and more!

Enter this doorway to the vast and fantastic: Get to know Nisi Shawl.

Order your copy at www.darkmoonbooks.com or www.amazon.com
ISBN-13: 978-0-9989383-4-9

ALSO FROM ERIC J. GUIGNARD AND DARK MOON BOOKS:

In this anthology, *DARK TALES OF LOST CIVILIZATIONS*, you will unearth twenty-five previously unpublished horror and speculative fiction stories relating to aspects of civilizations that are crumbling, forgotten, rediscovered, or perhaps merely spoken about in great and fearful whispers.

What is it that lures explorers to distant lands where none have returned? Where is Genghis Khan buried? What happened to Atlantis? Who will displace mankind on Earth? What laments have the Witches of Oz? Answers to these mysteries and other tales are presented within this critically acclaimed anthology.

Including stories by: **Joe R. Lansdale, David Tallerman, Jonathan Vos Post, Jamie Lackey, Aaron J. French**, and twenty exceptional others.

"The stories range from mildly disturbing to downright terrifying... Most are written in a conservative, suggestive style, relying on the reader's own imagination to take the plunge from speculation to horror."
—*Monster Librarian Reviews*

"Several of these stories made it on to my best of the year shortlist, and the book itself is now on the best anthologies of the year shortlist."
—*British Fantasy Society*

"Almost any story in this anthology is worth the price of purchase. The entire collection is a delight."
—*Black Gate Magazine*

Order your copy at www.darkmoonbooks.com or www.amazon.com
ISBN-13: 978-0-9834335-9-0

THE CRIME FILES OF KATY GREEN by GENE O'NEILL:

Discover why readers have been applauding this stark, fast-paced noir series by multiple-award-winning author, Gene O'Neill, and follow the dark murder mysteries of Sacramento homicide detectives Katy Green and Johnny Cato, dubbed by the press as Sacramento's "Green Hornet and Cato"!

Book #1: *DOUBLE JACK* (a novella)

400-pound serial killer Jack Malenko has discovered the perfect cover: He dresses as a CalTrans worker and preys on female motorists in distress in full sight of passing traffic. How fast can Katy Green and Johnny Cato track him down before he strikes again?

ISBN-13: 978-0-9988275-6-8

Book #2: *SHADOW OF THE DARK ANGEL*

Bullied misfit, Samuel Kubiak, is visited by a dark guardian angel who helps Samuel gain just vengeance. There hasn't been a case yet Katy and Johnny haven't solved, but now how can they track a psychopathic suspect that comes and goes in the shadows?

ISBN-13: 978-0-9988275-8-2

Book #3: *DEATHFLASH*

Billy Williams can see the soul as it departs the body, and is "commanded to do the Lord's work," which he does fanatically, slaying drug addicts in San Francisco... Katy and Johnny investigate the case as junkies die all around, for Billy has his own addiction: the rush of viewing the *Deathflash*.

ISBN-13: 978-0-9988275-9-9

Order your copy at www.darkmoonbooks.com or www.amazon.com

ABOUT EDITOR, ERIC J. GUIGNARD

ERIC J. GUIGNARD is a writer and editor of dark and speculative fiction, operating from the shadowy outskirts of Los Angeles, where he also runs the small press, Dark Moon Books. He's won the Bram Stoker Award (the highest literary award of horror fiction), been a finalist for the International Thriller Writers Award, and a multi-nominee of the Pushcart Prize.

He has over 100 stories and non-fiction works appearing in publications such as *Nightmare Magazine, Gamut, Black Static, Shock Totem,* and *Dark Discoveries Magazine.* As editor, Eric's published five other anthologies, such as *Dark Tales of Lost Civilizations, After Death...,* and *A World of Horror,* a showcase of international horror short fiction.

Additionally he's created an ongoing series of primers exploring modern masters of literary dark short fiction, titled: *Exploring Dark Short Fiction (Vol. 1: Steve Rasnic Tem; Vol. II: Kaaron Warren; Vol. III: Nisi Shawl; Vol. IV: Jeffrey Ford).*

Read his novella *Baggage of Eternal Night* (JournalStone), short story collection, *That Which Grows Wild: 16 Tales of Dark Fiction* (Cemetery Dance), and watch for forthcoming books, including the novel *Crossbuck 'Bo.*

Outside the glamorous and jet-setting world of indie fiction, Eric's a technical writer and college professor, and he stumbles home each day to a wife, children, cats, and a terrarium filled with mischievous beetles. Visit Eric at: www.ericjguignard.com, his blog: ericjguignard.blogspot.com, or Twitter: @ericjguignard.

ABOUT PSYCHOLOGIST, JESSICA BAYLISS, PhD

JESSICA BAYLISS is a fiction writer with a PhD in clinical psychology. Author of the young adult horror novella, *Broken Chords*, and her upcoming YA thriller, *Ten After Closing* (Sky Pony Press, September 2018), she has been a lover of thrillers and ghost tales since her days scanning VHS rental shelves—admittedly with eyes half-averted from the gory covers. She  also loves to eat, cook, and exercise—in that order—and is a firm believer that coffee makes the world a better place.

She has authored thirteen novels and several short stories that appear in anthologies such as *Beware The Little White Rabbit*, *Fright Before Christmas*, and *Zombie Chunks* and in such literary magazines as *Sanitarium Magazine*. Jessica is a Senior Editor for *Allegory Magazine*.

In the psychology world, she has more than fifteen years of experience in the cognitive-behavioral model. She's a psychotherapist, a teacher, and a researcher. One day it hit her: Why not combine writing and psychology? Just like that, PsychWRITE, her series of lectures, workshops, and coaching services for writers was born. Her blog features motivational posts for writers that combine her passion for writing with her love of psychology.

For more information about Jessica's books, blog posts, and resources for writers, visit: www.jessicabaylisswrites.com.

ABOUT ILLUSTRATOR, NILS BROSS

NILS BROSS was born in Germany in 1976, and since the days of early youth he's felt a deep love for all the arts, especially those with darker aspects. He has a general fascination for anything eldritch or occult, and learned early on to get used to the looks of worried school teachers when he filled his notebooks with crude sketches of ghastly ghosts and ghouls.

During the nineties he apprenticed as a graphic designer at the Neandertal trade school in Mettmann. Afterward, he joined the metal band SuidAkrA for some years as a bassist and became involved in historical Viking re-enactments. Today he's occupied as a freelance artist and author.

Ever since he discovered the writings of H. P. Lovecraft in teenage years, the influence of "cosmic horror" has played strongest on his work.

Further inspiration is found mostly in the gloomy well of folklore and mythology.

In addition to private customizations and art exhibitions, Nils Bross has also published at Pegasus Verlag in releases of the German version of the *Call of Cthulhu* role-playing game and has provided artwork for bands and numerous projects in the extreme metal and gothic community.

His portfolio can be viewed at: www.muninsheim.deviantart.com.

CPSIA information can be obtained
at www.ICGtesting.com
Printed in the USA
FFHW020005101019
55437352-61249FF

9 780998 827506